"We *need* this.
Grace and Mary
need this; all of the
kids do. It's for us...
...and it's for our
children."
– In the Dust

WHERE THE LIGHT STILL REACHES

JOURNEYS BEYOND THE KNOWN

ROBERT E. HAMPSON

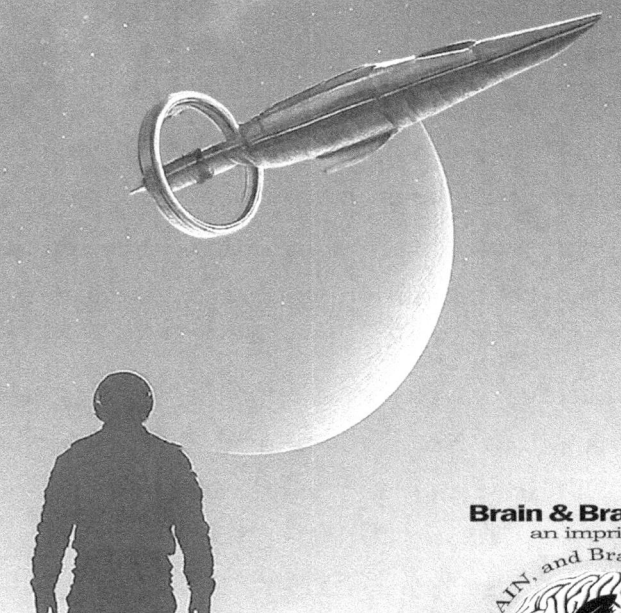

Brain & Brain Press
an imprint of
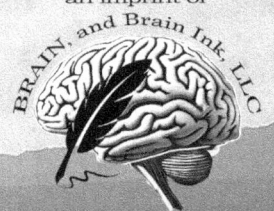
BRAIN, and Brain Ink, LLC

http://REHampson.com

Brain & Brain Press
an imprint of
BRAIN, and Brain Ink, LLC
http://REHampson.com

Copyright

Contents

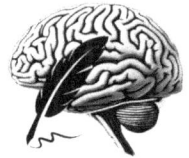

Dedication

FOR RUANN, THE LOVE of my life; for Mom, my first fan; and for Dad, my hero and role model.

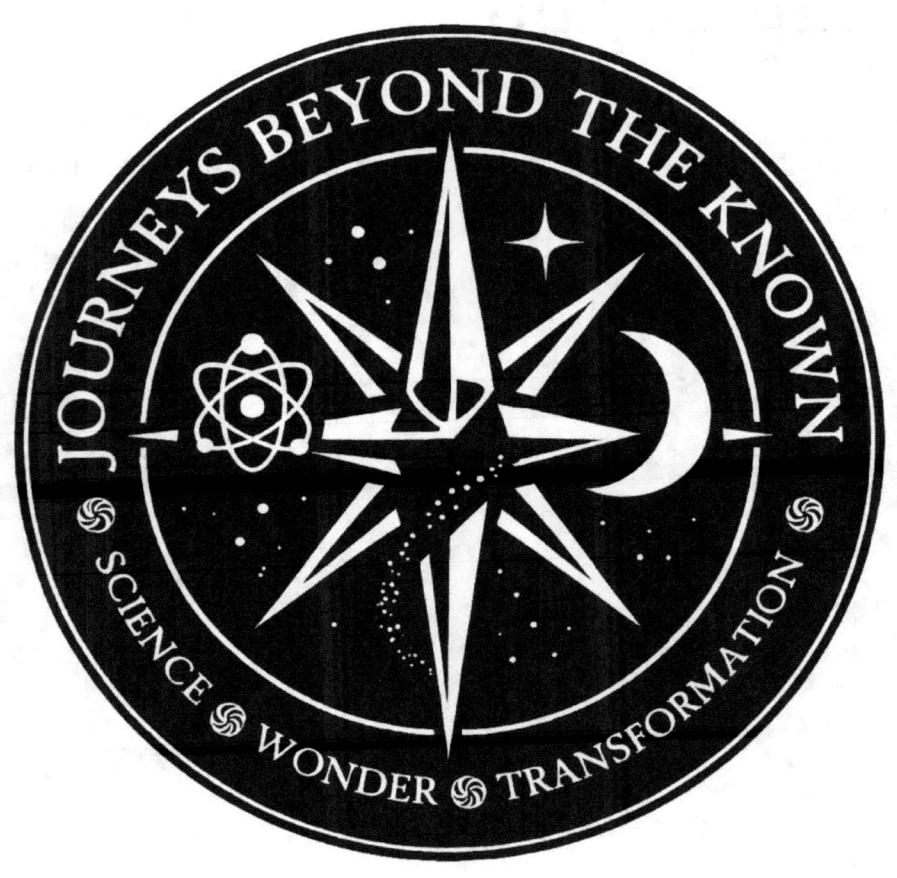

Journeys Beyond the Known

FROM NATIONAL BESTSELLING AUTHOR Robert E. Hampson comes *Journeys Beyondthe Known*—collections of science fiction and science fantasy exploring the human condition through the lenses of biotech, space exploration, strange futures, and uncommon valor.

What happens when biotech turns dangerous? When brilliant pioneers chase fading starlight? When strange magics emerge where science frays? When heroes rise to meet the impossible? From nanotech healing to bionic astronauts, from psionic children to zombie-ravaged worlds, from alien battlefields to acts of quiet defiance, come explore survival, transformation, and a spark that endures.

Hampson—scientist, educator, and master storyteller—blends hard science with heart, fusing cutting-edge research and richly imagined worlds to illuminate what it means to adapt, survive, and evolve.

The journey begins at the edge of knowledge—and ends where only story can take us.

- **Tinker, Tailor, Bio, Spy** delivers seven sharp and witty tales of biotech gone rogue, where stem cells, nanobots, and brain implants collide with military and industrial espionage. A place where ethics and integrity underlie unexpected heroism.

- **Where the Light Still Reaches** ventures into deep space and distant futures, chronicling the legacy of pioneers, the courage of survivors, and the quiet triumph of those who refuse to be forgotten.

- **When the Sky Forgot Us** wanders the borderlands between science and sorcery, offering seven visions of apocalypse, myth, and transformation—where magic rises, science fractures, and unlikely heroes carry the fire.

- **A Hero Rises** travels the paths of heroism, great, small, and everything in between—where people find a way to do the impossible—not because they want to, but because they have to.

Whether grounded in the hard realities of known science or lit by the strange glow of the fantastical, these stories invite readers to step past the boundaries of the familiar—and discover what waits just beyond.

Additional Copyright Information

our shared world anthology *The Founder Effect* (2020, Baen Books) although they appeared in different places.

All stories are reprinted here with permission of the copyright holder. This is the first published appearance of "Best Laid Plans."

Foreword

I'VE LONG BEEN A fan of science fiction—stories of space exploration, far-flung colonies, and the people in them. Stories about how those colonies were founded, and the ships that plied the space between the stars.

Volume 1 of *Journeys Beyond the Known* focused on stories of biotech—short stories directly influenced by my background in scientific research and academic credentials. These stories, by contrast, reflect much more of the young romantic who once thought about becoming an astronaut. Plagued with asthma and bad eyesight, I knew that avenue was closed to me, and I soon discovered a much greater interest in computers and scientific research.

In 2013, I became involved with a group called the Tennessee Valley Interstellar Workshop; later renamed the Interstellar Research Group, or IRG. This is a community of scientists, engineers, and—quite frankly—dreamers. It includes propulsion engineers, designers from the aerospace industry, and quite a few leaders in the field. We've had participation from members of the Air Force and Space Force, and from a number of space industry companies. There are people who work at NASA, universities, and private research firms, all investigating the challenges of long-term spaceflight. When

I joined in 2013, I was the lone biologist. Thankfully, that's no longer the case. Today, IRG represents a strong cross-section of science and engineering disciplines.

One of the important things about IRG is that it also includes authors, artists, editors, and publishers—because it's essential to keep the dream of a future in space alive. And who better to educate these creators on the realities of space than the people doing the work—so those creators can, in turn, turn it into inspiring stories that, just as in my own case, might inspire the next generation of scientists and explorers.

As much as I have a tendency to write hard science fiction, with principal characters who are scientists or science-adjacent, I also enjoy a good story in which the protagonist is a kid growing up on a world somewhere out there. I often muse on my time in Boy Scouts and imagine how that might translate to life on a colony world.

As always, I enjoy creating detailed characters and bringing them to life. So here are eight stories of space adventure and future frontiers—out where the light still reaches.

One

In the Dust

AUTHORS NOTE: To be perfectly honest, I have no idea where the idea for this story came from.

I'm a fan of movies, series, and books about the Apollo moon program, and I have to credit a lot of this story's inspiration to the HBO miniseries From the Earth to the Moon. Then, too, there are influences from various stories I've read. So, in many ways, this my version of a Golden Age or Silver Age of Science Fiction tale.

This story, though, has an interesting history. It was one of the first stories I wrote with the intent of submitting it to a national magazine and I was very, very disappointed that it didn't sell. As with many of my early stories, it needed editing and a fair amount of revision. But in 2019, I used this story for a convention reading, but needed to cut certain sections to make it fit the time allotted. It went pretty well, and I mentioned to my audience that I'd left a few sections out. In my audience were a publisher and contributing editor for a major science fiction imprint. They both told me: "The sections you left out? You don't need them. The story flows just fine as is."

A month later I learned of *Fantastic Hope*, the anthology being put together by Laurell K. Hamilton and Will McCaskey. They wanted fantasy and science fiction with a hopeful tone. I submitted the revised story—with the "skipped" sections omitted, and it was accepted.

I learned an important lesson: sometimes when a story doesn't sell, it's not that it isn't good enough. Maybe it just needs editorial refinement coupled with the right time and place.

Such as the perfect place to tell a story written in the dust.

"Three... two... one. Ready or not, here I come." Winnie thought he had the perfect hiding place, but looked up in annoyance as one of his classmates squeezed in next to him. "This is *my* hiding place," he hissed.

Jenny just giggled. She did that a lot.

"Quiet. You'll give us away," he whispered. "Why'd you have to come in here, anyway?" He was pretty sure he muttered that last part too quietly to be heard, but Jenny giggled and he heard the sound of footsteps coming closer.

The dark alcove was barely deep enough to hold one person, and Jenny squeezed in tighter. Winnie was eight and Jenny was seven-and-a-half. That half-year was important, and he thought of her as just a kid. She didn't seem to think so, and had an annoying tendency to follow him around. Like now.

Jenny squeezed past him to the back of the alcove. Although her movements were quiet, her squirming around threatened to push him out into view of nine-and-a-half-year-old, Chris, who was *Seeker* this round. His elbow bumped something, and he stifled a shout over the tingling pain shooting down his arm.

The game temporarily forgotten, he turned to examine the wall and the strange projection. A door! It was some sort of hatch, and there was a large lever instead of a conventional handle or door knob. He pushed on the lever and there was a loud metal-on-metal scraping sound.

"A-HA!" Chris was standing in the hallway, blocking the alcove. "Caught you."

Jenny quickly kissed Winnie on the cheek, then ducked low and ran under the older boy's arm. Once in the hallway she ran straight for the fire-house cabinet that they were using for Home Base. "*Olly Olly Oxenfree!*"

Darn it.

The older boy reached out and punched Winnie roughly in the shoulder. "Tag. You're it."

"DIDN'T YOUR PARENTS EVER teach you not to open a door until you know what's on the other side?" Jenny was tagging along. *Again.* Sometimes it was annoying, but he had to admit that he'd gotten used to it over the years.

"I heard my parents talking about it. They said it was special, once, but not anything of importance anymore. Aren't you curious what it is?" Winn had "borrowed" a can of lubricating oil from his father's shop, and was busy applying it to the latch and hinges.

"I heard it was a storage room of some sort, but Chris says that it's the door to summer." Jenny glanced around nervously, but she didn't leave.

"Hah! As if he even knows what that is." Winn snorted. He applied more lubricating oil to the mechanism and then worked the handle. The door creaked, but opened without too much effort. He reached up and switched on the light affixed to his headband.

"Oh. Wow."

"You realize that everyone thinks you are nuts," Jenny said. "No one else our age would *want* to spend time in a museum."

Winn thought about that for a moment. He knew his—well he wouldn't exactly call it an obsession—"hobbies" were laughed at by most of his friends. "I know. They think I'm weird. But somebody has to look after the stuff, or else the history will be lost."

"Well, I'm going to the movies, and then a bunch of us will be meeting for sodas afterward." Jenny was popular, and there was no doubt that there would be plenty of boys willing to escort her to both the movie and to the diner. The fact that she appeared to feel something for him was not entirely lost on Winn; after all, she'd been trailing after him for eight years. Unfortunately, he still had more work to do tonight. Otherwise, it would be weeks before he could get back to fix these displays.

Winn thought a moment. "I know. I wish I could go, too. But the longer these things stay out without a proper sealed display case, the harder they'll be to clean." Sure, it was a lame excuse and would just be more material for insults and teasing by the classmates who didn't get it. Only Jenny seemed to understand why he wanted to preserve the museum, particularly since the adults didn't seem to care anymore. The town of Armstrong was suffering, the mine was closed and it seemed like there was hardly a reason for tourists to come here. They used to come to the Museum, but there hadn't been a curator for at least twenty years. Some of the artifacts were in poor repair and the displays had more or less fallen apart. Winn had taken it upon himself to try to fix things up, ever since he'd started sneaking in here five years ago and became enthralled with the art and history of the place.

"Okay, suit yourself," Jenny said. "But if you have time later, why don't you come by for a soda or milkshake?" Winn wasn't sure what the look was that she had just given him, but it sure caused a shiver that couldn't be blamed on the cold workshop. He wasn't so oblivious that he didn't realize that he *really* needed to try to meet the others at the diner once their movie was over.

Jenny turned and left the museum, taking care to seal the door that she and Winn had discovered those many years ago playing "hide-and-seek." It was their own private entrance to the museum; a service entrance everyone had forgotten. The front door was locked and thermal sealed, with a formal sign that read "Museum Closed" over a hand lettered sign that read "probably forever."

Winn pulled his thermal hood up and went back to working on the display case. He had found two 70 mm Hasselblads and a Maurer in a broken case surrounded by dust eddies and ice crystals. The pressure seal had probably deteriorated recently when he'd been working on creating a new catalog of stored exhibits. Winn guiltily figured he needed to replace the case and get the cameras into an inert atmosphere soon, or restoration would be difficult if not impossible.

Fortunately, the cold temperatures in the workshop helped with the preservation even if it did make working in the Museum more difficult. He planned to restore all three. He didn't need two of the 70mm cameras, but there was a guy in Eugene who wanted a working camera and was willing to pay or trade for other supplies and collectibles. It was always a toss-up whether to work for payment or trade, considering he usually spent any extra money on new acquisitions. He could usually only afford non-working items for which there were no parts, but that was okay... he could make the parts himself. It took more time, but the only cost was for feedstock; he could earn extra money as a machinist, same as his father. The problem was, no one wanted to hire a 16-year-old these days, no matter how good he was with a programmable milling machine and three-dee printer.

For now, he worked on his online classes and spent enough time at the local school with Jenny and *her* classmates that they didn't have a clue about his college-level curriculum. In the off-hours he worked in the museum, and tried to pretend that it would make a difference. He couldn't explain why he wanted to study history, or why he was enrolled in courses such as archaeology, library science and cataloging, so it was easier just to not talk about it. That was one reason why he didn't socialize much, but Jenny knew what he was doing even if she didn't understand it herself. She liked him anyway, so he figured he'd better show up at the diner later. *For Jenny*; yeah, he supposed that was a good enough reason.

A couple hours later he stood up and took off the hooded parka. The cold and concentration left his muscles stiff, so he did a few exercises to loosen and warm up. Once he felt ready, he hung the parka co and left for the diner.

The look in Jenny's eyes as she saw him enter caused that same shiver, even though the diner was sweltering compared to the workshop.

"Hey Babe, I found that book you wanted." Jenny said as she entered their apartment. "A friend beamed it down from Lovell Station. I think he wanted a date, but I turned him down." That was fairly typical, Winn thought, every red-blooded guy and even a few girls wanted to date Jenny. Winn was constantly amazed that she seemed to reserve all of her attention for him: the geeky, bookish guy who worked in a machine shop and disappeared every evening. Jenny had been a friend, a rival, and a near-constant companion since they were seven and eight years of age, playing in the halls and corridors of Armstrong. She was the one person who could pull him away from the Museum, as well as the one who was closest to him now that he was all alone.

He had been working late that night. Jenny had come to tell him about the horrible transport crash, and sat by his side as Winn frantically checked the news channels and his parents' personal comms. Jenny had been the one to hold him through the night after his worst fears were confirmed; and Jenny had been the one to stand at his side and hold his hand throughout the memorial service.

The loss of his parents was devastating, but Winn had come face-to-face with just how he felt about Jenny; not to mention the realization of how she felt about him. She had encouraged him to speak to the owner of the machine shop where his father had worked, and been thrilled with him when he was hired as Journeyman Machinist—even though he'd only just turned 18 years of age.

Jenny also continued to encourage him in his less-frequent work at the Museum. Her contacts had led him to an actual Rover, and not just a model or holographic simulation. It wasn't necessarily period-accurate, but it would go in the collection with the camera timer, golf ball, feather, sun-bleached photograph and geologists' hammer he'd obtained over the past few years. He'd spent hours tenderly restoring the rover, including printing maps and fabricating clamps for the make-shift fender replacement. Jenny had been right at his side the whole time. She'd studied more chemistry than he had; that was definitely a benefit in figuring out the rover's antique silver-zinc batteries; however, even that knowledge wouldn't restore the photo-oxidized family portrait that originally graced the photograph.

With his work and her college classes, working in the Museum was the best way for them to spend time together. Jenny found a better solution to *that* problem when she informed Winn that even with his job, he couldn't afford to heat and power his parents' residence when he only returned home to sleep. Even though it hurt to put an end to that part of his life, Winn bowed to Jenny's practical wisdom. They now shared a small apartment midway between college and the machine shop, not too far from the Museum.

"So, why are you interested in *An Informal History of Liquid Rocket Propellants*?" Her question brought Winn out of his reverie with a start. Jenny recognized the shake of his head and smiled. "Are you planning on "Going to the Moon," Winnie?" she laughed. But her eyes twinkled and Winn knew she was only teasing.

"Actually, my friend in Eugene found an old Apollo engine pump, and I figured I needed to understand the principles better before I started on the restoration." He took the book reader, then laid it carefully on his workbench and folded Jenny in his arms. "So, how was class?"

"Ugh, well, the Botany labs are fine, but my lab mates simply will *not* do their own work." She grimaced, but then brightened up. "Oh! I have an interview with Melliere!"

"Um, is that a *who*, a *where*, or a *what*?" Winn pulled back slightly to look at Jenny—one eyebrow raised, and the side of his mouth crooked up in a grin.

"Melliere Corp is both a *what* and a *where*." Jenny returned the grin. "The company does agricultural genetics and they have a re-search station just north of Descartes. I'm interviewing for a lab internship two days a week and weekends. If I get the job, I can commute."

Winn's grin faded. Jenny recognized the look and the memory and emotion behind it. She hurried to add, "By tube, not hopper. It's cheaper, anyway." The worried look in Winn's eyes was one familiar to Jenny, so she reached out and held his chin. "It's only an hour commute, four days a week. Don't be a worry-wart. If they like my work, we can talk about setting up a test plot here after I graduate. Then I won't have to commute."

Winn forced a smile, but then the last thing Jenny said sunk in. "Really? Wow. That would be nice." His smile was genuine and he hugged her tightly. "It would be nice to stay right here."

"Don't count those chickens yet, Pooh-Bear. I still have to grad-uate, not to mention getting the job. It's at least a year." But Jenny hugged back and started thinking of a few plans of her own.

WINN SAT AT THE workbench, just staring at the components on the table. He'd been so lost in thought that he hadn't even donned his parka despite the cold. He really had no idea how long he'd sat there, ignoring the deep chill, not even shivering, before he grimaced and swept the video camera components off the table. They floated gently to the floor, depriving him of the visceral jolt of clatter and breakage.

He supposed it didn't matter; the video tube was fried, anyway.

Instead, he pounded the table with his fists. The cold had made them numb and he only stopped when he noticed the smear of blood from the bruised and cracked skin.

He laid his head down on the table, and for only the second time in his life, he cried.

His first indication that anyone was present was the parka settling over his shoulders. The lining was warm; Jenny had taken her own coat off and wrapped it around him, then gone to retrieve *his* parka from the peg by the pressure hatch. She gathered up the scattered camera parts and placed them in a covered plastic box—filled it with a shot of nitrogen to displace the air—then sealed the cover and placed it on a shelf.

Winn sat motionless while his not-fiancée cleaned up the mess he'd made. Even when she came back and sat at his side, he neither spoke nor moved.

"He's an idiot. You already knew that," she said at last.

Winn mumbled something unintelligible.

"He's a politician. First lawyer out of Armstrong in decades, and he has designs on mayor and then governor positions." Jenny reached out and lifted Winn's chin so that she could look him in the eye. "I told him that his petty prejudices were so twenty-first century and

Mom agreed. In this day and age, he'd have a bigger scandal if his wife and daughter denounced him than if his daughter married a "no-good" tinkerer." She wiped his tears and kissed him. "Then I told him that we'd just go to his arch-rival who actually *is* Mayor right now and have her perform a civil ceremony!"

Winn essayed a small smile and kissed her back. After a while he pulled back and spoke. "He hates me, though. I really don't want that hanging over our heads."

"He doesn't. Not really. That was just the politician speaking." She kissed him again, and they held each other for a while before she continued. "He's actually pretty proud of the work you did with the central water supply. Armstrong would be in a world of hurt if you hadn't machined the parts for the pumps. Mom reminded him of that and offered to let him sleep in the airlock tonight to rethink his words."

"Did you mean it? Do you really want to go to the mayor's office?"

"Sure, we'll go see Mayor Kubric tomorrow."

"Tomorrow?" Winn squeaked.

"Yes, tomorrow. You've already asked my father even if it wasn't the answer you wanted, and even though I told you it wasn't necessary. Tomorrow. Noon." She took his hand and guided him to his feet. "Now, let's go and see if your suit fits."

IT WAS ALMOST NINE years before Jenny was able to end the commute across the Sinus to Descartes. First came a few extra years to finish a doctorate in plant genetics. Then there was the part-time teaching job while she worked her way up through the research hierarchy at Melliere Corp. It also took time to select a location, build the greenhouse dome, and set up the experimental plot.

Winn was in the workshop at the Museum when Jenny came in, slightly dusty from her first official workday in the 'Garden of Eatin'.' "Hey, I thought you were supposed to wash all of that off at the dome to recycle the soil?" He called out as she stopped at a utility sink and wiped her hands with one of the ubiquitous shop towels before coming over to inspect the rake and scoop he'd set aside for restoration.

"I did," she muttered. "You of all people should know how that dust gets into everything. I have *got* to get some more organics in there, especially around the edge plots. They're the driest."

"Sure, I know. The dust gets everywhere." Here gestured at the cases around the room, each containing an artifact that he had painstakingly cleaned and restored. It was no longer a secret that Winn and Jenny both worked there. Winn set up an account to pay the utility bills, so what was once trespassing and a waste of time for teenagers was an eccentric, but acceptable, hobby for the supervising Master Machinist at Armstrong Tool and Die.

"By the way, I saw the doctor today." Jenny picked up a discarded shop towel and returned it to the sink as Winn packed up his tools and returned the latest items to their display case.

"Oh, yeah, I forgot you had an appointment." Winn sealed the case and filled it with nitrogen. "I hope you mentioned that stomach bug you've picked up. It sounded pretty bad this morning." Winn's attention was not on his wife, so he didn't see the sly look on Jenny's face. "I hope you'll be over it in time for that dinner your parents are planning."

"Uh, Winn. Pooh-Bear. Sit down and look at me." Winn leaned back onto his work stool and looked up in confusion. "I won't be "over it" for about seven more months. But I'm going to be just fine..."

GRACE WAS BEING FUSSY. The two-year-old had sinus congestion and was unhappy that she couldn't breathe properly. Colds were rare in Armstrong, but very uncomfortable since sinuses didn't drain properly. On the plus side, reduced sinus drainage meant fewer sore throats for the young ones.

Winn and Jenny's daughter wanted to be held and rocked, but Jenny had a meeting in Descartes in the morning, so Winn had drawn sick child duty. He stood in the middle of the nursery and held the squirming toddler, rocking back and forth and murmuring softly. Jenny was the singer of the two, and knew every nursery rhyme and song imaginable, even a few from languages other than English, thanks to her mixed-nationality colleagues. Winn didn't sing, but he did love to read aloud. Grace would snuggle up close and lay her head on his chest as his spoke.

Tonight, she wanted—no, needed—to keep rocking; it would help clear her head. Thus, it was difficult for Winn to read. Instead, he spoke softly, his voice rumbling quietly as her told her of his dreams.

"It's old, sweetie. Older than you or me or Mommy, or even Grampa and Grandma. They were brave men and women who made it possible, and even braver ones who made the trip. We have to tell people about it. We can't forget, and we can't let anyone else forget.

People need to be reminded not to give up on their dreams. It's *important*, Gracie. We must believe and remember for them."

"Mayor Harriman, please. It's an important piece of our history." Winn sat on the edge of his seat in the plain, but comfortable office. Armstrong's mayors had never gone in for luxurious appointments and displays of excess, but the office was appropriately furnished for both the current elected occupant and guests. The chairs were comfortable, but the comfort was lost on Winn at the moment. "All we need is the heat and light allotment; I'll take care of the rest. I can afford it."

"Son, I appreciate all you've done. Goodness knows Wright Fabrication has brought jobs back to Armstrong and Jenny's reputation has certainly caught on. If Melliere makes her a full partner, they'll probably move half of their research staff here." Harriman's tone was neither condescending nor dismissive, but it was clear he still had concerns. "It's just that we *had* tourists and they stopped coming. I don't see it happening again."

It was not the first time Winn had heard, or made, these arguments. In fact, he heard them every year. He had a standing appointment for July 20th every year.

"Don't think we don't appreciate everything you've done," the mayor continued. "Your family is the single biggest driver in our economy, thanks to the companies that have relocated here for access to you and Jenny. Think of it, Son, you've given us *hope* and growth again!"

"But hope is not enough, sir! We need to know our own history—we need to *share* that history as well." Winn had made this argument each year as well, but this year he added a new tactic. "Don't you want your granddaughters to grow up knowing the importance of this town?"

"That's a low blow, Son, especially knowing as I do that you'll teach them anyway. Am I right?" Harriman tried to glare at his son-in-law, but couldn't help but laugh at Winn's triumphant look. "Besides, a museum needs a curator." He held his hand up to forestall the protest. "A professional. I know you can handle the displays, but a proper museum requires professional management."

Winn looked down for a moment, and to all intents looked as if he was resigned to the same ending of the old argument. After a moment, however, he reached into the old-fashioned document case and pulled out several sheets of plastic wrapped parchment and laid them on the desk in front of his father-in-law. The mayor's shocked expression was almost worth it.

"Doctor Edwin Aldrin Wright?" Harriman carefully lifted the documents one at a time. "One... two... three degrees? Ph.D. in Archeology? Masters in Forensic Restoration and Library Science?" He looked up in shock. "But I... Jenny never said... I never knew."

"No one did. Well, except Jenny, but she's very good at helping me keep secrets."

"But... how?" Harriman still held the topmost document gingerly, as if afraid to touch it, but more afraid to let it go. "This is dated ten years ago. How... How did you manage to do this in Armstrong?"

Winn was relieved. Astonishment was easier to deal with than disbelief. "I finished the high school curriculum early, and my father set up the distance-learning college courses to keep me busy. I did everything online that I could, and the Museum provided all of my field projects. The worst part was that the Archeology professors had to inspect my documents and projects. Not to mention that the Restoration defense required a gallery showing. Remember those 'tourists' from Tycho who expressed such an interest in the machine shop when it was just getting started? That was my advisor and the external examiner. They are both clients, actually, and helped me set up a holographic gallery show in the Canaveral Museum in Florida. The 'honeymoon' over in Tycho before Grace was born was my defense. It still had to be done by virtual conference because we couldn't afford the recovery time it would take if I went Earthside.

Harriman sat stunned for several minutes while Winn waited patiently. "I had no idea," he finally said, as a new expression began to take over his face. "So. Why here? Why aren't you working at the Smithsonian or the Louvre? Instead of working at a machine shop?"

Winn reached out and placed his hand over that of his father-in-law. "Dad." Harriman looked up. "I *own* a chain of machine shops. I am married to a wonderful woman—your daughter—who is about to become Luna's top agricultural expert. Our children, and our family, are here."

Harriman finally put the sheets down and passed them back. It was clear that he believed the documents. That was never really the issue. The same was true for money, these days. Winn could tell that at this point, only one question remained. "Why now? What's so different that you brought out all of—?" He waved his hand at the documents. "—all of this. Why today?"

Winn placed the documents back in the case, closed it, and looked up. "In five years, it will be the bicentennial. Two hundred years since the moon landing. It will take that long to get the Museum ready, certified, and registered as an official event." He paused, and then continued. "Besides, we *need* this. Grace and Mary need this; all of the kids do. It's for us... and it's for our children."

"Huh. Yes, it would be, wouldn't it?" Harriman thought for a moment, and then continued. "Very well. I will take it up with the council. As for this..." He pointed at the document case. "You need to show this to your mother-in-law. She's going to be angry you didn't tell her. Dinner. Sunday. Bring it all, she's going to want pictures!"

THE THERMAL SEALS ON the outside doors had been removed. In fact, six months ago the original doors had been removed and replaced with the latest technology from Wright Fabrications for the unofficial opening day. For today's official opening, a small crowd was waiting for the curator, docent and owner of the museum to open the doors on history: July 20, 2169.

The city council had wanted to name it the "Wright Museum", but Winn successfully argued that *that* museum was in Ohio. Jenny convinced them that the "Armstrong-Aldrin Museum of Lunar History" was much more appropriate, and Winn agreed.

Winn opened the doors from the inside, and the crowd held back while fourteen-year-old Grace and eight-year-old Mary solemnly stepped up and showed their guest passes. Their mother had coached them in "formal" behavior for the event, but their father was determined to break the mood. He scooped Mary up in his arms and hugged Grace tight as he led the way in to the central display. A custom polymer case that Winn had designed expressly for this display enclosed a twenty-five-meter space, within which a blocky platform stood on four spindly legs. The one-hundred-seventy-five-centimeter-thick platform was nearly level with the floor, while the legs rested nearly one and a half meters below on exposed lunar regolith. It was the only place in Armstrong where the original surface was exposed, and Winn had carefully built the new, fully transparent casing around the original hull and viewports, then removed the hull so that viewers could see the entire site, including the two-hundred-year-old footprints in the lunar dust.

"What does it say, Daddy?" Mary asked, and pointed at the plaque affixed to one leg. Winn noted the hush that had come over the crowd as he quietly cleared his throat and recited the inscription he had memorized so many years ago:

"It says, 'HERE MEN FROM THE PLANET EARTH FIRST SET FOOT UPON THE MOON JULY 1969, A.D. WE CAME IN PEACE FOR ALL MANKIND.'"

Two
The Suit

AUTHORS NOTE: MY FRIEND Kevin Steverson created an in-credible universe with the book *Salvage Title*. In that series, a young man on a far-off colony world builds a suit of powered armor—a mecha, if you will—from scrap. He and his friends decide to try to make a living at salvage, given the abundance of technological debris from battle and things just plain wearing out.

Much to their surprise, they salvage an AI core that leads them to a cache of even better gear, including a warship just sitting there for the taking. They can't register it on their own, so they make a salvage claim and file a "salvage title"—and the series is born.

The stories reminded me of some of the old *Boys' Life* tales. Stories of Scouts who are inventors, tinkerers and adventurers, much like the old Heinlein juveniles, where someone builds a starship—or a mecha—out of scrap. In the *Salvage Title* universe, they build an entire society out of salvage.

When Kevin decided to create an anthology of short stories in that world, I quickly signed up. I wrote my version of Scouts on one of the *Salvage Title* worlds. **The events take place many years after the events of the original book, when salvaging, repurposing, and innovation are virtues, and incorporated into the Scout requirements. They even have a merit badge in which they make something useful using their scavenging and improvisational skills.**

In this story, young Pete Emil salvages something very, very rare, and gets it back into operation. Soon everyone will know of Pete and his suit.

"So, what are you going to do for your Maker Merit Badge?" Orlin was digging through the pile of discarded mech components. He'd told his companions all about his plans to build his own mech, 'just like Harmon Tomeral' and was now trying to figure out how much competition he was going to have from the other members of his patrol. Even though Tomeral had long left the Tretra system, he was still a hero, particularly on Joth, where he'd grown up under circumstances much like Orlin and his friends.

"I don't know," replied Pettekil—Pete to his friends—flipping his tail back and forth with nervous energy. "I think everyone wants to copy him and build mechs. I want to do something different." He turned back to his desultory sorting through burnt motivators, exhausted power cells and damaged sensors. "There's nothing of interest in this junk pile."

"We want to build..." started Jerry.

"... a fighter!" finished Jinx. The twins usually finished each other's sentences. They often talked about becoming fighter pilots because they assumed that their ability to coordinate their actions would provide an advantage in combat.

"Of course you do," said Orlin with a sigh of resignation. "It's all you two ever talk about."

"Hey J—" called Jerry.

"Yeah, J—" replied Jinx.

"There's a thruster..."

"...over here.."

"Wow, two..."

"...at a time? How lucky—"

"—is that?" completed Jinx

"Can you two please *stop that*?" asked Pete. "Do you know how annoying that is? Especially when the rest of us haven't found jack... uh... diddly."

"Just because—"

"—you can't look with four eyes—"

"—doesn't mean we can't!"

The irony was that 'Pete' was a Caldivar, an anteater-like creature with three eyes. He had an advantage over the human twins, and even Orlin, who was a lizard-like Prithmar. Joth was home to many races, and it was not uncommon for them to mix in both social and occupational settings. The four boys were all in the same Troop, and even the same Patrol—the Crockables, named for a leathery-winged scavenger bird common to the vast deserts of Joth.

"You have one more eye than I have, so I wouldn't call that much of an advantage..." he started, but was interrupted by Orlin.

"A-HA! Got another knee joint, here. Now I just need a couple of hip joints and the lower limbs are set."

"You guys have all the luck," Pete grumped.

"Alright guys. The troop as a whole is going to be working on the Maker Merit Badge this month. Since you're all on school break for the next three weeks, you should be able to spend all the time you need during that time period. Remember, merit badge rules say that you can work individually, or in teams up to the size of a patrol, however, to earn the badge, your team-mates must agree that you contributed significantly to the overall project. I've arranged for you to have access to the Farnog Corp printers, and the Rinto Scrap Yard will let you pick through the unsorted salvage. The rest of it is up to you. Build it, program it, salvage it... Just make sure that it is a functioning device of value to Joth society, because we'll be entering them in the Joth Maker Faire next month."

Troopmaster Zentto was Prithmar, like about one-third of the kids in the troop. Another third were human, and the remainder was a mix of Caldivar, Yalteen, Pikith and even a couple of Leethog. Xenophobia was rare on Joth given the number of different races present on the desert-like world. The variety also made the Crockables' troop quite successful in the various planet wide youth competitions like the Maker Faire. Residents of Joth were always inventive and self-reliant, but the popularity of build-it-yourself projects and competitions had really taken off after Joth's favorite son, Harmon Tomeral, had won the Top Fleet Marine competition. The fact that Tomeral ended up saving the entire system from the Squilla hadn't hurt either. Inventive, unorthodox, self-reliant, heroic—Tomeral was an example to all. Thanks to his example, every young resident of Joth wanted to be the next to make their mark on the universe.

The only problem was that Pete still didn't know what he was making for the competition. Orlin had most of an exoskeleton together and was starting to fashion armor plates. Even if it wasn't a full mecha, he'd already proven its worth by using the augmented strength to improve the searches in the salvage yard. Jerry and Jinx had affixed their thrusters and motors to a hover frame that the quartet used to transport their finds back to the workspace that the troop had arranged for their members to finish projects. The other three were well on their way to completing the merit badge and even had a chance of scoring well at the Maker Faire. Pete was the only one without a project of his own.

Of course, he could always work with his patrol-mates on their projects. He was helping them with programming anyway, so there was no question but that he was contributing significantly. It's just that he wanted something of his own.

"Hey, what's this—" started Jerry

"—it looks like armor—"

"—but soft—"

"—and no joints," ended Jinx.

The device in question did look vaguely like something a bipedal could wear. There were four tubes roughly the size and shape of humanoid arms and legs. There was also a much larger, clamshell that looked like it would fit the torso of Yalteen. It was much too large for a human, let alone a Caldivar or Human. There didn't seem to be anything joining the separate pieces into a suit or armor, although there were some damaged tubes that *might* have connected the various pieces at one time. There was also no evidence of a helmet or joint protection.

"If it's a Mecha, it's missing anything practical," observed Orlin. "I suppose it might be some sort of an add-on, like ablative armor."

"Not armor—"

"—too soft." Jinx held up one of the tubes. It might have been a sleeve, with a semi-flexible elbow joint, but Pete agreed, it was much too soft. The material was almost a fabric, it seemed as if the only reason it even held its shape was more tubing inside.

"Could it be some sort of reactive material that can be programmed to be rigid in one state and flexible in another?" Orlin had picked up another of the sleeves. This one bore a similarity to a leg, with a large diameter opening at one end, a narrow opening at the other, and once again, a slight flex where a knee joint might be located.

"If that's the case—"

"—where are the shoulders—"

"—and hips?"

"You would think—"

"—that it would be important—"

"—to protect them, too!"

"If it's programmable, there should be a controller. Look around for anything that looks like a processor that has those tubes coming out of it. We'll take it back with us and I'll hook it up and see what it does. If we can figure it out, maybe Orlin can add it to his exoskeleton." Pete might not have a project of his own, but if he could figure out programmable armor for Orlin's mecha, that would be a worthwhile contribution. "Jinx, Jer, help me put this on the H-frame."

"Here is a box—"

"—the same shape—"

"—as the discoloration—"

"—on the 'chest.'"

Sure enough, the object appeared to be some sort of computer processor, and was exactly the same size and shape as a corresponding discolored place on the front of the clamshell. It even had indications of wiring connectors in locations that lined up between the two pieces. It didn't make sense to put a controller right on the front of armor where it would be the first thing hit. Maybe there was more to this "armor" than met the eye. Was there a reason why the builders weren't worried about the exposed control panel? Was it some form of energy shield?

Pete's imagination began to race. Maybe he wouldn't have to treat this as simply a part of Orlin's mecha. Maybe he could make this on his own.

THE MAIN WORKSHOP WAS noisy. Orlin alternated between heating metal plates in an electroforge and hammering them on an archaic iron anvil to make hardened plates that would cover key components of his mecha. He'd decided to proceed with hip, shoulder and neck armor while Pete tried to figure out the mysterious components they'd pulled out of the salvage yard. Jerry and Jinx were arguing in their strange style while the remounted the hover thrusters with vectored nozzles to transition from vertical lift to forward thrust.

Meanwhile, Pete worked in the quieter clean-room to one side of the workshop, cleaning and rebuilding the wiring connections between the controller, torso and limbs of the strange armor. The most unusual feature of the device was that the tubing appeared to be able to fill with some form of fluid to form a rigid frame. Unfortunately, he hadn't figured out if there was a way to make the fabric itself become less flexible.

Perhaps it had something to do with what fluid was pumped into the tubes? Maybe this wasn't armor. Was it a cooling system? If so, why did it even need the fabric covering?

So far, he'd only worked with one of the suit limbs, experimenting with providing electrical current, then air pressure to the tubing, then fluid pressure in the form of water, hydraulic oil and liquid refrigerant. None of them seemed to make a difference, but he hadn't tried hooking up the complete system yet.

Still, before doing that, he needed to figure out what fluid the suit used. There was one long piece of tubing that had been attached to the clamshell at shoulder height, if there was still some trace in there, perhaps he could have someone analyze it.

"This is unusual; you don't see these molecules very often. Lots of fluorine and carbon, usually called a 'perfluorocarbon.'" Pete's cousin Bereketil showed him the diagram on the slate of a number of carbon molecules bonded to fluoride molecules. "Breck" was a graduate student in Materials Engineering at the new branch of the Tretrayon Academy that had opened on Joth in the last few years. It didn't completely eliminate the history of inferior treatment of Joth and its citizens by the system capital, but it was a start.

"Wasn't that used in refrigeration units? So, this *is* some kind of cooling suit." Pete picked up the tubing he'd asked his older cousin to analyze for him.

"Not really. Refrigerants usually contained chlorine as well. Chlorofluorocarbons were banned millennia again, and frankly, there's better ways to cool than letting a liquid evaporate, absorbing heat, then compressing it back to a liquid and venting the heat somewhere else. No, there were several other uses as well, such as fire suppressants and electrical insulation. If it was pumped through your suit, perhaps it was worn by shipboard damage control. It would probably be fire-proof and shock-proof." Breck tapped on his slate some more. "Oh, this is interesting." He showed Pete a diagram of a molecule that looked like two six-sided rings that shared a side. "Perfluorodecalin. Ten carbons, eighteen fluorines. There were some attempts on Earth at using for a blood substitute."

"For humans, then. That won't help me much."

"Actually, it helps carry oxygen, so most races with closed circulatory systems can use it." Breck handed the slate over to Pete. "Show me those pictures you took again."

Pete placed his own slate on top of his cousin's and initiated the transfer, then pocketed his own and handed Breck's slate back to him. "That's what we're calling the torso unit. It looks like it would fit down over a neck and then close at the sides."

"Big, isn't it? Not human sized. Not Caldivar and certainly not Prithmar. Yalteen?"

"Tall enough, but much bigger in the chest. More like the Withaloo who settled in Salvage." Pete tapped the slate again. "These are the sleeves. Near as I can tell there are two fluid tubes and a wiring harness supposed to connect each one to the torso unit. There's also four wiring connectors—one at each corner—connecting the control unit to the torso. Those were intact, and I have just about gotten them clean enough to re-attach."

"Wait, how much of this have you done on your own? You're still in Upper School, right?"

"Actually, Jerry and Jinx's father helped a bit with the electrical. You know we do this for fun in the Troop, right?"

"I remember you took apart my watch when you were just a pup. I never did get it to synch back up with my slate after that."

"Um. I've *built* watches, since then, Breck. From a kit, true, but they work."

"Huh. Think you can do something with this one, then?" Breck extended a claw and popped the catch on a black band he wore around one leathery wrist. "It hasn't worked right since I started working in this lab."

Pete took the watch and held it up to look closely with his lower, left eye, the one he usually used for fine detail. "You know this has been etched, right? Looks like acid of some sort."

"Oh, damn. That's what it was. I'm still catching grief from the professor about that spill. Okay, never mind." He held out a paw to take the watch back but Pete kept it just out of reach.

"Actually, it's fixable. I can open it up, clean the moly's, lay down new traces and print a new case for it. I owe for doing this, at least." He nodded toward the bench-top analyzer Breck had used to analyze the residual fluid in the tubing.

"Hey, thanks, cuz. This? This was no trouble, and I appreciate the watch. Good luck figuring out what your suit does."

"Pete—"

"—did you notice—"

"—these ports—"

"—on the back?"

Jerry and Jinx had the torso of Pete's "firefighter suit" in a cabinet where it could be sprayed with a fine abrasive to remove contaminants and polish metallic surfaces. Each of the twins pointed to a line of small fittings along each side of the back plate. They had previously been covered in a hard crust of some sort of resinous material. The boys had offered to let him use the cleaning chamber once they finished cleaning their thruster nozzles. They must have finished early, because the suit fittings positively shone with a blue-green glimmer in the artificial lighting of the shop.

"You guys are done with the nozzles?"

"Well actually—"

"—one of them was so worn—"

"—the abrasive cut a hole—"

"—right through the chamber wall—"

"—we need to go—"

"—back and find a new one—"

"—so, we decided to—"

"—help you!"

Pete pulled out a monocle magnifier and held it up to his left-low eye to inspect the ports. At least two on each side looked like fluid or gas ports, and the area surrounding those looked exactly like the quick connect system used for the fuel containers on Orlin's mecha. Several other ports looked like they would have held some sort of fixture, but there was no opening in the socket to suggest either electrical or physical connection with the device.

He realized that the twins had continued talking to him as he was lost in inspecting the newly revealed features of his project.

"—so, we're headed back—"

"—and we rigged—"

"—a scanner—"

"—to identify—"

"—the same components—"

"—as your suit."

Jinx—or Jerry, it was hard to tell since they were both covered in the powdered abrasive from the cleaning station—held out a device with a paw-grip and small screen. Material scanners were pretty common on Joth. They were used for everything from finding buried minerals to identifying sophont remains. He wasn't entirely sure he wanted to know where the human twins had gotten the device, but he wasn't going to turn it down.

They wouldn't have the hover sled this time, not with a missing thruster, and besides it was being refitted into something much more like the fighter profile that Jerry and Jinx had proposed for their merit badge. Instead, they'd talked their big sister Jenny into flying them over to the Rinto yard in her flitter. Pete supposed that having siblings whose names all started with "J" must be one of those family identification things, such as the "-etil" part of his own name. He didn't really understand Human naming, even though he'd grown up in the mixed-race society of Joth. Most sophonts went with whatever name their Human friends called them, especially since Humans were known for shortening names.

At least they wouldn't have to worry about Jerry and Jinx's sister sticking around to take them home from the scrap yard, either. The boys said that she was sweet on the human operating the big Grappler scrap mover at Rinto's. The problem would be convincing her to leave when they were done.

"Okay Jerx, go have fun, I'll be talking to Roland," Jenny had said when they arrived at the scrap yard. The twins immediately ran off to hunt for thrusters in a large pile of material that was new since the last time they'd visited, leaving Pete to go to the sector where they'd found the "fire-fighter suit." When he got there, he found only a patch of bare ground and a few scraps of metal. He went to find Ronnie, and earned a dirty look from Jenny in the process.

"Sorry, Pete, but that pile's been sorted. Boss said you can pick through all of the unsorted scrap, put once it's been sorted, it's in the inventory." Ronnie looked apologetic, and he probably was. He'd actually helped them load up their salvage on the first couple of trips, before the twins had assembled the hover frame.

"But, Roland, there might have been parts there for my suit! I just need to look at the stuff from that pile."

Roland looked at Pete, then at Jenny, then back at Pete again. "Okay, kid. That sector has been scanned and sorted for useable salvage, but it hasn't been category sorted, so it's still all in one place. I can let you take a look, but I gotta warn you, if it's been entered into inventory, you're going to have to buy it. I can't just let you have it or the Boss will skin me alive."

Pete tried to imagine a human with its thin dermal layer peeled open. It wasn't something he wanted to dwell on. He totally missed the wink Roland gave Jenny. He swallowed and pushed the thought out of his mind.

When Roland showed him to the container with the tagged and labeled salvage, Pete pulled out the scanner and started running it over the piled-up components that would eventually be sold to sophonts needing specific parts. None of the pieces in the collection triggered the scanner, so Pete started over, this time looking closely under and behind the stacked components, but he never saw anything that looked like it went with the suit he'd found.

There certainly were not enough items here to account for the entire volume of the pile they'd originally explored—even given the items they'd salvaged themselves. Troopmaster Zentto had ensured that few of the troop members would get into fights over the same pieces. Each patrol had been assigned different sectors, and told to stay within them at risk of being disqualified. Since it would be another two years until Maker Merit Badge came around again, it was a serious threat. So, it was unlikely that another patrol had gotten to "their" salvage.

The problem was—where was everything else from the pile?

Pete hunted down Roland yet again. He'd heard that Roland had gone on break, and had last been seen on the far side of the open-sided roofed shelter where some of the larger pieces of obviously good-condition salvage were stored. He knew that Humans of Roland and Jenny's age liked to engage in what Jerry and Jinx called "snogging"—he'd certainly heard enough details of the practice from the twins—so he made sure to make a lot of noise as he approached the area where the Humans had last been seen.

Sure enough, he heard giggling and low talking from just beyond a large object that looked like a complete airlock assembly. Pete kicked a piece of debris into the airlock door, making a satisfying thunk. He waited a moment, and then Roland came around the corner, putting his eye protection and hat back on.

"Okay, pipsqueak, what do you want now?" Pete realized he was a bit small for a Human his age, but he would be nearly two meters at maturity. The scrapyard worker was probably about as tall as he would get, and would barely come up to the Caldivar's chin once he was fully grown. There was simply no need to be insulting.

"I'm sorry, Mister Roland, I really am, but… where is the rest of the scrap?" He looked around, and extended a claw to gesture with. "Each of these piles is mixed scrap. The sorted items you let me look at are only about half of the original pile. What happens to the rest?"

"Oh. Oh! Sorry kid, I guess I should have told you. If it's not sorted for labeled salvage, it gets put over there." Roland pointed to an absolutely huge pile of scrap on the far edge of the yard.

Pete's spirits fell. There was absolutely no way he was going to find anything in that pile. It was many, many times the size of the original, and looked like it had years' worth of scraps.

"Although," continued Roland, "we just finished sorting your stuff this morning. The scraps are probably still in the hopper of the Grappler…"

Pete didn't hear the rest as he took off in the direction of the bull-dozer-like mecha. Roland watched him go, then muttered "whatever" and took off his hat and sunglasses and he headed back behind the airlock assembly. "Jenny, I've got another 10 minutes and then I've got to get back to work."

As soon as he reached the Grappler, he knew he'd found the right salvage. There was the burned relay and cracked power cell that Orlin and the twins had rejected on their first salvage trip. He pulled out the scanner and started to run it over the items. He was rewarded with several beeps immediately. He dug into the pile and pulled out two bottle-like objects made from the same blue-green metal as the suit. Another ten minutes yielded a total of seven items—two long bottles, two short ones, one large, *heavy* rectangular object that was exactly the size of one of the unusual sockets on the suit, and two smaller, lighter cylinders. The cylinders looked like some sort of power cell. The cylinders probably contained liquid or gas. A larger one sloshed slightly, while the smaller ones seemed to be mostly full. The heavy rectangle appeared to be solid, with no openings or obvious connections. That they went with the suit was highly probable based on the size, fittings and the unusual metal.

As for what they contained, he might have to go back to visit Breck.

"Yes. Perfluorodecalin." Breck declared, holding up the bottle that still contained liquid. "The trace from the other bottle is the same, and they're an exact match to a variant called 'Flurodec.' The bottles are designed to hold pressurized liquid, and Flurodec is pretty dense in liquid form. It's probably a pretty good supply for fire-suppression and cooling. Are you going to want to refill them? I can synthesize some in the molecular printer. Carbon and Fluorine can be scavenged from dirt, air, water, so it will be pretty cheap. I can make a run and fill the bottles once you clean them up."

"What about the other pieces?" Pete asked.

"Well, as you said, the cylinders are power cells. They're exhausted, but it shouldn't be hard to power them up. It looks like a standard capacitor array. As for the small bottles, the pressure and weight suggests that they are probably between half and three quarters full. I can't tell what the stuff is, though; it's a complex organic mix that doesn't match anything in our database. This..." He held up the dense rectangle. "...is interesting. Its density suggests heavy metals, possibly even rare ones. The closest density match is osmium, but it's the wrong texture—this feels like a polymer, not a metal. However, I can't scan anything in the interior. It seems solid all the way through, so it's unlikely that this is just a plastic shell over heavy metal. Given the scan, this is either made up of nanometer sized or smaller components, or it's a heck of a lot better shielded than anything I've ever seen."

Breck looked at Pete expectantly.

"I'll take that refill. And thanks. Oh, by the way..." Pete reached into his coverall and pulled out Breck's watch. "Cleaned, serviced, and in a brand-new case, courtesy of the Farnog student workshop."

"Wow, thanks." Breck put the watch back onto his wrist and closed the clasp. Immediately the face of the device lit up with the time and a list of the Caldivar grad student's appointments and reminders. "Yeah, no problem. I'll start the synthesizer. Bring back those bottles with the fittings cleaned up and I'll refill them for you."

THE DAY FINALLY CAME to assemble the components of the suit and see what it did. Pete first attached each of the limb sleeves to the clamshell via the hiring and tubing harnesses. He then attached the four bottles—two large and two small—and inserted the heavy block in the matching receptacle on one side of the shell. He then attached what he assumed was the control module to the front of the clamshell. Orlin, Jerry and Jinx clustered around as he inserted the first power cell into the back of the suit.

Nothing happened.

"Are you sure—"

"—it's charged up?"

"Shut up, I charged them myself. They're not that different than the power cells for my mecha. They both registered peak charge when I tested them," answered Orlin.

"So, what—"

"—do we do now?"

"Insert the other one." Orlin nodded at Pete, who felt a prickling on his long tongue, a sure sign of anxiety. It was the Caldivar equivalent of a nervous sweat.

"I <choo> want <choo> to do <choo> a test <choo> first," Pete said. He had sneezed a couple of times since arriving at the workshop; now it seemed as if he couldn't stop. He'd felt the first signs of a respiratory infection the night before, but he'd hoped the medicine he'd taken that morning would suffice until they finished the day's testing. There was only one more week to complete the project and register it for the Maker Faire. He *needed* to test it today.

"Are you okay, Pete?"

Pete stared back at Jerry, dumbfounded. It was the first time in his experience that one of the twins had spoken a complete sentence on his own. Jinx looked on with a concerned expression. "It's okay, 'just a head cold' I think you'd call it."

"Sounds like more of a 'nose cold,' Jinx corrected. Pete was used to his friends teasing him about his long flexible snout, but Jinx seemed genuinely concerned. "That has got—"

"—to hurt," finished Jerry.

The surreal moment had passed. The twins were back to splitting sentences. "I'll be okay. Let me run this test, then plug in the other power cell."

He had a multiband spectral analyzer plugged into his slate. A check of the suit showed no activity. After pausing to sneeze a couple more times, he plugged in the second power cell. Again, the scanner showed no activity.

"It doesn't work," Pete muttered.

"Wait—"

"—look at this."

Jerry pointed to the odd rectangular block. A seam appeared in the otherwise solid block and was lit by a faint orange light. Meanwhile, the rectangular socket on the other side of the clamshell was pulsing with the same orange light. Jinx reached out to touch the block and it came apart at the seam.

"Maybe you should—"

"—plug this in—"

"—over there?"

Jinx handed the half block to Pete, who looked it over carefully. It was just like the original block, only half the size. There was no evidence it had ever been part of a larger object, yet strangely, it felt just as heavy as the original. He shrugged. "Might as well."

Once the block was plugged into the open socket, the light stopped pulsing, and a brief flicker showed on the screen of the control module. The multi-band scanner showed that there was some electronic activity in the control module, and a faint electromagnetic field emanating from torso of the suit.

Aside from that, there was no other indication or response from the suit.

"You have to—"

"—put it on."

"Yes, Pete." Orlin nodded concurrence with the twins. "This is the last part. You have to put it on to see how it works. You've done all of this work re-assembling and restoring it. Don't you want to see how it works?"

"To be honest, <choo> I been waiting <choo> to see what it does on its own, first." As soon as Pete got the last words out, he started a sneezing fit that lasted for almost a minute.

"Are you sure you're okay?" Orlin looked at him with concern, but then his expression turned into a smirk. "Or is this just an excuse to back out?"

"No balls," whispered Jinx.

"No balls." Jerry repeated the taunt with a bit more volume.

"Eff you, Lizard Face!" Pete managed between sneezes. "And you too, Monkey Twins!"

The sneezing and now the taunting were giving Pete a splitting headache. With a glare, he stomped over to the bench set up at the foot of the assembly table. The suit was attached to a rack that would lift it upright off of the table and over the bench, so that he could sit and just pull the clamshell down over his torso. It was too big around and too tall for him, but his hips were still slim enough at his age that the suit would settle over his shoulders and just hang halfway to his knees.

It was almost anticlimactic.

Almost.

The one unexpected occurrence was that as the clamshell slid down over his body, the surface separated into plates and readjusted to perfectly fit him. Then it just seemed to sit there.

Jinx ran the scanner over him while Jerry took a bunch of pictures with his slate. Orlin had been taking a continuous video recording, but the Human used a close-up setting to capture the details of the now-perfectly-adjusted suit.

"That's a whole lot of nothing," complained Pete.

"Yes, but now—"

"—your suit fits."

"You probably have to put the sleeves on." Orlin handed Pete the first of the four tubes, which now seemed to be sized exactly right for Pete.

Even with the full suit on, it didn't seem to do anything. On the other paw, it was now obvious that their earlier surmise that the suit would leave the hips and shoulders unprotected was incorrect. The torso appeared to have pauldrons to cover the shoulders right up to the top of the sleeves. The torso also extended over the groin and buttocks while the legs extended from ankles all the way over the pelvis and hip bones. The comparison with armor was apt, given that it seemed to cover everything except head, paws and feet, but it wasn't actually *protecting* him. They'd already determined that the fabric couldn't be cut by anything in their shop, but when Pete challenged Jinx to hit him in the stomach, the suit did absolutely nothing to block or lessen the blow.

That *hurt*!

At least, it hurt briefly. There was a slight flash of the chest display, but nothing else aside from a single green light at the top of the panel.

The suit was also hot. Caldivar didn't sweat like Humans, but he did start to pant from increased body temperature. Yet, almost as soon as he started, the suit seemed to cool off.

"It's cooling."

"Maybe it goes—"

"—under a spacesuit?"

"Whatever it is, it needs to wait until tomorrow," Pete said. "I've been feeling bad all day, and now I'm pretty tired. I just want to go home and sleep."

"Go ahead. We're headed out to Beggar's Canyon to field test Stomper and Zoomer tomorrow." Orlin used the names that Jerry and Jinx had applied to the mecha and two-seat flyer, respectively.

"Thanks." Pete sat back down on the bench and started pulling off the sleeves. He hung them on the rack, and almost before he could reach for the catches on the clamshell, it shifted back to the original, oversized configuration. Jinx hooked the storage rack to a loop just inside the collar of the torso while Jerry released a weighted arm that lifted the suit right off of the young Caldivar.

"Hey, did you—"

"—see that?"

"Some words—"

"—on the panel."

Pete turned to Orlin. "Did you get that on the video?" When his friend nodded, he continued, "Zip that over to my slate. I'll try to look at it later." The headache was receding, and it felt like he'd be able to manage not sneezing for a while, so he'd try to look at the video of the test when he got home. In fact, he wasn't feeling quite as tired, but he wasn't sure why.

As one last step for the evening, he and his friends removed the bottles and power cells from the suit. The rectangular blocks, however, did not want to come loose. In fact, it wasn't possible to detect the seams at the edges of the sockets. It was strange that the block had divided in tow, and now couldn't be removed—almost as if the suit had decided that those sockets needed to be filled and stay that way.

He'd worry about that tomorrow.

"Have you ever seen this script before?"

Cousin Breck was studying for his comprehensive exams, and made it clear that he was not to be disturbed, so Pete took the video still images to Troopmaster Zentto. The adult troop leader didn't recognize the symbols that had appeared on the control module of the suit, so he had referred the scout to an older human professor at Tretrayon Academy.

"It's an older machine script known as 'Roman,'" said Professor Gannon. "One of the variants of Earth Common from a few thousand years ago. Every once in a while we'll make contact with one of the Lost Colonies and their systems will use Roman. I have a book here somewhere."

The professor's office had something that Pete had never seen before—real, physical books. There were floor-to-ceiling shelves filled with the rectangular objects of various heights, lengths and widths. The professor carefully stood up from his desk and slowly moved to select one such book from a shelf. He laid it open on the desk and opened it to show the symbols printed on the individual pages. Unlike the classical books sometimes shown in old vid'tainment, these weren't actually made from the cellulose pulp that used to be known as "paper," but rather from a thin polymer not unlike the screen of a slate. The images weren't all static, either. Several pages contained searchable indices, and optical fibers displaying colored prompts helped identify locations with the book where searched text could be found.

The book was remarkable, but he hoped that the professor wasn't expecting him to take it and perform a translation by paw. The thought must have shown on his face, because Professor Gannon laughed and reached into a drawer, pulling out a long, thin cylinder, about one-half centime by eighteen centimeters. He tapped one end to the binding of the book, and both binding and cylinder pulsed green for a moment. He then took the cylinder, grabbed it in the middle, separating it lengthwise, revealing a thin membrane stretched between the two half-cylinders. The membrane was approximately the dimensions of as slate screen, and sure enough, the membrane adhered to the screen when placed over it.

"That's a translation filter. I programmed it with the Roman symbology. It will translate the symbols for you, and may even be able to interpret some of the words, but I must caution you." Gannon looked at Pete sternly, and lifted one eyebrow. "It may not be a dialect of Common that you are familiar with. If these symbols come from a Lost World Artifact, there's no telling how much the language has drifted. Good luck, son."

Pete thanked him and headed back home from the university. He was tempted to visit Breck just to see how he was doing, but he got a "Do Not Disturb" response when he tried to text his cousin. Well then, he'd just have to inform Breck of his results on another day.

ONCE BACK IN THE workshop, Pete started to work on the translation. In all, Orlin had captured five different video sequences where symbols appeared on the screen of the control module. Pete had begged off on the testing today, and his patrol-mates had headed off to the canyon on their own. They still had five more days, so Pete was going to get this translation done this afternoon while his friends were out.

The professor was correct, the translator overlay converted the symbols, but the words were unfamiliar. They seemed as if he should know them, however, and a couple of hours on the 'net searching thousand years-old Earth Common dialects gave him some rough translations.

The first text had appeared when the rectangular block had split. The translation didn't make a lot of sense:

Nanite source unbalanced.

The next sequence occurred when the clamshell resized itself to his body:

Biomorphic adjustment, species 1732, juvenile.

The third message was quite a bit longer, and appeared soon after he'd finished pulling on all of the sleeves:

Allergen detected.

Imidazole-ethanamide levels elevated.

Eicosanoid PgI levels elevated.

Administer antihistamine and cyclooxygenase inhibitor.

He didn't know all of the words, but Pete knew that some of them were medical terms. The fourth message was more of the same:

Blunt impact trauma. Tissue damage. Organ bruising.

Administer hematoma nanites 1732.42.

Temperature imbalance. Cooling.

The final message put it all in perspective:

Treatment complete.

If Pete was interpreting these messages correctly, he had actually been seriously hurt when he had Jinx punch him in the stomach.

The suit had treated the injury, and all he'd felt was a brief pain from the impact. A few more minutes on the 'net revealed that he'd been in the middle of an allergy attack when he'd first donned the suit. It diagnosed and treated his sneezes and headache.

No wonder he'd felt better by the time he finished testing that day.

He still wasn't sure what was meant by "nanite source unbalanced" but apparently both sockets needed to be filled with the dense material, so maybe that was the nanite source. As for "species 1732" that was likely a reference to being a Caldivar. After all, he *was* a juvenile and hadn't reached his full adult height yet.

With this new knowledge, Pete decided to put the power cells back in and don the suit to see if he could get any other responses. Sure, he was healthy now, but the only time he'd really gotten a response was when he was wearing it.

He propped his slate up on the workbench where he could see it, and detached the video pickup so that he could place it in position to view the chest readouts. He then sat on the bench and pulled the clamshell down over his head. Once again it configured himself to his body, and he saw "Biomorphic adjustment, species 1732, juvenile," followed by a new message that read: "Health check complete, no treatment needed."

Okay, so he was healthy. Now he needed to see if he could get any other response. After about an hour of trying to get a response from the control module—and succeeding to a limited extent—he translated a message that read:

Enhanced Medical Technician Operator Interface (Y/N)?

Pete figured there was nothing to lose, so he tapped on the symbol that was being translated as the letter "Y" in Earth Common. Almost immediately he noticed a prickling sensation in his paws and that his vision was sharper. He looked closely at the mottled gray skin of his paws, and noticed a very fine network of fibers, terminating in what looked like sensor pads on the tips of his digits. Looking in the video playback from this slate camera, he noticed a similar network on his cheeks, and leading up to his lower two eyes. When he touched the skin of his face to see what the fibers were, he immediately began to see a readout of skin temperature, moisture content, hydration, pulse, respiration rate, and other body conditions. The test showed up directly in his vision.

More surprisingly, it was in Caldivar Upper, the technical language of his people. All Caldivar learned to read Caldi-Up at the same time they learned Earth Common. Even if their particular community mostly most Caldi-Low, Caldi-Up was used for all scientific, technical and engineering communication. If you were educated, you knew Caldi-Up. He supposed he shouldn't be surprised. This had to be another feature of the Suit. It knew he was Caldivar, thus it was communicating in the appropriate language.

He noticed that it was getting dark. Orlin and the twins weren't back yet. He wondered why they were out so long. It would have long since been dark down in the canyon by now, and if they had left when the light failed, they should be back by now.

He no sooner had the thought than he heard the whine of an approaching flyer. It *sounded* like the thrusters the twins had mounted in Zoomer, but it also sounded like they were unbalanced. There was a vibration that he could almost feel, and one of the thrusters seemed to be sputtering as if it had an uneven fuel feed. He stepped outside to greet his friends and find out what had happened to the flyer, and was shocked at the appearance of a badly damaged vehicle with only one occupant. One of the twins was in the cockpit, and from the appearance, he was having difficulty controlling the vehicle.

"Jerry? Or Jinx? What happened?"

The Human, Jinx—as evidenced by a small scar on his chin, the only distinguishing feature between the two—was smeared in blood and was holding his left arm close to his body. It didn't look right, and Pete noticed a new set of symbols appearing in his vision. He didn't have time to pay attention to those just yet, as he tried to pay attention to what Jinx was saying.

"Pete come quick—" He paused, as if waiting for his twin to finish the sentence. He gulped as he realized that he was alone for one of the few times in his life. "Jerry's hurt, but Orlin's hurt *bad*. Stomper crashed into Zoomer and we both hit the canyon wall." We need your help to get Orlin out of his mecha so we can get him to medical help."

Pete took in the information, and then noticed the text flashing in his lower right vision:

Probable osteo fracture. Contact diagnostics needed.

"Hold on, Jinx, let me help you." Jinx was trying to slide out of the pilot position. He winced every time he had to move his left arm. Pete touched him on the shoulder and was rewarded with more diagnostic information:

Compound fracture, left radius, simple fracture, left ulna.
Subcutaneous hematoma. No internal injuries.

He felt his left sleeve begin to loosen, and then it split lengthwise down the middle.

Limb component L1 configured for independent operation.
Place splint on injured limb and activate.
Continue? (Y/N).

He tried to concentrate on the text in his vision. How was he supposed to respond to something projected directly at his eyes? There was no physical symbol to touch or tap?

The sleeve was threatening to fall off, so he grabbed at it with his right paw. The fabric, tubing, wires and all, easily came loose from the clamshell. The ports in the edge of the carapace appeared to have come with it, since the connections terminated in a small rectangular block similar to the "nanite source" blocks.

That must be the "independent operation" part. He carefully placed it over Jinx's left arm and attempted to seal it. It appeared to have dilated to even larger than its resting state, so Pete just settled for overlapping the two edges. It must have been enough, because the moment he did so, the sleeve tightened and the embedded tubing became rigid, forming a hard splint to realign and support the broken bone.

Jinx gave out a quick "Agh!" of pain as the sleeve stiffened, then a relaxed sigh.

Pete saw:

Fracture immobilized.

and:

Analgesic administered.

in his vision.

"Okay, let's get moving." Pete climbed into the pilot station of the flyer. Yeah, it was rough, but he'd assisted the twins with the assembly—they'd each helped each other with the projects—so he should be able to fly it out to the canyon. "Beggar's Canyon, right? Where in the canyon?"

"Down by the thermal ports."

It was a region of turbulent winds, fueled by geothermal vents that vented hot gases into an already narrow stretch of canyon.

"What the hell were you fools doing down there? You were supposed to stay up near the moisture extractors!"

"Everything was going so well, we decided to step up the testing to the next level. Stomper was so stable and Zoomer so responsive that we thought that a little bit of wind wouldn't hurt."

Pete just shook his head.

During the twenty-minute flight out to the canyon, Jinx continued to talk about the testing, never once mentioning—or noticing—that Pete was wearing the suit and one arm was currently serving as a cast on the Human's arm.

Pete just thought about what he would do... what he *could* do... once they were at the canyon. He'd brought his slate. In fact, as he had been trying to figure out where to carry it, a pocket opened up on the front of the clamshell. Before leaving the workshop, he'd triggered the emergency locator beacon on the slate, sending it to his parents, Troopmaster Zentto, and Cousin Breck. He'd used a code that indicated that he, personally, was okay, but that he needed assistance. The adults could track his slate to find them. Hopefully they could get there before it was too late.

When they reached Beggar's Canyon, Pete set the flyer down a cautious distance from the Thermal Ports and walked the rest of the way with Jinx. They found the wrecked mecha with Jerry sitting beside it. Orlin's face was barely visible through the open visor of the combat armor. His face was very pale, the normally blue-green scales tinged with gray, and his eyes were closed. Jerry was pale as well. He tried to stand when the pair approached, but his right leg wouldn't support his weight.

A red circle appeared in Pete's vision superimposed over Jerry's knee, but it was when he looked at what he could see of Orlin that the display was filled with alerts and flashing indicators. Since he already had an inkling of the suit's response, he stepped up to Jerry and placed a paw over his knee.

Ruptured right anterior cruciate ligament.

The right leg sleeve loosened, and as he had anticipated, his visual display said:

Limb component R2 configured for independent operation.
Place splint on injured limb and activate.
Continue? (Y/N).

It occurred to him that he still didn't know how he was supposed to respond to the query. On Jinx, he'd simply put the sleeve on the injured limb and the suit did the rest.

Once again, he removed the expanded sleeve. He wrapped it around Jerry's leg, but this time he was able to mate the edges together. The sleeve sealed itself up and inflated. He saw the confirmation message and the information that medication had been delivered.

Now for Orlin. One of the arms of the mecha had come loose at the shoulder joint. Pete and the now-mobile Jerry carefully removed the mechatronic limb, exposing the Prithmar's scaly skin.

Pete touched Orlin's arm, and the display started scrolling a large amount of information. It stopped and then flashed an instruction to remove the right arm sleeve and apply it to his badly injured patrol-mate. This time he noticed that the fittings for the large and small bottles on that side also came loose from the clamshell when he pulled off the sleeve. Once the sleeve was on Orlin, his vision displayed several long messages. Each paused in his vision just long enough for him to see and understand it before the next message appeared.

Severe trauma and shock.

Concussion.

Multiple internal injuries.

Internal bleeding.

Multiple compound fractures.

Blood pressure low, administering Flurodec volume expander.

WARNING: Leak in FLURODEC reservoir.

Leak is within tolerable limits. Continue? (Y/N)

There was a vaguely sweet smell in the air, and he could hear a slight hissing. It was the fluorocarbon tank. There must have been a hidden crack. He concentrated on the Yes/No query, and saw the Y flash green. The readout continued:

Multiple internal injuries.

Medical stasis required. Trauma nanites required.

Remove central somatic unit and place on patient.

Continue? (Y/N)

Central somatic? Oh. Soma meant body. He needed to put the clamshell on Orlin, but they needed to get him out of the damaged mecha first. He concentrated on N and saw it flash ready. The question remained in his vision.

"We have to get him out of there. Jerry? Jinx? How do we get him out?"

"There's an emergency eject—"

"—under his chin. But I didn't want to do that before help got here. I think a piece of the hatch is sticking into him. I didn't want to him to start bleeding when I pulled it out."

Pete looked at jerry, surprised at the long speech without his twin's interruption.

"You mean 'start bleeding more...'" Jinx added.

Jerry looked down at the blood on his shirt, pants, and on the front of the mecha.

"Well, we have to get him out. I can't say for certain that he won't start bleeding some more, but the only way to treat him is to get him out of there, and get this," Pete rapped his knuckles on the chest plate of the suit "onto him."

No sooner had he uttered the words, than his display signaled:

Patient stability limited. Current blood loss within acceptable limits.

Place central somatic unit on patient within the next fifteen minutes.

Additional Flurodec blood substitute being administered to compensate for removal of primary impalement.

Proceed with patient extraction.

The last sentence wasn't a question. It was a command.

"Okay, guys, let's pop the lid. Once it's open, you lift him out and I'll slip the clamshell over him." The moment he said it, the catches on the torso of the suit popped open, and the plates rearranged into a larger volume to accommodate their injured friend.

There was indeed a projection of the suit hatch penetrating Orlin's body. The moment the cover came open, there was a spurt of blood, and the hissing sound increased.

Pete pulled the clamshell over his head and was surprised to see that a small ring of suit material remained around his neck, connected to the network of fibers on his paws and face.

Okay, I guess that's how he would continue to control the suit.

The three youth managed to get Orlin free enough from the mecha to get the clamshell over his upper body. Once lowered over his form, it configured itself to whatever parts of the Prithmar's body that it could contact. A continuous stream of diagnostics and treatments scrolled through Pete's vision and stopped with one final message:

Trauma Nanites type 2460.9 administered.

Medical stasis achieved. Transport patient to medical facility.

EMT Mk XI service required at conclusion of independent operation.

The text blinked for a minute, and then was replaced by a graphical readout of Orlin's pulse and respiration rate, blood pressure, body temperature, and oxygen saturation rate. A new displayed appeared in his upper eye, depicting a map of the region with a flashing icon moving toward the canyon. Pete knew that somehow, the suit had interfaced with his slate and was tracking the adults racing to their position.

Now that all three boys were treated, and help was on the way, Pete stopped to look around at the crash site.

It was completely dark.

It had been maybe an hour since Jinx had arrived at the workshop—dusk up on the plains, but well into night down here in the canyon. It would have been completely dark even before they arrived, but he'd been able to see perfectly throughout the whole rescue. Caldivar had good night vision, after all, they were a burrowing species, but it didn't explain the fact that the only reason he knew it was dark was because of the color of the sky.

His own vision might have been a result of the suit's optical fibers enhancing his vision, but what about Jerry and Jinx? They seemed to be able to see pretty well, too.

"Now that your body—"

"—isn't glowing like daylight—"

"—can we turn on a light?"

ZERITH FARNOG HAD RETURNED to Joth as a special guest presenter for the Joth Maker Faire. The Prithmar was one of Salvage System President Tomeral's closest friends, and had been an important part of construction and innovation that had helped President Tomeral defeat first the Squilla threatening Tretra and Joth, but also the Squilla home world, not to mention the Krith and the Gritloth. He was one of the principal shareholders of Tomeral and Associates, and shared the company's reputation for hating bullies, but supporting sophonts struggling to be self-reliant. It had once been rumored that he was responsible for establishing the Maker Faire, but it was just that, a rumor. On the other paw, his parent's company, Farnog Corp, was one of the main sponsors for the youth category.

Zerith had to stand on a platform to be able to place the Special Award medallion over Pete's head. Troopmaster Zentto had already pinned on his Maker Merit Badge and his new Senior Class rank insignia, as well as recognition for lifesaving. Now it was time for the *big* moment.

"Pettekil Emil. It is my pleasure to award you this Special Award for your discovery, restoration and most importantly, analysis of the Trauma Suit. While Maker Faire awards are generally for sophonts who make their entries from components, the Maker Faire Council has decided that your work in restoring the Emergency Medical Technician Mark XI support garment is worth recognition. The last of these suits was thought lost more than two thousand years ago. To find one and recognize what it was—not to mention restoring it to working order *before* you knew what it was—is a remarkable achievement. Thanks to your work, we not only have a working suit, but also the information we need to duplicate it.

"For that, Joth, Tretra, Farnog Corp and Tomeral and Associates thank you."

The audience started to applaud, and Pete felt a flush of embarrassment. He suppressed the urge to sneeze. There was no point in starting that again, although...

About thirty seconds in The Suit would take care of that.

Three
Cheating the Odds

Authors note: For the second *Salvage Title* anthology, Kevin asked me to continue the story of Pete, Orlin, Jerry, and Jinx. We jump forward a few years after the events of *The Suit*. The boys are now in military training, undergoing a survival exercise.

Pete is not allowed to bring the full suit along. This is supposed to test their ability to survive and improvise without tech. But Pete believes in the old adage: "If you ain't cheating, you ain't trying." And sometimes, when the odds are against you, a little cheat may be exactly what saves the day.

"This-s is most definitely *not* my idea of camping. It'ss too wet, it'ss too cool, it'ss too... foresssty." Orlin was complaining, pretty much the same as he had ever since the drop pods had deposited them in Tretra's equatorial jungle. "I thought s-survival training was done in deserts-s? I can *handle* deserts-s."

"Actually, that's why survival training for Joth natives is conducted on Tretra," replied Pete. "Tretra natives complete the Extreme Environment Survival Exercise—EESE School on Joth, we do it on Tretra. The whole *point* is to push us to an environment we are adapted to."

"Besides it's not—," began Jerry.

"—supposed to be just 'camping,'" finished Jinx.

Jerry and Jinx were human twins, and had a very bad habit of finishing each other's sentences. It was enough to give a sophont whiplash. They were also the youngest of the quartet.

Orlin was a Prithmar, lizard-like, and technically the oldest of the group, but his kind didn't count the year spent as an undeveloped newt, before their neural ganglia differentiated into their species' equivalent of a brain. As it was, he realistically edged out the twins by about six months in developmental age, even as they held the height advantage.

Pete—only his mother called him Pettekil—was a Caldivar, anteater like with a long flexible nose and three eyes. He was also older than the twins by more than a year, and older than Orlin by two months, as long as one didn't count the latter's year as a newt. For that sin, and one other, he had been named Squad Leader for this exercise.

The "other sin" occurred just under two years ago when he had been working on Maker Merit Badge, discovered an odd protective suit in a salvage yard and reconditioned it. Thinking it to be a protective garment for firefighters, he had been surprised to discover that it was a product of a Lost Technology—an emergency medical technician's field wearable aid kit. For his ingenuity and level-headedness in rescuing his companions when all three were injured testing their own Maker Badge refurbishments, Pete had been awarded many honors, including a guaranteed place in The Academy run by Tomeral and Associates. After graduation next year, he would train with the Tretrayon military for two years, then transfer to Salvage System for the rest of his study. Pete had a guaranteed spot, but Orlin, Jerry and Jinx still had to earn their own—but with a considerable boost from their own Maker projects as well as their roles in helping Pete with the EMT suit.

The past two years had been uncertain, but as of the end of the most recent school year, they'd learned that all four would be heading to The Academy on graduation. Thus, they had to spend the summer preparing for the physical challenges of Salvage System's unique service, and one of those preparations was Survival School. Pete's seniority both by developmental age and his incoming-cadet ranking put him in charge of their cadet squad for this training exercise.

Most of the Tretrayon Academy cadets did their survival far from the urban and temperate climate of home, in other words, on Tretra's sister world of Joth. However, those who grew up in the sparsely-populated hot, arid deserts of Joth were sent to the forests and jungles of Tretra to learn emergency survival skills; hence why Pete and his squad found themselves in a high-elevation cloud-forest, dealing with chilling wet conditions and unable to see much of the sky or horizon.

"I'm cold," said Jerry and Jinx simultaneously, for once not speaking in tag-term fashion.

Pete checked his wrist-comp. "Well, we're at twenty-four hundred meters elevation. We might be pretty much *on* the equator, but the altitude means it's going to get chilly tonight. Let's go ahead and make camp, it will be night in about an hour. The instructors said we should always make camp when there was enough light for not just pitching shelters, but also for anything else we need to do afterward.

The "need to do afterward" meant trying to fix a meal, and that meant trying to find something to eat. All four of the "boys" could eat fruit, nuts and berries. Prithmar were largely vegetarian, and like many of his race, Orlin was constantly snacking on a particularly crunchy or juicy fruit or vegetable at home. He'd been grumbling about the lack of snacks for the past day. Jerry and Jinx were omnivores, and it had been said that humans would eat anything that wasn't tied down. As a Caldivar, Pete was also an omnivore, but a little fussier about where his protein came from. At home they had Tretrayon vat-meat, as well as domesticated herds of small Joth desert animals and cool-house-raised agriculture. When traveling, there were always full-calorie meal bars. The Tretrayon version were pretty bland, but the new ones coming from Salvage System were said to be nutritious *and* delicious.

Unfortunately, this was a survival exercise and none of that was available. They had water purification systems and electrolyte tablets, vitamins suitable for several species, and had been allowed one supplement. Naturally, Orlin had chosen Joobla Oil for his supplement. The incredibly spicy oil was much too strong for Pete and the twins, but Orlin said it made most food "just barely palatable." Pete had opted for a concentrated protein paste. He and Orlin gathered local fruits, nuts and berries. That would save his delicate stomach the indignity of eating grilled forest rodent—or worse, raw forest rodent—for a few more days. Jinx and Jerry had packed something called "curry" and were currently cooking a fragrant stew from scavenged roots and the meat of an arboreal rodent with a large bushy tail.

After they cleaned up the remnants of their meal, Orlin snuggled into his insulating thermal shelter. The exothermic Joth native was at a distinct disadvantage in this environment. Jerry and Jinx should have fared much better, humans had adapted to every environment, as long as they had breathable air. Unfortunately, the best way to described the twins was "spoiled." They'd lived on hot, arid Joth all of their lives, and were shivering even in their heavy garments. It surprised Pete that of the quartet, he felt the least discomfort, even though the air was much wetter than his race's desert home-world. Dry air produced extreme temperature swings, so the cold wasn't an issue, just the humidity, and even that could be handled with the appropriate clothing.

It might be a survival experience, but it was a challenge, and Pete was in his element.

THE EARLY MORNING SUN filtered through the trees and started a chorus of chirps, trills, squeaks and caws. Orlin was still in the warm embrace of his shelter. Pete could hear him snoring. Jerry and Jinx were moving around in their tent, the mosquito netting at the entrance still firmly closed, so they were probably applying insect repellant. Orlin and Pete didn't need it, none of the Tretrayon insects could penetrate the Prithmar's scales or the Caldivar's tough skin.

Pete had chosen to hang a hammock from two sturdy trees. The airflow above and below his nesting place had helped keep the humidity tolerable, and it also helped him keep an eye on the rest of "his" squad. He looked up and saw motion in the tops of the trees—birds from the sound. There was a slight rustling sound off to the south. That was likely another of the arboreals like the one Jerry and Jinx cooked last night.

Speaking of which...

"Uh, my stomach—"

"—doesn't feel right."

The boys quickly unzipped and raced out of their tent to the bushes over where they'd dug the hygiene trench the night before. The sound of retching was quickly replaced with groans, and then with argument.

"I told you to cook the *skwirl* some more."

"—and I told you it was too tough and stringy. Well done would have been impossible to chew."

"Not if it makes us sick!"

"It wasn't the *skwirl*, it was the *mushrunes*. I warned you they were poisonous."

"It wasn't the *mushrunes*, but those *toobers* were questionable..."

"Actually, I think you both ate too much." Pete climbed down from his perch, his long nose wrinkling at the smell from the hygiene area. "Now I know why your sister always refers to you by a single name... 'Jerx.' You're both acting like it. Besides, you used so much curry powder, there's no way anything could have survived. In fact, I can still smell it." He held up a paw and pinched the end of his long, anteater-like proboscis.

Jerry turned to look, and his skin paled. He turned for the hygiene trench and retched again, soon followed by Jinx.

"We can't have you two doing that. You'll be weak and dehydrated before we get to the extraction point. It's only two more nights and fifteen kilometers, but you're not going to be able to make it this way.

"If only you had—"

"—your EMT suit!"

"Y-You kn-know th-they'd n-never h-have l-let h-him k-keep it," came a new voice, teeth chattering in the cold morning air.

"Well, good morning, Orlin. Did you sleep well?"

"F-F-Fargle y-you, P-Pete, I w-was n-nice and w-warm in there, but I couldn't s-stand listening to Jerx-ss argue!" Orlin's shivering seemed to calm down, but his species' characteristic lisp came back in its absence.

"You're right, the suit is at Farnog Corp, back on Joth." He started rummaging in his pack, and pulled out a pair of heavy gloves custom designed for Caldivar paws. "But everyone brought their own pair of gloves, right?" He held up a pair of gloves made of a dull gray fabric. The cuffs were wide and thicker than the opening of the cuff. He put them on and they shrank to fit. A fine thread of silver extended from each glove, climbed his arm and joined just at the base of his neck. Another thread climbed from the junction up to the side of Pete's head and formed a small cluster at the base of his lower right eye.

"Ooh, me first!" said Jerry. "I'm sickest."

"No, me," responded Jinx.

Pete turned his third eye, the uppermost one, toward Orlin and rolled it. It was a talent he had perfected over the years of friendship with the human twins.

"How about two at a time?" Pete placed one gloved paw on the arm of each of the boys. "Ooh, it's not the *skwirl* or the *mushrunes*. You've got a water-based bacterium. Were you drinking water straight out of the stream?"

"Well, sure—"

"—it's so clean—"

"—we didn't think—"

"—it would be a problem."

"You didn't think. Why did we expect anything less of you, *Jerx*?" interrupted Orlin.

"I wouldn't talk," Pete addressed the Prithmar. "You've got scale-rot at the base of your neck. Did you use your antifungal spray last night?"

"No" Orlin looked about as sheepish as a six-foot tall lizard could manage.

"Well, let me get everyone fixed up so that we can finish packing camp and get moving to the extraction zone."

"Isn't that cheating?" Orlin pointed to the gloves.

"Well, we're expected to carry a first-aid kit, and before we do the advanced EESE school on Salvage, we'll be trained in a lot more so-phisticated treatment. Besides, they're talking about deploying EMT Mark XIs with all Salvage teams before we even *get* to the Academy. I understand the Bolts will even have a version with fluorescent blue lightning all over it."

"Good. Me first then—"

"—no, me—"

The twins went back to arguing. Pete motioned to Orlin. "Let's treat that scale fungus, okay?"

BY MID-DAY THEY HAD descended almost a thousand meters, and the temperatures were rising quite a bit. They were approaching a small river that they were supposed to ford, then ascend another five hundred meters to their evening camp near the summit of a ridge separating the outback region from their extraction point. The final day would have them descend almost two-thousand meters to the edge of the equatorial plain. Temperatures by that point would be approaching that of some of the cooler regions of Joth, but with nearly one-hundred percent humidity. Dehydration would be one of their major concerns, along with the possibility of falls and twisted ankles from the rapid descent. They had one more night at high elevation, and then one nearly at sea level.

After sun-up on the third day, they could safely activate their emergency locator beacon without washing out of the course. If they were within two kilometers of the base camp when they activated the beacon, they'd be given directions to the extraction point via the two-way radio in the beacon. That would earn them the maximum points for the course. If they were further away when the beacon was activated, extraction could come to them, but they'd lose points. If they encountered a true emergency at any time, the beacon would summon rescue, but whether they failed out or had to repeat would be determined by a review of the emergency itself. Pete was determined that his squad would earn the highest possible score for this exercise, and kept the beacon locked away in its protective box. He knew it tracked and monitored them anyway, but he wasn't about to risk accidently triggering it before the appropriate time.

Which made it oh, so difficult when Jerry almost fell over the injured man.

He was human, middle aged, so he wasn't one of the EESE students. He was lying near the edge of a small stream that joined the river about twenty meters from their chosen crossing point. He was unconscious, most likely due to the large discolored bruise on his left temple, and had bled a fair amount from a scalp wound just above his left ear.

"Do you think—"

"—he's an examiner?" asked Jerry and Jinx.

"He's-ss too old to be a s-student, and not in an EESE-ss insstructor uniform," Orlin replied, coming over to investigate.

"He seems to have fallen here. There's blood on this rock." Pete pointed to a red and brown-stained rock the size of two human fists. He poked at it with the stick he'd been using to steady himself during the morning's descent. "He didn't fall on it, though. There's blood on the underside."

"...Unless-ss it fell with him," supplied Orlin.

"Or that. Hmm." Pete bent and examined the man with all three eyes. "He's breathing a bit slow, and there's no sign of other injuries of broken bones. He's not lying in a position that suggests he was moved, though. There's not much disturbed vegetation, so he hasn't moved on his own since this happened." He reached over and touched the scalp laceration, and peered closely with his upper eye, the one with greater acuity. "He's been here long enough that the insects have gotten into the wound."

"S-so get out your magic gloves-ss and fix him."

"But what if—"

"—this is a test?"

"Maybe, but this might also be too much for just the gloves. After all, it took half of the suit to stabilize you," Pete looked pointedly at Orlin.

"True, but I had internal injuries-ss, too."

"Point." Pete crouched down and pressed a paw to the man's neck to check the man's pulse. It was slow and weak. He touched the skin of the man's cheek, and there was no twitch. He tapped his fingers in the inside of the elbow and saw a faint muscle twitch. He then took hold of one hand, extended one of his claws and pressed down right in the center of a fingernail. He held it long enough to watch the skin turn white, then released the pressure and counted how long it took for the skin to turn pink again.

As the other three boys watched in amazement, Pete switched sides and repeated the tests with the other arm and hand, and then again with both legs. Instead of taking the man's boots off, he did the pressure test on the side of the leg just above the boot-top.

"Where did you learn—"

"—to do that?"

"You've been s-studying."

Ever since Pete had found the EMT suit, he'd gotten interested in medicine. His cousin Breck was a graduate student and had helped him with the materials for the suit. After they'd been recognized for the restoration job on the rare medical mecha, Breck had also introduced his younger cousin to several of the professors, many of whom had asked about future educational plans. Despite still being in high school, he'd wondered aloud about studying and becoming a flight surgeon. That had led to more introductions, and some "extracurricular" lessons and reading assignments. He still wasn't sure if that's what he wanted to do after The Academy, but he'd learned a lot over the past two years.

"Okay, his breathing and heart rate are slow and faint, but steady. Reflexes are good, so it's unlikely he has a neck or back injury. Reperfusion is delayed, so his blood pressure is low. He's certainly not faking it."

Pete took off his pack and reached for the gloves. In doing so, he touched the housing with the emergency beacon. He could activate the transmitter and call in a rescue for the injured man. He supposed he could ask the rescue party to allow his squad to continue and finish the exercise, but he wasn't sure if they'd be allowed.

Let's just see what the diagnostics say, first.

The familiar display formed in front of his right-side, lower eye. There was a flashing yellow message instructing him to touch one glove to the injured man for more complete diagnostics. He blinked and shifted his focus several times to dismiss several "helpful" offers to put an alert on the EMT network to call in assistance. Pete had to likewise cancel queries for retrieving additional EMT Mark XI components, and to refer the patient for immediate medical assistance.

Finally, he convinced the limited artificial intelligence of the gloves to list the standard, unassisted first aid that they could administer on their own. The nanite reservoir in the cuffs of the gloves was severely limited, and all that could be administered was a pain reliever and a drug to maintain blood pressure. If and when the man woke up, they would have to get him to eat and drink to restore his strength.

Now, how were they going to get him out of here?

"It's called a TRA-viss—"

"—no, a tra-VOYSE!"

"Technically, it is-ss a tra-VWAH."

"Guys, I know what a travois is." Pete held up a paw to stop the argument. "However, I don't think that bumping this man along a mountain trail is going to be good for his injuries."

"So, we pull it on the smooth dirt trails—" began Jerry.

"—and carry both end over the rocks," finished Jinx

"Oh. Okay, that makes more sense."

"Besides, it's no different than the stretcher relay we ran at last year's Scout competition." Orlin was busy trimming side branches off of two long poles while the twins skinned some vines to use as rope.

"You guys *do* realize we each have rope, right?" Pete held up a coil of brightly-colored rope. The thin synthetic line was issued to each EESE student along with their camping gear.

"Actually, we should save that in case we have to lift or lower the travois," Orlin said as he started to lash sticks together to form the litter.

"Don't worry—"

"—we know—"

"—what we're doing—"

"—mostly."

It actually seemed as if they did know what they were doing. Their patrol, the Crockables, usually won troop competitions and had represented their troop many times in the regional games. When they weren't bickering, the boys worked well together. Pete decided he should gather some wide, flat leaves, and once the litter took shape, he and the twins wove a mat to cushion the injured human.

The travois worked the way it was supposed to, and the human twins, being the tallest of them, took turns pulling or lifting the litter as they headed for the ridge where they'd spend the night. When the trail became particularly steep, one of the twins would place the poles of the litter on his shoulders, and lift the downhill side while Orlin or Pete, being shorter, would take the uphill side. In this manner, they kept the still-unconscious stranger relatively level and free of bumps and jolts.

As evening approached, they found a campsite and set up much as they had the previous night. Jerry and Jinx donated some mosquito netting, and they rigged a tarp and netting around the litter for the night.

The next morning, the man stirred for a bit, and spoke in an odd language that their translators didn't recognize. His eyes didn't focus, and didn't really seem aware of his surroundings, so they weren't entirely sure that he wasn't simply delirious. The twins did manage to get him to drink some purified water and Pete contributed some of his protein paste.

"Do you think—"

"—we should break out The Brick?"

It was a concentrated emergency ration issued with the rest of their gear. The Marine who'd briefed them mentioned that it was the "only food supply they'd ever need to carry," mostly because "an intelligent being will eat *anything* before resorting to The Brick!" It was heavy and textured like an extremely dense bread or cake, and filled with small bits of fruit and nuts. It was extremely shelf-stable, and there were rumors of Bricks that had been handed down in certain families for generations.

"Ugh. No. Anything but the Brick. Besides, I don't have a chisel to break it into small enough pieces."

"We just thought—"

"—since we're using—"

"—your protein paste—"

"—that you might need something else!"

Pete shuddered. "No. No thanks, I can manage for another day."

"I wonder—"

"—does Brick go with curry?"

Pete shuddered again, and looked over at Orlin, who was doing his own version of rolling his eyes at the twins. He went to his pack and pulled out the EMT gloves again. He put a paw on the injured man, but noticed that he didn't see the normal head's-up display in his lower, right eye. He touched his cheek and the customary trace of nanites wasn't there. There were red lights flashing on the cuffs of both gloves, and he bent his left, lower eye—the one he usually used for fine detail—to read the tiny display.

Nanite supply exhausted, seek immediate medical attention.

That wasn't good. They still had today's descent to the equatorial plain, and then one more night before pickup. If he got any worse, they'd need to use the emergency beacon no matter what that did to their scores.

THE SUN WAS ALREADY down as they approached the location for the night's camp. They'd lost time when the stretcher lashings failed and they had to rebuild it. The downhill hike had been difficult. It was too rocky to drag the litter, so Orlin and Pete took turns carrying the uphill end, while the twins traded off with the downhill end. In the afternoon they'd come to the bank of a wide river. Pete's record of their course said that their goal was downstream, but across the river. There had been nothing in the briefing about crossing something that deep or swift, so they decided to follow the riverbank downstream for a while and hope that the river turned away from their direction of travel. After all, there was no sense in crossing the river only to discover they would have to cross back.

Sure enough, the river turned, and Pete recorded their position in his log. The destination should now be straight ahead, so even though it was getting late, they had a relatively clear path along the riverbank. They decide to press on to get absolutely as close as possible for the morning pick-up.

Much to their surprise, just as the last light was fading from the sky, they noticed artificial lights ahead and emerged from the densely forest of the past few days to an open plain, with the buildings of a large city on the far horizon. That must be Forest City, where they'd arrived four days ago. The lights they'd seen were from several military vehicles that appeared to be setting up a camp of their own.

Was this the extraction point? Had they accidently found the exact *spot they needed?*

A Prithmar Marine looked up and noticed the quartet walking out of the woods carrying the litter. "Well, well. You're early, but it looks like you've had a casualty."

Pete came to attention and saluted. "Cadet Corporal Pettekil Emil. We found an injured human and packed him out with us."

The soldier laughed. "At ease, Cadet. I'm a private, you don't need to salute. Private First Class Makk." When Pete relaxed, she approached and looked at the litter. "Hmm, well, you're here, so I guess that's good for him. Let me get a couple of stretcher bearers to get this one over to the medic trailer, I think they're just about set up. You might as well head over to the blue trailer. It's the check-in point. Not sure if being early is going to count against you, but no-one can fault your navigation. If you'd gotten here an hour earlier, you would have beaten us to the spot."

Ah. That explained it. Pete thought to himself. *They move in after dark when we're all supposed to be in camp. That way they don't give away the target coordinates.*

After a moment's thought, Pete figured he needed to stay in character as squad leader. "Cadets Orlin, Jerry and Jinx. Take the stretcher to the medic trailer. I will check us in."

The boys brought themselves to attention and saluted, much to the amusement of the Marine private. She nevertheless directed the boys toward the medic, and turned and saluted Pete with a smile. "I believe Top would say 'carry on' at this point, Cadet."

If the First Sergeant was surprised to see cadets in his camp one night early, he didn't show it. He took Pete's report, then examined the navigation logbook. He reached for his slate and tapped a few comments, then grunted. Looking up at Pete, he said, "Son, I've been running the EESE school of cadets for five years, and SERE school for Marines for the past decade. I have *never* had a squad turn up on my doorstep early. I *did* have to move the extraction point one course because a squad was camped about 50 meters away. They didn't have a watch set, though, and they woke up with our trucks and trailers surrounding them. It cost them a few points."

Pete felt his face begin to flush—despite his leathery skin—as he thought of the past two nights when all four of them had slept through the night. He continued to stand at attention, trying not to look directly at the first sergeant.

A faint hint of a smile appeared on the NCO's face. "I thought so," he said, "but that's a Marine thing, we don't worry about that too much with you cadets. Now, let's talk about your casualty…"

The next hours turned into an extensive debrief about when and where they'd found the injured human, and the decision to carry him out. Orlin, Jerry and Jinx were summoned to give their version, then the Marine doctor came in and questioned Pete about his first aid and field diagnosis. Pete didn't reveal that he had used the gloves from his EMT suit, but he was able to justify his decisions with the advanced first aid and field medicine he'd been studying on his own with the professors his cousin had introduced him to on Joth.

It was approaching midnight when the first sergeant and the captain-doctor seemed satisfied with the debrief. "Ok, Cadets. Private Makk will show you to the bunkhouse. You're here and you've had an unusual experience, so you might as well skip the tents for the night. I think there might be some chow in the mess tent as well. Dismissed." With that, the four headed for some welcome food. The mess tent had a plate of sandwiches suitable for humans and Caldivar, and a selection of pungent fruit for the Prithmar. They ate sparingly despite the long day, and stumbled off to their bunks.

THE NEXT MORNING THE four squad mates ate a leisurely breakfast in the mess tent while listening to the sounds of increased activity in the camp. A few of the early EESE students staggered into the mess tent looking as if they hadn't eaten in three days. There was an increase in the general background noise as the ground-effect trucks moved out to pick up the squads that were more than a few kilometers away. They could also hear a flyer from time to time, and Pete didn't want to think about the number of points those squads would lose being so far off-course they needed to be picked up by air.

There was a roar of distant rockets. They went to one of the openings and looked out to see a drop-ship taking off.

Then again, there was off-course, and there was *Off. Course.*

Private Makk came in and headed for the coffee dispenser. She filled her canteen, then added lots of creamer and sugar. She smiled as she turned back and saw Pete and his squad.

"Was that—"

"—a dropship?"

Her smile slipped a bit into confusion at the twins' characteristic of finishing each other's sentences. Orlin and Pete were used to it, but it tended to take others by surprise. "Uh, yeah. Squad didn't make it past the valley. Three casualties out of a squad of five. Rescue's headed in to pick them up and transport straight back to Forest City." She took several long swigs from her canteen and topped it off from the coffee dispenser. "Oh, and Top told me that if I saw you four, to tell—let's see, how did he put it? Oh yeah. 'Send the med student to doc, he's gonna be short-handed. The other three might as well come over and help with check-in.' He also recommended that if you've got clean uniforms, put them on. All of the top scoring teams are already in, there's a few regular Marine squads out there that are still struggling. He gave me these for you to put on your uniforms to put the Marines in their place." She grinned, showing a mouthful of sharp teeth and held out a scaly paw holding four gold pins.

Those were EESE Honor Squad pins!

"I, I don't know what to say..." Pete trailed off, uncertain how to respond to the award.

"We do—"

"—we take it!" said Jinx and Jerry, immediately reaching for the pins.

Orlin reached for his pin, and Makk moved her paw just slightly, to make him fumble, then smiled and winked at him. Orlin's scales turned a faint yellow as he retrieved the pin, a Prithmar equivalent of a blush. Jinx—or Jerry—elbowed him in the ribs.

"...w-well, thank you," Pete finally said. "But I'm hardly a med student. We're all just finishing Upper."

"I heard Top and the Doc talking last night after you guys racked out. They were mighty impressed. Besides, Doc had to send two of his medics in the drop shuttle. You wouldn't believe how many cases of stomach upset and scale rot we see in the squads that come staggering in."

At that, all four of the squad flushed, and Makk just laughed. "A-HA! Yes, I see you know what I mean. Good thing you dealt with it before you got here. That's another point in your favor, you know."

Pete would have loved to accept the compliment, but he worried that using the EMT gloves would be considered cheating. It nagged at him that he might have actually endangered their standing in the guise of helping. He spoke quietly, trying not to betray the turmoil inside. "Uh, okay. We do have clean uniforms in our stored gear."

"Good, head over to the orange cargo units. They have your cubes, then report." She winked at Orlin again, and laughed once again at his discomfort. "Get going, heroes."

Pete felt even more conflicted. They weren't heroes. Even two years ago when he'd discovered The Suit and restored it, he was just a Scout trying to earn his Maker Merit Badge. Today he felt like a kid pretending to be grown-up, while still making all of the mistakes of childhood.

After changing and putting the honor pins on their uniforms, Orlin, Jerry and Jinx headed off to the blue trailer to help with the check-in. There was already a line, and several Marines were setting up tables outside the mobile command center to handle the arriving squads.

Pete went over to the medical facility. The previous night it had been just a trailer pulled by a ground-effect truck. Today it was a complex of pop-up buildings and tents, and there were cadets and Marines standing, sitting, and lying on stretchers waiting for treatment. He was immediately put to work, although it was just minor stuff such as dispensing anti-fungal ointment and applying it to scale rot in places that the sufferer couldn't reach.

He wanted to ask the doctor about the man they'd brought in with them, but he didn't actually see the doc for a couple of hours. He heard the rockets as the dropship returned, and the two medics that had been dispatched returned and went to find the doc. The casualties had been delivered to the Forest City hospital, but Pete could see that one of the medics had blood on his uniform. A few minutes later, the medic and doctor—Captain Grisham—returned and came over to Pete.

"Son, we need you and your squad to come with us right away. Where is the rest of your squad?"

"O-over at the check-in. We were t-told to help out." *Was this it? Had they been found out and were about to be punished? Did something happen to the person they'd rescued?* "W-What's wrong, s-sir?"

"One of the other squads was attacked near where you found your casualty. We need to check over your log and pinpoint the exact location. We also need to find out if you saw anything else."

"Oh." It wasn't his worst fear, but it was still serious. He abruptly remembered his training. "Sir, yes, sir. Cadet Pete Emil at your command, sir." As he saluted, he saw a faint change in the doctor's expression, as if trying to remember something.

The doctor, medic and Pete headed over to the HG trailer, retrieving Orlin, Jerry and Jinx when they arrived. They could see the stern look on Pete's face, and kept their normal exuberance toned down. When they entered the office at the back of the trailer, Pete was surprised to see Top and a Caldivar wearing Colonel's insignia. Even with the efforts to end the xenophobic history of the Tretrayon military prior to the Salvage Fleet battles with the Squilla, non-humans were still rare in the upper levels of command.

The boys came to attention and saluted. The doctor and NCOs stood stiffly, but did not salute. Pete was worried that they had done something wrong, but the Colonel simply returned the salute and instructed them all to sit.

"Gentlemen," the senior officer began, "I am Colonel Alanatto. Doctor, I received your report, but I've just learned there is even more to the story." He turned and addressed Pete and the squad. "Boys, I have just learned that the human you found is wanted for kidnapping."

Pete, Orlin and the twins were shocked. Murmurs of "oh, no" and other words of dismay were exchanged.

Captain Grisham just nodded. "So, the shooting is probably related?"

The Colonel confirmed the doctor's statement and continued. "It happened within half a kilometer from your estimate of where you found the injured man. Your logbook, the tracker in your emergency beacon, and satellite surveillance gives us a kilometer radius as the likely site where he was hiding. The squad we airlifted out were Marines, and one of them said he'd rigged a sling and scored several hits while they were under fire."

"He had several contusions in addition to the scalp laceration. It's possible he was disoriented and wandered a bit before falling and hitting his head," the doctor supplied.

"The marine with the sling confirms that he heard an impact and a cry, then some thrashing about as the firing stopped. He would have given chase, but he had three wounded and only one other squad mate. They stayed in hiding for a day while they treated the wounds they best they could. When it proved impossible to make it to the extraction point today, they punched the rescue beacon."

For the next half hour, the boys were questioned about what they had seen in the area. Pete couldn't recall seeing any kind of shelter, but they *had* been approaching a stream, so perhaps the kidnapper had left his hideout in search of water.

The consensus was that they would simply have to mount a search and rescue mission. The man was accused of kidnapping the teen-aged daughter of local Caldivar councilman. He hadn't been identified as associated with known xenophobic organizations, but he had a record of petty crime that had advanced through extortion to armed robbery and now, kidnapping. There was a young lady, hidden out in the forest, and her food, water and health status were unknown.

The Colonel called for a fresh platoon of Marines—ones that had not been on the EESE course, as well as the Marines and cadets that had arrived earliest and had a chance to eat and rest. "That means you four will need to go back into the field. You found him, which means you hiked right past where he was likely hiding. We've got one of the Marines from the other squad. I don't dare put you in the front line of the search, it's too dangerous, but I want your eyes in the area." He looked directly at Pete and smiled. "All three of them."

The next item to plan was medic support. The later a squad arrived, the greater the number of injuries in the EESE students. In many cases, the reason for the delay *was* the health of the squad members. Captain Grisham would need most of his medics, and could only spare the one that had accompanied him to the meeting. "Besides, Cadet Pete has proven himself equal in skill to a basic medic. He seems to be a natural."

"Um, sirs." Pete hated to interrupt, knowing that what he was about to say could jeopardize their good standing with Top and the Colonel. "Do you have access to an EMT suit?"

"What? Why? We don't have anyone trained in them." The Colonel looked puzzled, but Captain Grisham got that same look that Pete had seen earlier.

"You do know that they have to be custom-fit and adapted to the wearer, right?" Top added.

"Yes, sir." Pete didn't even realize he'd called an NCO "sir" but no one else seemed to be paying attention. "But if you can get one, I can operate it."

Captain Grisham snapped his fingers as a look of understanding replaced the confusion on his face. "Pete Emil. Of clan -ekil, right? Pettekil Emil?"

"Yes, sir," Pete replied sheepishly.

The doctor turned and addressed his medic. "Specialist, there is an EMT Mark XI suit at Medical Command. Get on the horn and have them send it in a drop-pod. It's worth the expense." He turned back to Top and the Colonel as the medic saluted and left the office. "Gentlemen, this young Cadet is Pete Emil. The 'Emil' in 'Emil Medical Tool.' He *invented* the EMT suit!"

"Actually, sir, I just recovered it."

"Recovered, discovered, identified, reassembled, reconditioned, decoded and then demonstrated field capability on first use." He laid a hand on Pete's shoulder. "Once my suit gets here, Pete will be as good as any doctor or field surgeon." He paused a moment, then continued, "the only problem is that I don't have gloves for a Caldivar."

"I, uh, might have my own."

"*I knew it!* Specialist Murphy owes me a beer. A squad that comes in with no sign of bad water or fungus? You know they cheated the odds somehow."

"I'm sorry, sir, does that mean we're disqualified?" There was an ache in Pete's stomach right now.

"The captain said *'cheating the odds'* Cadet, not 'cheating.' This is supposed to be a realistic exercise, and Marines are all about every edge we can get. Just ask President Tomeral." The Colonel laughed, but then turned serious. "Still, I have to ask you. Cadet, are you up to this?" He stared at Pete intently with his upper eye.

Pete stood as straight and tall as he possibly could, executed as precise a salute as he knew how, and replied, "Yes, sir."

The Colonel nodded and returned the salute. "Then make it so."

THE DROPSHIP DELIVERED THE augmented platoon of thirty marines, plus Top, the Marine EESE student, and Pete's squad to the side of the river a bare fifty meters form the point they'd found the injured man. Each of the five EESE students was pared with an NCO, and Pete had drawn the First Sergeant—or Top had drawn Pete, he wasn't sure which was which.

"Okay, Cadet, show me where you found him." Pete noted that Top and the regular Marines were armed and armored. The Cadets had been warned to stay down and undercover if any shooting started. Pete student pointed out the slight depression where they'd found the man, the blood-stained rock was still there. Top called over the Marine EESE student who confirmed that the rock was *not* one that he'd launched from his make-shift sling. It was too big to be slung, but a bit small for the man to have simply fallen on.

However, it was not too big to have been wielded by hand.

"Okay, Cadet. You'd better suit up." Pete was wearing the carapace, legs and sleeves of a new manufacture EMT suit. It was certainly cleaner than the one he'd refurbished two years before. This one came with a display monocle built into a pair of goggles, since most users were discomfited by nanites crawling up their cheek and forming interface nodes in the ear and eye. The monocle was designed for a human, though, so rather than don the headset to activate the suit, Pete merely donned his gloves, and allowed them to tap into the seemingly limitless nanite supply of the never-before-used suit.

The head's-up display in front of his lower, right eye made an interesting overlay with the close-up view from his lower, left eye, and the distance view of his upper eye. Not only did the display identify two types of blood on the rock, it indicated two trails of blood leading away from the site, one downhill toward the river and one uphill.

"First Sergeant, there's two blood trails leading away, which one should we follow?"

"We follow both, Cadet. That's why we have a platoon with us."

"Oh, yes, sir."

The NCO turned and looked at the cadet intensely, raising one eyebrow.

"Sorry, s—First Sergeant!"

"Cadet, you have certainly earned the right to call me 'Top'—just so long as you don't call me 'sir.'"

"Yes, Top. Understood." Pete thought a moment. "Top, I can track one trail with my head's-up display, but no-one can see the other trail. I can charge the human-interface monocle with nanites and then they can follow the other trail."

"Good thinking." He motioned the other senior NCO over. "Gunny, take a squad. Detail one man as tracker and have them wear the goggles. Your squad heads..." He looked at Pete, and the latter pointed down toward the river bank. "...toward the river. We'll go up this way."

The platoon separated, with squads heading in the two directions *not* associated with a blood trail as well, and formed up in search lines to make sure there was no-one else in the area besides the one who had been bleeding. Orlin was with the gunnery sergeant's squad, and Pete was amused to see Private Makk wearing the tracker as they moved out. Jerry and Jinx had been separated and would each be in one of the teams paralleling the river. Pete led the way as Top's squad moved uphill away from the river, back in the direction from which his team had come just two days ago.

For an hour, they moved carefully through the forest, both on and off of the trail that Pete's squad had traveled. The nine members of their squad spread out in a line perpendicular to their direction of travel. They were spaced about ten meters apart, except for Top, who stayed glued to Pete's side. Pete could still detect faint traces of blood, when Top's radio crackled. Gunny's team—and Orlin—had found a shack with signs that someone had been held there. That person—presumably the councilman's daughter—had apparently cut through her restraints with the sharp edge of a rock, probably the same one she'd later used to knock the kidnapper unconscious. The blood trail ended there, although the squad would continue to search that area just in case there was another kidnapper waiting to see if anyone returned.

That meant that the girl had to be in the direction Pete was tracking.

It was another hour before Pete lost the blood trail. He backtracked and picked it up again, then lost it once more as he headed back uphill. He turned around and carefully searched the edges of the trail.

"This way," he called, and headed off the trail.

They found her ten minutes later, a female Caldivar, maybe a year younger than Pete. Her clothes were torn, and her tough skin was scuffed and scratched. Her upper eye was bruised and swollen, and she was curled in a ball at the base of a tree. It appeared that she had attempted to climb the tree, as her claws were extended, and there were scratches in the tree bark. Alas, Caldivar were a burrowing species, and tree climbing was something that took considerable practice—Pete knew how only because he'd grown up with the human twins. Even if she'd succeeded in climbing the tree, she would not have been able to get her bearings this far into the forest.

As soon as Pete looked at the girl, his EMT display started showing yellow and red caution indicators. She was dehydrated and malnourished, it had apparently been three days since she had eaten. Her left ankle was sprained, and there was a broken bone at the wrist joint of her left paw. Either she'd injured both at the same time, or the wrist injury had occurred when she broke free of her restraints. She also had lacerations at the wrists, and they appeared to be infected.

With Top's help, Pete got the unconscious girl uncurled and got the carapace of the EMT suit onto her. Top grunted in surprise to see it shrink and conform to her. Even though she was close to Pete's age, she was quite a bit smaller. He'd seen it before with members of his extended family that lived in the city. Country boys grew to almost the height of a human, but city Caldivar tended to be shorter.

Pete's suit interface also instructed him to remove his left leg sleeve and place it on the girl, whereupon it inflated into a cast and immobilized the ankle. He examined her wrists, and the gloved exuded antiseptic-anesthetic nanites into the wounds.

Once Pete indicated that treatment was complete for now, Top gathered the girl up in his arms and carried her back to the trail, then downhill to where they'd started. The other three teams reported that there was no-one else in the area, and Top summoned everyone back to the muster point. The last arrived just as the drop-ship arrived.

They flew directly to the hospital in town, delivered the girl to her family and the doctors on-site, then headed back to the EESE camp. Pete and his squad mates were due to catch a shuttle back to Joth at midnight, and they still needed to pack and catch a meal before heading to the spaceport. Top came to see them off, and apologized that he was unable to escorted them himself, but he assigned Private Makk to fly them over to Forest City. Pete noted that Orlin managed to snag the front seat, so that he could talk with the female Prithmar. Pete rode in the back with a couple of other EESE students and the twins, Jerry and Jinx, who were unusually subdued, although they got into an argument with the other students about the latest video by a band called Cypress Spring. He sat back and closed all three eyes, thinking of a young female Caldivar who would have been quite pretty if she hadn't been so sick and injured.

WORD GOT BACK TO both their Scout troop and their classmates in the Upper school that they had scored Honor Squad in the Extreme Environment Survival Exercise. There was a commendation from Colonel Alanatto and a personal letter of recommendation for Pete signed by Captain—Doctor—Grisham and Top. Pete was surprised to see that Top signed the letter 'Edward Stacey.' It turned out that Top was a cousin of Evelyn Stacey—head of Salvage System's Navy and President Tomeral's fiancée. The boys had gained a lot of attention, but thankfully, it passed, and they were able to get back to work and finish their final year of Upper on Joth before heading off to the Academy.

One week before graduation, the class was supposed to report for Award Assembly. The various academic and sport awards would be announced, along with the class rankings for valedictorian and honors. They had been instructed to wear their cadet uniforms, but that was because their entire cadet class had earned honors from the drill exhibition earlier in the spring. Thus, it was a surprise to Pete when he saw First Sergeant Stacey and Colonel Alanatto file in behind the school officials and representatives of the various awarding agencies.

Something was up.

The sight of Doctor Grisham, and an unknown Caldivar clinched it. The Marines were all in dress uniform, and the Caldivar was in a formal suit that looked almost military.

Near the end of the assembly, but before the valedictorian announcement, Colonel Alanatto got up and called for Pete, Orlin,
Jerry and Jinx. Understanding that military decorum was in order,
they marched in formation to the stage and lined up facing Top.

"Last summer, these four cadets distinguished themselves, not
only by earning Honor Squad at the summer Extreme Environment
Survival Exercise on Tretra, but also demonstrated courage and com-
mitment by rescuing and extracting an injured civilian while earning
that honor." Colonel Alanatto addressed the assembly, while Top
marched to the table at center stage and retrieved four flat, black
boxes. "In addition, these young men participated in the search and
rescue effort for Susanatto Onid, a young girl lost in the same area
used by the EESE school."

*Lost. That was interesting. No mention that it was a kidnapper
or that the man they 'rescued' was the kidnapper*, Pete thought to
himself. *Wait, Susanatto? Clan -atto, just like the colonel?*

The colonel had continued speaking, and Pete's attention was
caught by his next words, "...upholding the best tradition of both
Cadets and Marines. For these actions, Cadets Orlin, Jerry Garcia,
Jinx Garcia and Pettekil are awarded the Cadet Star." The assembly
applauded and the Colonel waited until it died down before continuing. "And for the record, not only is this the first time the Star has
been awarded *on* Joth, Cadets Orlin and Pete are the first Prithmar
and Caldivar to earn this honor."

The assembly came to its feet as Top pinned the miniature stars to
their uniforms and Colonel Alanatto came over to salute and shake
their hands. As the audience was seated, Top dismissed the other
three, but motioned for Pete to remain.

Captain Grisham stepped to the microphone. "Cadet Pettekil Emil. Your home world of Joth surely knows the role you have played in finding the lost technology of the EMT suit and bringing its capability back to our troops and hospitals. Ladies and Gentlemen, we have an additional award to present today. Councilor Cubinatto Onid."

The civilian Caldivar stepped up. "Cadet Pete, when my brother, Colonel Alanatto informed me that my daughter was rescued by a Cadet from Joth, I was interested. When Doctor Grisham told me that Susa's rescuer was the Caldivar who had discovered the EMT suit, I was intrigued. When I further learned of your aptitude for medicine, I asked my family what we could do for you in return. Alan tells me you are headed to the Academy, but have not yet chosen a track. Doc says if you don't choose flight surgeon, it would be a waste, so clan -atto has established a scholarship to Forest City College of Medicine, to commence in your second year at Academy." Once again, the audience stood and applauded.

The councilman stepped back and motioned to a young female standing just off the stage. She stepped up and handed over a large rigid folder. She then turned toward Pete and winked her lower left eye.

It was her!

Her father continued, "...This certificate with my family's thanks." He bowed to the audience, then father and daughter stepped over beside Colonel Alanatto and Top, and all four bowed to Pete.

Pete returned the bow, and as he straightened, he noticed that Susa was staring at him again. Once she knew he was looking, she winked at him again. He caught a very stern look from her uncle, the colonel, but that, too, dissolved into a smile and a wink.

Pete's head was spinning, he barely noticed that the Principal didn't allow him to sit down before they announced the valedictorian. He was a good student; he just hadn't realized he had done that well.

I wonder if it's the nanites? Is that cheating? No, it's just cheating the odds!

Four
Rescue Ops

Authors note: Once more into the *Salvage Title* universe—and we see Pete and his friends now fully integrated into the Salvage System military. By this point, it's clear that Pete's mission in life is one of caring and treating. He's graduated medical school and joined the Rescue Ops division of the Salvage System military.

One of the best compliments I received came from Kevin Steverson, the series creator, who said: "There's no Rescue Ops division in the Salvage System military—but I'm going to have to create one for you. I like the idea."

I wrote this after watching the movie *Greenland*, which follows a family trying to reach survival shelters as comet fragments approach Earth. The visual effects were stunning, and the story struck a chord—particularly a scene where a meteor storm suddenly strikes the region. I wanted to capture that sense of danger and desperation, because in situations like that, your only hope might just be a rescue ops team.

*Join **Medical Command**. **Travel** the Universe. Meet new people... and **HELP** them!*

Pettekil Emil stared at the sign for several minutes before continuing into the multistory building labeled Salvage-Coalition Medical Command. Pete was a Caldivar from Joth, the "minor" planet of the Tretra System. For hundreds of years, the human inhabitants of Tretra had dominated the system's military and professions. That all changed when the Squilla invaded, and the Tretra military were rescued by a group of misfits from the desert planet of Joth. It was an eye-opening experience, and Tretra soon learned that the humans, lizard-like Prithmar and anteater-like Caldivar had much to offer—particularly since Harmon Tomeral, leader of those misfits, forced the Tretra leadership to face—and demolish—their own prejudices.

Following the example of independence shown by Tomeral, Pete and his best friends, Orlin—a Prithmar—as well as Jerry and Jinx—human twins—had been looking for spare parts they could assemble into working machines of their own design for their Maker Merit Badge when he discovered a piece of Lost Technology—an Emergency Medical Tool mecha—also known as the EMT Mark XI. Two years later, Pete, Orlin, Jerry and Jinx were undergoing an extreme environment survival experience as cadets training for the Tretrayon—and eventually Salvage—military academy. They encountered an unconscious human, treated his injuries, and carried the injured man for several days to their extraction point. Upon learning that the man was wanted for kidnapping, and that his victim was likely still up on the mountainside where he'd been found, they joined in the search party to rescue the daughter of a local Caldivar politician.

He was hailed as a genius for the first event, and a hero for the second, but in the Academy, he was simply "not half bad." The scholarship to Forest City Medical School on Tretra, a reward courtesy of the family of Susa, the girl he'd rescued, resulted in his recent graduation as a Doctor of Trauma Medicine, and a captain in the Salvage Marines Medical Command.

Through this door would be the career that would shape the *rest* of his life.

If only he could convince himself that he was ready.

His orders said to report to Colonel Suminto, and he was directed to a door at the far end of the room. He made his way through the busy office, knocked on the door, and heard a voice inviting him to enter.

"Captain Doctor Pettekil Emil, reporting for duty." Pete stood at his best parade-ground attention and snapped a sharp salute, the digits of his right paw just barely brushing the lid of his long-distance eye, centered above the two eyes he typically used for near-field and fine-focus purposes.

Colonel Suminto was a Rincah, a member of another humanoid race with ram-like features and curved horns on his head. Salvage System, and the Coalition they'd formed, was unique in the outer worlds by virtue of the sheer diversity of the society—and in particular, it's armed forces. It made learning to be a flight surgeon all that more challenging, but Pete had a slight advantage in that his EMT suit had a near artificial intelligence programmed to recognize and diagnose over one-thousand races. He didn't let that stop him from learning as much as he could without "cheating" through the use of his own compact EMT-link.

Suminto stood as Pete came to attention. He walked around the desk, returned Pete's salute, and offered his hand to shake. Pete was surprised to see that he towered over the commanding office. "Captain Emil. Welcome to Rescue Ops. I've heard good things about you. Top of your class, quick thinker, hard worker. I trust the Academy disabused you of those 'hero' notions the popular media like to throw around."

"Yes sir, the Academy and medical school showed me just how much I didn't know."

"Good." The colonel told Pete to be at ease, and gestured to a chair beside the desk. Suminto took a chair where he could sit in a comfortable conversational manner. "You'll find out that Rescue Ops views you in a slightly more favorable light. We want you here precisely because of the qualities you've shown us. Part of your time will be spent developing the Mark XII EMT and part of it will be continuing your education in order to become fully board- and flight-certified.

"I'm telling you this, because you're getting dropped right in the thick of it. I know you have your own personal Mark XI EMT, reconditioned from the original parts, so you'll need some updates. In two days, you're going out on a mission."

"A mission? Already? I thought I was supposed to spend two years in residency?"

"You do, and you will. The two-year practicum cannot be waived, but with your experience, we can rotate you in and out of assignments that complement the battlefield and emergency medicine training you're supposed to be getting. We need you, more importantly, we need your suit and your experience with it."

"Sir, uh... thank you, sir."

"I'm not so sure you should thank me, yet. We provide assistance to those who've gotten a raw deal from the Galaxy... and it's in those circumstances that Rescue Ops plays a major role."

"Disaster relief?"

"Got it in one. The Akea system is having a comet problem. A rather large, rocky object entered their system, headed toward the sun, then broke into smaller pieces. They've already had several large strikes as their planet passed through the tail of the comet on its way sunward, and they're likely to get hit by more fragments. Akea will be right in the comet's path as it heads back out."

Pete thought for a moment, considering parabolic and elliptic trajectories, interplanetary speeds, and other variables. It was the sort of thing Jerx—Jerry and Jinx, that is—were very good at. Pete was no slouch at math, but the exercise made his head hurt. "That's... highly improbable, sir. A comet on a parabolic trajectory should round the sun much faster than a planet on round or even elliptical orbit."

"Ah, good. Your record said you were sharp. We don't know if it's natural from the outgassing, or something else. Either way, we have two months to rescue, relocate or assist the Akeans. Floods, earthquakes, volcanic eruptions, acid rain... lots of injured people, and we don't know enough about the race—they're not in any of our databases. We're hoping they're in yours."

"Uh... thank you? Sir?"

Suminto laughed. "Oh, you're going to love it here, son. Never a dull moment!"

AFTER PETE LEFT COLONEL'S office, he proceeded down to the laboratory on the twelfth level. As he walked into the lab, he noticed one of the technicians was a Eitom –an eight-foot-tall humanoid with heavy build and three arms. The biology of the Eitom showed that they'd once had four arms, but the upper and lower arms on the left side had fused together. On the right side, a normal sized upper arm concealed a delicate lower arm that generally folded in underneath the upper.

Pete had met an Eitom from one of the early years in his medical training. Eddie was one year ahead of him in medical school. Much to his surprise, the Eitom looked up as he entered the laboratory and addressed him by name. "Hey, Pete, glad to see you finally made it!"

"Wow, Eddie, I'm surprised to see you here!"

"Don't be, we always talked about your EMT, and this is the best place to work on one. I get to do medicine and fiddle with gadgets at the same time. Did you even *read* your assignment orders?"

Pete's three eyes opened wide, and he pulled out the thin plastic sheet that constituted his official orders. He snapped to attention and spoke a tight, "Yes, sir, Major Niveen, sir!"

"At ease, Pete. We are pretty informal, and this is just the lab. You can still call me Eddie unless there's a superior officer present, like the Colonel."

"Uh. Thanks, Eddie." Pete put his carryall on a benchtop and pulled out silvery cloth and a hardshell chest plate. "The Colonel said you need my EMT for something—but not a whole lot else about what to expect other than this urgent rescue operation."

"Okay, well, Rescue Ops is just what it sounds like. We provide search and rescue support to Tetra, Salvage System and Coalition worlds. It's just like an emergency medicine residency. " Eddie pulled over a computer link cable and plugged it into the primary interface console built into the hardshell. He then unlatched small cylinders attached to the backplate and connected them to a machine against one wall of the laboratory. "*This* is where we finally put it all to use. We go out in the community and into the galaxy, working rescues, disasters, and recovery. *This* is when it gets fun."

"Wow. I'm not sure what I was expecting. Classrooms, simulators, maybe bandaging training injuries or other minor stuff. This is ... fast, I guess is what I want to say."

"Well, the planet we're headed to, Akea—actually, the major race calls themselves Carico –caused a stir because they're not in any of our databases. That means we're going in on a rescue without detailed medical knowledge. Med Command is hoping that we can get some translations once your suit recognizes the Carico and that might just help us pull out more translations from your database."

"Aye-aye, Major Eddie!" Pete threw a quick salute and smiled.

"Not under cover, soldier," Eddie replied, but grinned as he said it. "Yeah, you'll fit in just fine."

Pete was billeted in the visiting officer's quarters. That seemed strange, he certainly didn't feel like an officer. After dinner, he returned to quarters, pulled out his slate and started re-reading his orders and dealing with a large number of comm messages he'd received since officially arriving. Once all of that was done, he sent a quick text to his mother, letting her know he'd arrived and all was well. She'd appreciate that. Next was a somewhat longer text to Susa. They'd seen a lot of each other when he had breaks in med school. He missed her already, and knew that she was waiting for word whether he'd be returning soon, or she should come join him.

After composing and sending a lengthy message with lots of reassurances, but carefully worded to keep her from racing to join him, Pete laid down on the strange bunk and tried to sleep... not that it would do any good, he could seldom fall asleep immediately with such an important day ahead of...

... He was awake before his alarm. The yellow-orange light of Salvage System's primary had awoken him the moment the sun cleared the distant hills. Every morning on Tretra at the Academy and med school, he'd awoken with the dawn. Growing up on Joth, residents were up several hours before dawn to take advantage of the relative coolness—sleeping until dawn always seemed like a luxury...

This upcoming mission gave Pete a strange feeling in his stomach. It took a while to recognize it—but eventually he realized that it was the same feeling he'd had twice before—the first time when he'd worn the newly refurbished Mark XI EMT to rescue his injured friends on Joth, and the other time when he'd been tasked with locating Susa when she'd been kidnapped. Anticipation, excitement... whatever. It was time to knuckle down and do the job he'd been training for the past seven years.

PETE MET THE REST of the team the next day. Rescue Ops was a large organization with hundreds of members working all across the galaxy. The Salvage office was largely research and headquarters support, but the evacuation of Akea would require every possible technician, medic, doctor and rescuer. While waiting for Pete and his EMT Mark XI, Colonel Suminto had sent everyone else off to Akea. In addition to Pete, Eddie and the colonel, there was Ralph, a cyber-canid from Earth; Walicta, a platypus-like Otreme; and Serena, a human female who was their Marine security specialist.

Walicta—Eddie called her 'Wally'—just nodded and waved a clawed forepaw in Pete's direction. Serena stuck out her hand to shake Pete's paw with a quick, forceful motion. Ralph, however, walked up to Pete on all fours, stood on his back legs and embraced him in a hug. " Glad you could join us, Pete," the cybernetically-enhanced canine spoke through a translator positioned over his throat.

"Ralph is our 'digital nose.' He can sense the chemicals given off by living creatures with a sensitivity much greater than any race could manage without assistance. He's also our practical joker and comic relief. Wally is the penetration expert. She can explore small spaces and carry relief supplies to anyone trapped in collapsed buildings, cave-ins and wreckage. Serena will run security, although we'll be augmented with at least one mecha." Eddie handled the introductions since the Colonel had been called back into a conference call. "We'll also have a couple of dropships we can call on. We'll be needing one for our team, and another will deliver the Marines that will work with Serena."

Pete wondered if those marines might include his friends Orlin, Jerry and Jinx. Orlin had gone into mechanized infantry. The nearly inseparable twins, Jerry and Jinx, had entered flight school. It would be nice to see them, but he knew the odds did not favor it.

Colonel Suminto returned from his office and addressed the group. "Our departure has been moved up. We leave this afternoon. I just got off the comm with Admiral Lurvel who is in command in the Akea system. That comet has a lot of fragments. There have been some major meteor strikes in the past day, and they need all hands, immediately. Our gear and the three EMTs are on the way to the transport as we speak; you have one hour to collect personal gear, and another thirty minutes to get to Yatarward Field. We lift in one-hundred-twenty minutes. Now go."

FORTUNATELY, PETE HADN'T REALLY unpacked, so he was able to grab a clean uniform, some utilizes, and one of the new lightweight, reinforced jumpsuits to wear under the EMT. He still had time to spare, so he decided to hit the 'fresher himself, and get to the field early.

There was a drop ship on the field displaying a logo of an angel holding a globe. The shuttle itself had its numerical designation and name—347-38D Cunningham—but was also emblazoned with the name of its parent ship—CRO Takur Gar. Standing at the cockpit door was a human with red-hair and a familiar freckled face. Although he'd grown taller and thinner, Jerry still had the irrepressible smile that Pete remembered from his younger days.

"Jerry!"

"Pete! Hey, Jinx is not going to believe this!"

"Wow. That's not right, you finishing your own sentences."

"I know—" Jerry paused for a moment then grinned and continued, "—strange, isn't it? My worse half went for fighters, I had the aptitude for dropships, the Navy finally managed to find a difference between us."

"But, do you still see each other?"

"Oh sure, we're both stationed on the Mayaguez. I'm just on loan to the Takur Gar for this mission. The only real difference between the bomb truck he drives and the bus I drive is that the weapons I deploy can think for themselves."

"Hah! And what does Jinx say to that?"

"Usually something about not having to worry about shaking up the cargo if he does a barrel roll."

"Yup, that sounds like Jinx."

"C'mon in and get your gear stowed. We've got some Caldivar seats up near the bulkhead."

Eddie was the next to show up, followed by Wally, Ralph, and then Serena. Colonel Suminto showed up at exactly ninety minutes after he'd sent the team to pack. He was wearing a commander's comm helmet, and seemed to still be in conference as the dropship spooled up its engines and lifted off.

The Takur Gar was typical for a naval support ship—lots of cargo and shuttle space, tiny crew quarters. In fact, the quarters had to be allocated according to species' size. Thus, Eddie and the Colonel would be one deck up on the Rincah-Yalteen deck, while Pete and the others were quartered on the Human deck. Pete shared a half-compartment with Ralph, while Serena and Wally shared the other half, behind a flexible divider that Wally insisted would be kept closed to "keep the boys out." The massive cargo decks were almost completely empty—reserved for whatever was needed to evacuate anyone and anything from Akea.

There was barely enough time to secure their carryalls in the restraint webbing and strap into their bunks before the acceleration alarm sounded and they began a three-gee burn to get to the stargate, and thus to Akea as fast as they possibly could.

"ALERT! ALL PERSONNEL TO duty stations. Alert!"

Pete jumped up out of his bunk and hit his head on the low bulkhead. He rolled over and slid down to the floor, eliciting a yelp from Ralph. "Oh man, I'm sorry. I didn't mean to land on your tail!"

"It's okay, Pete. I'll be sure to return the favor." Ralph grinned with a very doglike expression and cocked his head sideways. The action was accompanied by laughter from his collar-mounted translator. "Seriously, though. It was my fault. I was asleep and jumped up like a newbie."

Pete rubbed his head and didn't say anything. Ralph looked back at him, then cocked his head to the other side and 'yipped' in time with the laughter coming from the miniature speaker.

"We'd better suit up. Our duty stations are right here until the Colonel tells us otherwise—but if the alarms are going off, we need to be ready to deploy when he does call."

Pete was already in the silky skin suit he'd packed in the top of his carryall. All personnel onboard ship were required to wear some form of vacuum-resistant clothing. Most wore shipsuits, a type of skin suit with light insulation that could be sealed to a variety of footwear, helmets and gloves. Pete's was meant to be worn under his EMT and only worked with custom gloves and helmet that were extensions of the EMT itself. He'd made his own gloves for the cadet survival school, and customized a helmet for his three eyes and elongated snout. It also had an interface for the EMTs specialized nanites that formed visual and auditory display interfaces over his eyes and ears.

Pete suited up, then turned to assist Ralph. The cybernetically-up-lifted canine found it almost impossible to sleep in any form of body covering, and needed to get into a garment with reinforced weave that served as both pressure suit and armor. Eddie had offered to shave him prior to deployment, but Ralph preferred to keep his thick gold-and-white-colored fur. That made getting into the skin suit more difficult, especially in a hurry, so he'd made his bunkmate promise to assist since Pete didn't need as much time to suit up. The worst part—for Pete—was that Ralph's tail wagged when he was excited, making it all the more difficult to get him completely encased in the suit.

Once Ralph was safely suited, with no fur caught in the seals, Pete finished donning his EMT. The main body plate was a clamshell that fit over his chest and back, plus arm and leg sleeves that connected to tubing and wiring sockets on the clamshell. The suit morphed itself to fit his body, then cover shoulders, hips and groin, leaving no portion of Pete unprotected. He felt nanites assembling a diagnostic monocle in his lower right eye, and a display formed in his vision that echoed the heads-up display in his helmet.

It only took two minutes for Pete and Ralph to be completely sealed and armored. Almost as soon as they finished, the partition retracted to reveal Wally was in a small cylinder with tank treads and articulated external arms, and Serena in a shipsuit with added marine scout armor.

Their Rescue Ops squad looked ready. His helmet comm activated, and he heard Colonel Suminto's voice. "Team, report to shuttle bay twelve. SKYWATCH is reporting cometary fragments in the emergence zone. We are sending out all dropships immediately."

At that very moment, they felt and heard an impact shake the ship. More alarms started to go off, and the external atmosphere indicator in his helmet started to alternate green and yellow. The four looked at each other for a moment, then—as they had practiced in the drills, Pete reached down and picked up Wally, tucking her little tank under his left arm, while Serena picked up Ralph and hoisted him up to drape over her shoulders. With the smallest—and slowest—members of the team now riding, they set off for shuttle bay twelve as fast as they could.

IN THE SHUTTLE BAY Pete could see mecha-suited marines loaded onto two largest shuttles, while EMT suited medics and various scouting species loaded into smaller dropships. There was a sense of urgency, and many support personnel were added to the vessels at the last minute.

The Takur Gar shuddered under an impact, and Pete's ears popped. Emergency alarms started and sounded a depressurization warning. More impacts were felt and the loading crews forced people onto the shuttles under the strobing red light of emergency evacuation beacons. Eddie led the team to the Cunningham, where the pilot didn't even wait for all of the occupants to get strapped in before closing the hatch and moving to the bay exit.

Another impact shook the Takur Gar as Jerry's voice came over the compartment speakers and suit intercoms. "If you're seated, stay there, anyone standing, either sit on the floor or strap yourselves to the cargo rings on the walls. This is going to be rough."

Pete felt the shuttle rotate relative to the direction that had been "down" on the Gar, then the shuttle's belly-mounted thrusters throttled up and pushed everyone toward the floor of the compartment. He gave a silent command consisting of subvocalization and muscle twitches to his EMT, and a display opened in his view, courtesy of the nanites now concentrated in front of his lower right eye. He selected a visual feed from the external sensors on Gar and Cunningham.

The view of Gar was shocking, with obvious impacts glowing a bright yellow from heat. As he watched, another bloom appeared right over the shuttle bay and he could see shuttle jets firing erratically and fragments coming off of a ship that had been directly behind them exiting the bay. Pete wanted to scan around to find the source of the projectiles impacting the ship, but Jerry came over the comm to warn the passengers to expect evasive maneuvers. Pete commanded the display to turn off, sat back, and tightened his straps. The next ten minutes were harrowing, as their pilot put the dropship into spins, abrupt changes in direction, and alternating high acceleration and braking. As the violent movements began to slack off, the comm channel chimed with a high priority incoming transmission.

"All Rescue Ops personnel. Please switch to Command Channel Alpha-Seven for a message from Admiral Lurvel." The EMT comm system automatically switched, but Pete knew that some of the additional persons who'd been packed onto the dropship might not have been tuned into unit-specific comms.

"All personnel—if you are listening to this broadcast, you know that the Takur Gar is currently under emergency and has initiated evacuation protocols. Gar emerged from gate transit into a debris cloud that has been attribute to the rogue comet threatening the planet Akea. The cometary debris is small in size, radar transparent and low albedo. It was not detected until the Gar was right in the debris cloud. We have loaded as many of the support personnel onto the dropships and shuttles as possible, and all unattached personnel should report to Base Green for assignment. Rescue Ops operational squads will receive assignments via chain-of-command once you are groundside.

"Rest assured, the Takur Gar is not out of this. We have offloaded Coalition personnel for resource and safety reasons. By the time we are ready to complete the evacuation of Akea, we expect to have the Gar back in operation." There was text information about the assignment of the bases and attaching the various shuttles and dropships to the and different operational groups. Base Green would act as the main hospital and processing center for Carico that needed to be evacuated from unsafe or heavily damaged areas. There were bases for urban rescue, suburban and rural operations, and high-latitude polar regions. Base White served as a headquarters unit for the marine commanding general and Colonel Suminto's team.

As Pete was reading, he felt the aft engines throttle up for the transition to Akean orbit, and then landing. He figured this was as good a time as any to refresh his information on Rescue Ops procedures and any information they had on the Carico. It seemed like there would not be any time to spare once they landed. Thus, it seemed no time at all until atmospheric buffeting began, and then suddenly seemed to stop as the engines wound down.

He was seized by a moment of panic.

Had the engines failed? Were they dropping from a great height to end of crushed on the surface?

It was only when he noticed the other occupants unbuckling their restraints and beginning to move around the cabin, that he realized they had landed. Once more, he was caught up in the seeming chaos and haphazard process of getting all of the additional persons off of the dropship but soon found himself joined by Serena and Ralph—Wally's tank was still secured above his left shoulder—and then by Eddie and Colonel Suminto.

"Follow me. We need to get comms and databases set up in headquarters first. Billeting will come later—we're likely getting cots in a back room, because we're going to be *busy*!" True to his word, the Colonel had them working integrating communications with all of the rescue teams and setting up the computer systems and medical databases until well after local nightfall. Given that Base White was located at a northern latitude during local summer, that was late indeed. Pete estimated that it had been at least thirty hours since they'd awoken to alarms on the Gar. It was the first of many long days, and each night he laid down on his cot and fell asleep without delay.

PETE WOKE TO MOVEMENT near his cot. The entire headquarters staff—including the colonel—were bunked in a large room behind the main staff room. The females were on the other side of an opaque curtain, although shadows indicated that someone was also moving on that side.

Eddie touched him on the shoulder and whispered, "Time to get moving, Pete, you are headed down to base Green today to see if we can get some more information about the Carico out of your EMT."

He blinked several times, and the nanites in front of his eye reconfigured into a messaging display. Sure enough, he had new orders telling him to report to Base White's airfield at o500.

He checked his chrono. It had been local midnight when all but the night watch had headed to their cots. It was now 0430—what doctors and marines commonly call "oh-dark-thirty." He had thirty minutes to get ready. Fortunately, he'd started sleeping wearing a glove, leg or sleeve of his EMT, so that he had nanites available in an emergency. A silent command started them performing perform basic hygiene. It had been very useful in medical school to have flush fatigue toxins from his body after a long procedure or late night of studying.

He was surprised to learn that Serena was going to be accompanying him to Base Green. When he asked Eddie about it, he was told that she was assigned as security. He and his suit were considered high-value assets—well, technically, his suit had the high value, but as the most knowledgeable user, he came in a close second in value. Therefore, he merited an escort who would do her best to keep him out of trouble whenever he was out of HQ.

He was even more surprised to learn that he would be traveling to Green not in a shuttle or dropship, but in the back seat of a fighter. Two Marine Q-114 were waiting for Pete and Serena at the landing pad. Their engines were spooled up to a fast idle, and as soon as the airfield technicians strapped him into the back seat, the canopy closed and they rolled out to the runway. He was pushed back into his seat by g-forces as the pilot pointed the nose at the sky and accelerated straight up, followed by a loop and barrel roll. The comm crackled, "quit showing off, Red Five. Captain Emil is not going to be impressed."

"Hey, that was just evasive maneuvers, Red Leader," said the pilot. The voice sounded familiar.

"J– Jinx?" Pete asked.

"At your service, Pete. Red Flight delivery, you spy 'em, we fly 'em."

"Not that I'm not happy to see you—but, why you? Why fighters—wouldn't a shuttle make more sense?"

"Not really, not for two people, plus the orbitals are pretty busy right now. Atmospheric is better, faster, and appropriate for single or double cargo."

"So, I'm cargo now?"

"Hey, do I look like a trash hauler... no, don't answer that. Yeah, you're cargo. Valuable cargo. They need you at Green A-S-A-P."

"I TOLD Jerry that it was odd to hear him speaking in complete sentences. I think it might be even stranger from you."

Jinx laughed. "Yeah, basic broke us of a lot of things. Okay, hold on, we've got some bad weather ahead and we've been vectored through instead of over or around. It's going to get rough, but Red Leader and I are going to pour on some speed and bring up the combat shields. That should take the extreme edges off of the turbulence."

True to his word, the ride got extremely rough. Mach-plus flight through the center of a super-sized thunderstorm, with lightning flashing in the pre-dawn darkness, was not an experience Pete necessarily wanted to repeat. He was certain he would have lost his lunch if he'd had any... or breakfast.

Jerry kept up a constant patter—clearly he wasn't experiencing any discomfort—but Pete found himself wishing for an airsickness bag for the first time in his life. He blinked and called up a self-check menu on the EMT's ocular. The suit recommended a peristalsis inhibitor and mild muscle relaxant. He'd have to increase his vegetable and grain intake later or pay the consequences with gas and cramps, but it certainly made the ride less nauseating.

After they cleared the storm, Jinx poured on yet more speed, and it only took another thirty minutes until they were taxiing up to a hanger half a continent's width away from where they started. Base White was located in a rural region on the northeast coast of the principal continent on Akea, but Base Green was located on the edge of an urban center on the southwestern shore of that continent. The city itself had been hit by several cometary fragments more than a month ago, and the craters still glowed a dull orange as they continued to dissipate the massive heat of impact. A badly damaged and nearly abandoned metropolitan hospital had been located at this site. Repaired and expanded with multi-species medical teams, it now served to supplement the native Carico doctors and care staff.

After reporting to the chief of staff, Pete was ordered to assist in the overtaxed Emergency Department. It was hoped that the wide variety of injuries and ailments might trigger the ancient database built into his original EMT. The Carico were a "new" race in the experience of the Coalition, and neither the standard medical databases, nor the various EMTs in service, had been able to reveal specific medical information. The docs were falling back on standard practices and universal precautions in handing the Akeans.

The sun was just coming up as Pete reported to the Intake and Triage area. He scanned his first patient and waited for an identification by his EMT database. He was wearing the full suit, and the ocular display all of the information it had:

Species... unknown, humanoid, probable subtype 42xx

Height—one point three four meters,

Weight—62 kilograms

Sex—male (85% probability)

Compound fracture, left forearm (92% probability)—possible identity: left radius

Subcutaneous hematoma (35% probability). Internal bleeding - unknown

Internal injuries and/or organ damage—unknown

Hematology—unknown

Immunology—unknown

Unconscious (98% probability), Mental status—unknown

Dehydration and exposure (67% probability)

Shock (55% probability)

Volume expander—unknown risk, recommend Flurodec minimal dosage

Rehydrate with local fluid sources

Nanites—contraindicated.

Pete had never seen the EMT respond with probabilities, instead of definite diagnosis and treatment orders; it was somewhat unsettling. He marked the chart for secondary priority—urgent but non-life-threatening injuries—and moved on to the next patient. He worked triage for the next four hours. After a brief meal break, he was sent to the emergency surgical bay—minus his full suit. We kept his gloves, and the nanite ocular interface. Again, it was hoped that exposure to the alien's internal organs (again, roughly human standard, but with at least three additional presumably endocrine organs, and no pancreas) would trigger recognition in the EMTs artificial intelligence.

Throughout all of this, Serena stood guard, either at the corner of the triage tent, or just outside the door to the surgical suite. She joined him at meal breaks, and while she didn't say much, Pete welcomed her company. The other doctors and medical staff were just too busy to do much more than acknowledge his presence.

"I don't understand it, Serena, how can the Carico not be in the EMT database?"

"Maybe they were completely unknown to the inventors?"

"Possibly. The colonel said that the Coalition didn't know of the Carico before they contacted Tomeral and Associates for assistance. Still, they have a stargate, so the Bith knew of them. The tech level of this world suggests they had communication with the rest of the galaxy."

"Maybe they invented the suits and hid their own data?"

"No, I don't think so. We're pretty sure humans invented the first EMT. The Mark XI's database lists Human as Species #1."

Serena grunted and went back to her salad of hydroponic greens and vat protein. Pete just nibbled on a protein bar. Back on Joth or Tretra, those were pretty tasteless, but these tasted like real food. It had been ten hours since Pete had reported for duty, and he had yet another four-hour shift to complete before finding his temporary quarters. He went to the dispenser and ordered coffee—triple strength—and sat back down to drink it in silence as he cross-referenced his EMT database with a network information search for more data on races similar to the Carico. He found a link that referenced some very old Earth idents that were labeled as "probably mythological." Called "large greys" and "small greys," they were similar, but didn't really fit the natives of Akea. The Carico had the same gray skin, large wide-set eyes and elongated heads, but also a pronounced midline ridge extending from the back of the head to the face, ending in a prominent nasal flare. Their mouths were slightly protuberant—not quite a muzzle, but not flat-faced like the "greys." The Carico were also covered in a fine fur that was gray with hints of iridescent blue and green. It was frustrating to be seemingly so close to a described species, and yet have no exact reference to the people he was trying to help.

AFTER A WEEK OF fourteen-to-eighteen-hour days providing triage, surgery and emergency care, Pete was called to report to the hospital chief of staff. Admiral Lurvel and Colonel Suminto were on video link and took turns quizzing Pete about the information obtained from his EMT that week.

After hearing Pete's report, the chief of staff addressed the others. "Gentlebeings, that's pretty much the same as what we got. There's no sense in keeping Doctor Emil here. We're well staffed and have people experienced with treating Carico now. I say we send him back to Base White to see what he can do with those research facilities."

Research facilities? Pete thought to himself. *There are research facilities? Are they medical? Perhaps I can find a clue there!*

As if reading his thoughts, Colonel Suminto nodded and answered Pete's unspoken question. "Indeed, we're sited near the Akean government's major scientific research institutions. There is a medical research facility about thirteen klicks from base. We've been excavating with some local help. Major Niveen is the lead on that project. I'll assign Pete to work with Eddie. How soon can you send him back?"

"Well, there's no urgency, so we won't subject him to the fighters, besides, that squadron is being reassigned to comet-chasing duty. You're too close for a ballistic hop, so we'll put him on the shuttle that's headed up to Mayaguez tonight and then back down to White in the morning. He can have a berth and get some sleep on the way."

Sleep. That would be nice!

THE SHUTTLE TO MAYAGUEZ left base Green at local midnight, but Pete was allowed to crawl into one of the bunk-like crew berths about an hour before departure. He slept through liftoff, rendezvous with the flagship, and through most of the unloading and reloading. Just before re-entry, he emerged from the tunnel-like sleeping space and took a seat in the passenger compartment next to Serena. She'd been sitting in that exact seat since he had gone to sleep—did she stay wake all night? She looked... pretty much the way she always did: Competent, alert, on guard. He looked at his own reflection on a seat-back screen. Nanites were crawling at the corners of his three eyes cleaning away dirt and dried mucus. He looked terrible—he'd need a 'fresher visit before he dared go back to the HQ.

It was noon before he reported back to the colonel. The entire operation was running short of time, but orders to get fed and cleaned up had come over his comm before they landed back at White. He entered the HQ facility to find only Eddie and the clerks. The colonel, Wally and Ralph were working a salvage and rescue site nearby.

"Good to see you, Rock Star! Did you have a nice beauty rest?" Eddie laughed and winked as he delivered the mild insult, so Pete didn't take it *too* seriously.

Pete yawned and stretched theatrically. "I don't know, Eddie, you ever sleep in one of those crew bunks? ... Oh, wait. You wouldn't fit, would you?"

"I can fit a Yalteen bunk just fine, but I know what you mean. Those things aren't much more than a shoulder-width tube." Eddie shuddered. "I'm not claustrophobic—can't be in this outfit—but I don't like them."

"Yeah. Same here. Okay, let me get some coffee and then you can point me to my next assignment."

"Here, I've got a cup for you already. Drink up and read this." Eddie handed over a slate with a diagram of a building.

"What's this ... underground? This is what, a bunker?"

"Nope, a lab. The Carico we talked to didn't know of it. It's old and buried underneath a farm about fifty klicks away. We've been doing ground-penetrating imaging to make sure we don't miss people in caves or bunkers. Colonel asked the folks at the main research complex, and they said there was a rumor of an old lab somewhere, but no-one knew the details."

"...and they found it?"

"Yes, they did, or rather, a team of mecha-suited marines found it while trying to evacuate some folks from a collapsed farm building. A Prithmar ended up falling down a hole and reported an underground structure. I think you might know him—a kid from Joth named Orlin."

Pete laughed. "Yes, that sounds like Orlin, always falling into trouble, but coming out the better for it."

"Indeed, the Admiral recommended a commendation, because he was in the process of rescuing one of the locals, who fell in first. He did rescue her, and had already gotten the family out. Once everyone was safe, he volunteered to explore, but the Colonel wanted Rescue Ops in there first, and then to get you down there." Eddie gave Pete a wry smile. "I hope you're rested; we're headed out in ten minutes."

"My EMT is right here..." Pete patted the wheeled case at his side. "... and I'm wearing everything else. Let's go!"

ALTHOUGH ONLY FIFTY KLICKS away, it still took nearly an hour to reach the site via aircar. It was well away from the small urban concentration adjacent to base White, and up a box canyon filled with ranches and farms. "We think the lab is built under the mountain range. This access appears to be an emergency exit or air shaft," Colonel Suminto told Pete once they'd reached the site. "That makes this pretty tricky. There have been lots of ground movement and shocks. Ralph and Wally are currently in there mapping places where it's safe for us to access."

Pete and Eddie were taken over to view a couple of screens displaying scenes of the underground lab. One screen was fed by a camera attached to Wally's protective armor, while another showed the feed from Ralph's harness. There was a lot of debris on the floor, and a few places with cracked walls or ceiling, but for the most part, the facility seemed to be accessible.

Two other screens were clearly from larger sophonts, approximately Caldivar size, although bulked out much more in mechanical suits of armor. "One of those is Serena, the other's your friend, Orlin,"

Suminto said. "He asked for permission to remain with the survey once we gave approval. I'm having them scout out access to what we think are the main labs before I send you and Eddie in."

He was interrupted by a shout of surprise from the comm. Orlin's screen showed a new room, filled with unusual equipment, odd chairs... and a skeleton.

"That's—" Pete began.

"—Not a Carico," Eddie finished.

"Suit up, you two. Time to go in"

Pete and Eddie, in their respective EMTs with full armor supplement to protect their limbs and joints, were met by Ralph, who led them to where Orlin and Serena guarded the entrance to the lab.

"The ceiling's not particularly stable, so the two heavies are going to play 'Atlas' and make sure the sky doesn't fall on you." Ralph yipped a bit in laughter, then continued. "Seriously, they are your rescue. Try not to move anything that is next to a supporting wall or touching the ceiling. I know we can't convince you not to touch anything, but just use some common sense. If the wall or ceiling collapses, Wally and I are going to have to dig you out, and it takes *ages* to get the dust out of my fur!" Pete laughed, but assured Ralph that he would be careful.

The room was indeed a lab, and there were not one, but two skeletons in the room. The first was seated in a chair, the other laid out on a medical or surgical platform. The one on the table was—mostly—Carico, but with a more of a snout shape to the skull, and a vestigial tail extending from the bottom of the vertebral column.

The other skeleton, though, was amazing! If standing, it would be as tall as Eddie—over two meters in height. It was bipedal with very long limbs and short torso. The hips were positioned such that the legs would contribute more than half the total height of the creature, while the long arms extended almost to the knees. Most amazing was a humanoid skull with a flat face and very long cranium that extended back much further than a human.

Pete had seen this creature lately. The EMT reported:

Species... 5. "Large Grey"

Deceased.

Height—two point three meters,

Weight (estimated)—80 kilograms

Sex—female (62% probability)

"Not so mythological after all." Pete muttered to himself.

"What was that, Captain Emil? You have an identification?" Suminto asked over the comm.

"Yes, sir. The EMT database identifies the seated skeleton as a 'Large Grey,' Species number 5 in the database. I read that they are considered to be a myth."

"Interesting. Number five, eh? This is a very ancient species."

"Yes, sir." Pete paused a moment. "Sir, do we have any idea how old this installation is?"

"I think I can answer that," Eddie responded. He was in the next room over, and Pete could see him holding up a dust-encrusted instrument in his left hand, pointing sensors at it with his upper right hand, and tracing an engraving on the bottom surface with his lower right hand. "This is a pre-gate Earth language, and my instruments suggest it's about seven thousand years old."

"But this facility can't be that old... can it?"

"No, the construction reads out as about two-to-three-thousand years old."

"So, either someone was collecting old lab equipment, or ... *using* old equipment?"

The comm crackled. "Hey guys, we're starting to get some indications of movement. Just being in there seems to have caused something to shift." That was Orlin. Pete had spoken only very briefly with him when he entered the facility. He looked around and could see some streams of dust and dirt coming down from the ceiling.

"Confirmed, it's unstable. Finish taking pictures and get out of there," Suminto said.

"*ALERT. ALERT. Meteor Swarm Alert.*"

A synthesized voice came over the comms and could be heard echoing from locations and outside.

"*This is an Emergency Alert over Coalition and local channels. SKYWATCH has confirmed a meteor swarm impact zone extending fifty kilometers either side of a line extending from forty-two point six-seven north latitude, seventy-three point eight-eight west longitude, to forty-four point two-seven north latitude five by seventy-two point six-zero west longitude. Expect impacts of molten debris ranging from point one to two point zero meters in size. Seek immediate cover and avoid structures in danger of collapse. Ground all aircraft and take immediate cover.*"

The message repeated several times. Pete checked the compact slate attached to his left arm. The impact zone was approximately one-hundred by one-fifty kilometers, and almost exactly on their current location! Before he could move he felt the ground jolt. The comm emitted a sharp squeal, but cut off as Serena's agitated voice came over the local comm circuit. "Major, Captain, Sergeant Ralph, get out of there. We had an impact almost on top of the Command Center vehicle. It's been tossed and overturned. Wally and I are going over to check it out. Lieutenant Orlin will keep your route open. Get up and to the surface, that complex is ripe for cave-in."

There was another impact shock, and Pete lost his balance. He put out a hand to stop his fall and inadvertently touched the skeleton on what he'd come to think of as an examination table. Suddenly, the ocular display started to scroll text.

Species... 114. "Ocaricoso"
Deceased.
Height—one point one meters,
Weight (estimated)—36 kilograms
Sex—female (79% probability)
Age at death—thirteen years
Cause of death—agathic decay, accelerated aging
Probability of epigenetic modification—100%

The display paused for a moment, then the next row began to blink as additional text filled the display.

UPDATE PENDING.
Redesignating unknown species as 114 uplift variant
New Designation Species 114.1X—uplifted.
Emergency Medical Tool network update push pending connection.
Network connection... paused
Master server core detected,
Beginning download.
Download completed... resuming EMT network push.
External link authorized and activated.
Case Indigo.
EMT override Five-Alpha, priority one.

DANGER! EXTREME DANGER! Facility Collapse Imminent! Emergency core dump in process.

Ralph yipped in surprise. "Uh, Pete, what did you do? These machines are all starting to light up!" There was a thud, and Eddie could be heard cursing in Eitom in the background.

"Captain! What the *hell* did you do? This damned machine turned on and shocked me, causing me to drop it on my foot!"

Pete was completely unable to respond, because his EMT display stopped scrolling text, everything went blank, and the suit became rigid. Pete was unable to move, unable to see through his nanite ocular (or at all, since his helmet-mounted lights turned off) and the leg and arm sleeves puffed up to immobilize him. He tried to waddle, but the overlapping armor at shoulders and hips seemed to have locked in place.

All he could do was shout. "My EMT has shut down and locked me in place. Leave me and get out of here. I'll try to take it off and join you."

"Not without help, you're not." Eddie came in to the room. Clearly his EMT was still functional. "Ralph, head to the entrance and tell the marine we'll be late."

Ralph yipped in acknowledgement and took off on all fours.

"*Dammit*, Pete, what did you do?" Eddie started pulling at the sleeves, but Pete's suit seemed to be locked together at the now-inflexible joints.

After several minutes of trying in vain to remove the suit, Eddie was ready to pick Pete up and carry him to the exit. They could hear yipping as Ralph returned.

"Sergeant, you were supposed to get out of here." A vibration in the floor indicated the approach of one of the marine mecha.

"You can't carry him, but I can, Major." Orlin had come into the complex to retrieve his friend. "No man—or Caldivar—left behind, sir!"

"I'm not going to argue, Lieutenant. Pick him up and let's go."

"No!" Pete protested. "My suit was communicating with these machines! I can't leave!" There was another distant impact, and a portion of the ceiling fell on the examining table, shattering the skeleton that his suit had briefly identified as *Ocaricoso*. "There's a server here somewhere and we need to find it."

"No, Captain, we're going. Pick him up, marine, we're going now."

Pete felt tethers being attached to his limbs, and then he was picked up and slung across Orlin's back. Ralph led the way as the four of them moved as quickly as they could through the collapsing underground facility. He would have yelled and protested, but in his heart, he knew his Eddie was right.

At the entrance, Orlin attached everyone to a thick cable running down the center, touched a control on his wrist, and they were all yanked from their feet and hauled to the surface. A couple of technicians tending the equipment at the wellhead helped them off to the side and disconnected the lift cable. The narrow walls at the head of the canyon would be less prone to collapse, so the entire team headed for shelter. Pete was still slung across the back of Orlin's mecha, and he saw a large cloud of dust and dirt rising from the wellhead.

They made a shelter at the narrowest part of the canyon—the ceiling was basically Orlin's mecha, supplemented by an emergency survival tent found in one of the technician's packs. There were still minor rock falls with each impact, but they were not in immediate danger of being buried or hit. They stayed sheltered in place for over an hour, until the emergency comm announced that the meteor shower was over.

A few minutes later, they saw Serena coming their way, helping a limping Colonel Suminto and carrying Wally under one arm. They were greeted with relief and a bit of nervous laughter, but Pete just sat silently. His EMT was dead, and he had no idea what caused it, other than the fact that it had identified a new species right before everything went wrong.

He'd finally managed to get his helmet off with Eddie and Serena's help, and went to wipe the dead nanites off of his face when he noticed that the ocular was not completely black. There was a single red dot, and as he watched, it gradually faded to orange, then yellow, then green.

A second green dot appeared next to the first, then a third, then a fourth.

"Hey, uh, guys? Colonel? I think my EMT is booting back up."

Eddie came over to look and said, "Yes, I can see a line of dots on your chest display. Huh, now there's words, but it's that weird old-earth script."

Pete's ocular showed the same script. Fortunately, he'd learned to read it many years ago courtesy of a translation overlay used to view the original displays. "It says 'Memory usage 99.9% - add external storage.'"

"Hey, tech, you got a memory cube in that backpack of yours?" Eddie asked the technician who'd had the survival tent.

The answer was no, but Serena offered to go back the command vehicle and retrieve supplies. With Orlin's help, she got it right-side up and running, and a few minutes later they heard the hum and crunch of the command vehicle approaching on ground wheels as Serena brought it back to their temporary camp.

Pete's EMT did not continue its boot-up process until a technician came back with a storage cube and plugged it into a receptacle on Pete's clamshell. The memory usage message went away, and the green dots continued to fill the display. After another twenty minutes, the suit asked for another storage unit. In all, they filled five storage cubes before the display was filled with green dots, then cleared.

The familiar start-up symbols filled his ocular, quickly replaced by a message Pete had never seen before.

Founder diagnostic interrupt encountered.

Offline storage complete.

Heuristic content rebuild pending transfer to master server.

System broadcast awaiting superuser credentials.

Local broadcast pending playback.

Initiate playback?

"Colonel? My suit seems to want to play a message. It says it encountered a 'Founder diagnostic' and has stored 'heuristic content' on those offline storage cubes."

"Heuristic? Oh, we're going to need to buck that all the way to President Tomeral. His AI, Jayneen, probably needs to analyze those before we dare plug them into anything. Go ahead and play the message, though. See if you can broadcast it."

Pete queried his EMT, and it confirmed that it could broadcast using nanites to form Tri-Vee pixels. Once he acknowledged playback, an image started to form in the middle of their group. The figure was nearly identical to the 'mythological Large Grey' he'd seen in his searches.

Much to their surprise, when it spoke, each of them heard it in their species' native language. Pete heard in in Caldi-high, the technical language, which surprised him, since Caldi-low was used as the universal communications medium.

"Sophonts. If you are viewing this, you have found my laboratory. Hopefully I have finished my work.

"Call me Ozmin. It is not my name, but one you can all understand and pronounce. I have been working on the Ocaricoso—number one-hundred fourteen in my catalog. A natural disaster changed their genetic structure, causing them to age very fast, and they are in danger of extinction. They have such beautiful artworks, poetry, and music, but all will be lost if I cannot restore their lifespan and reproductive ability.

"I fear that I may have to introduce so many changes that they will be unrecognizable. I only hope that in so doing, I do not affect their art.

"I offer to you a gift. The servers in this laboratory are filled with all of my data, but also all of the art I have been able to collect. Look upon my works and rejoice, for I dare not allow such as these to be lost for all eternity!"

"So, HE SUCCEEDED," HARMON Tomeral said.

Pete was a bit nervous being in the compartment with President Tomeral and his top assistants. The AI Jayneen had just finished presenting her analysis of the memory cubes—they were exactly what the recording said. The Salvage System President and Coalition Commander had invited Admiral Lurvel, Colonel Suminto and his team to the briefing and was now open to comments.

"As far as we can tell," the admiral replied. "We have managed to shelter most of the population of Akea, and swept the system of the worst of the cometary fragments. The EMTs all updated even before Colonel Suminto's team got back in contact with us. With the updated EMT database, we can see that the Carico are indeed genetically derived from the Ocaricoso, only with a one-hundred-year lifespan and an effective thirty-year reproductive range. The data from the laboratory suggests that this was all Ozmin's work, since the Ocaricoso only lived twenty years and didn't become fertile until a year before they died of old age."

Eddie and Pete had been busy examining as much of the data as possible once it had been certified not to pose a cyber-security risk.

The Admiral turned to Pete. He knew what was coming, because they had been over it so many times, but he knew they needed to repeat it for the coalition leader. "And it was specifically your suit that triggered the data."

"Yes, sir. Eddie—um, I mean Major Niveen, sir—was in the lab before I was, and he was within visual range when my EMT received the download." Pete responded, then took a sip of water to soothe his very dry throat. It wasn't his first time coming under the scrutiny of President Tomeral, but he had hoped not to have it happen again.

"You do seem to make interesting finds, Doctor Emil. First the EMT, then a kidnapped heiress, now the laboratory of one of the individuals who likely invented that suit."

"Yes sir." It was all Pete could get out without risking a coughing fit. It had been two months, but he still felt as if he was breathing the dusty air of the laboratory.

Harmon smiled. "Be at ease, son. That's a compliment. I understand you have to finish your residency, but I think we'll be talking again."

The President invited them all to remain and enjoy a good meal and hospitality, but all Pete could think of was that he was overdue writing to his mom and Susa. He'd have to break it to her gently that he'd be on Salvage for quite a few more years. It would be all he could do to keep her from insisting on joining him while he was still going to be too busy to spend any time with her.

He was so preoccupied with his thoughts that he didn't even realize Colonel Suminto was standing next to him until his commanding officer leaned over to whisper in his ear. "Tell the young lady to come to Salvage, Major Emil. Majors can marry, after all!"

Five
Unto the Last, Stand Fast

AUTHORS NOTE: THIS WAS the first of three stories I wrote in the Four Horsemen Universe. The other two are included in Volume 1 of *Journeys Beyond the Known*.

I'm a big fan of the Swedish metal band Sabaton. Their songs often tell of heroes and historic battles. I've used a couple of their songs as inspiration to dig into historical events and use them as templates for my writing.

In 1527, Rome was under siege. The pope had to be smuggled out through a secret tunnel to Castel Sant'Angelo before enemies could discover him, resulting in imprisonment, or worse. This was the famous Last Stand of the Swiss Guard.

I had just the right story to make use of this.

While the other two 4HU stories I wrote featured biotech, this was strictly a planetary exploration and colony story. It features humans and an alien race that share a common faith. When their home churches declare them heretics, they band together to smuggle a religious leader to safety. On San Pietro,

the Custode Sviss demonstrates courage and resolve. That unto the last, they will stand fast.

"Father Salvatore. You have a message?"

"Yes, Your Excellency. My contact says they can get me into the Arritim city. They don't guarantee that I will get out."

"Indeed. The Zuul. They have besieged the city."

"My contact says that the Zuul are not much of a threat. Their lines have too many holes and only one hundred mercenario to fill them. They are unable to use the heavy equipment that was liberated from Zaragossa. They are little better than bounty hunters...eager but not very competent."

"Then we still have a chance to get the Holy One out?"

"Not likely. The Arezzo General Pompe'oCo has brought his own troops, but they are restless. They threaten to sack the city, but for now, Pompe'oCo holds them in check with the Zuul. My contact is not sure how that will last, the mercenario are outnumbered ten-to-one."

"Dire circumstances, then. We are not a rich colony, and Nuova Roma can only authorize a small amount. We have found an agency from Schweiz that specialize in 'Executive Protection.' We cannot afford them, although we have someone who may assist. Even one company is beyond us, for they are Terran and use 'CASPers,' as I think they are called."

"If we cannot afford them, then it matters not if they are even Zaragossan discards, which the Zuul possess, but cannot use. My fear is that the Arezzo might."

"We have a chance at the Schweiz Company, Salvatore. I will send a gentleman with you to Commu'neDi. Mr. Jefferson has been helpful in negotiations with the mercenario. You should have two weeks. The mercenario cannot be here before then."

"Wait, you said we could not afford them!"

"There is more than money of interest to warriors. We have arranged a 'deal' if you will."

"A deal? No, I will not inquire further, you would only dissemble. Yet may I ask how many? I will have the Arritim prepare a passage for them."

"Ah, you wound me, Salvatore!"

"Merely the truth, your Excellency. No more than is right for the Church."

"It is good that you understand, Salvatore. More mercenario than the one hundred Zuul, but not by much. Around two hundred."

"One-hundred eighty-nine, perhaps? Of the Mercenario Sviss? I have heard of this legend. Perhaps the Heavenly Father makes a joke at our expense."

FRANK JEFFERSON TURNED so that he did not have to see his wife's face as he packed. It was only a small bag; where he was going, he would need only lightweight clothing. If the plan worked, the rest of his gear would meet him on-site. If the plan didn't work, it wouldn't matter, so either way, there was no point in taking too much.

Betsy was crying now, silently, except for the occasional sob. As he sealed the final pouch and applied the device to the valve which would suck all of the excess air out of the package, he turned and took her face in his hands.

"I have to do this, my love."

"No, you don't. Franklin Washington Adams Jefferson, you told me you gave up that. You gave it up for me and to 'buy the farm' you said."

"Betsy Jefferson, I am doing this for you. If this goes badly, there will be no farm, and you will be in danger."

"But it's not your job to defend the Stars or their church!"

"I swore an oath, Betsy."

"Not to them! It's not even your Church!"

"No, my love, I swore it to you. Love, honor, cherish, defend and protect, 'til death do us part."

"If you love me, you'll say no!"

"Ah, but love is only one of the terms, my heart, I promised to cherish, defend and protect. I would not be protecting you if the War comes to San Pietro."

"What can one man do?"

"Not one alone, but my Company will be there."

"And you? Why do they need you if they have the Company? You promised me that you left that behind."

"It is duty, Betsy, duty and love. 'Greater love hath no man than this that a man lay down his life...' for his friends, for his love, for his God, for his home."

"Promise me you'll come back."

"I can only promise to Stand Fast, my love. Unto the Last."

"YOU KNOW, PADRE, I for damn sure wouldn't mind heading to the damned 'Star' city if it wasn't so damned wet!"

"Patience Mr. Jefferson, patience....and please temper your tongue."

Frank just gave a snort of disgust and sat down on the edge of the PlasForm dock attached to the last solid ground for miles. He took off his shoes and hung his feet down into the warm water. He didn't see any crocagators floating in the still water, and this close to the Stars' waterlogged city, there would be few aquatic predators with a taste for human.

Aside from the long peninsula they'd walked in on, they were surrounded by wetlands—bogs, marshes, swamps, trees and open water. On Earth this might be called 'bayou' or 'canali.' On San Pietro it was simply called 'The Wet.' Any human traveling to The Wet knew to dress for heat, humidity and frequent rain. Thus, Frank wore short pants, a loose sleeveless shirt and a hat with a floppy brim to keep the sweat and water out of his eyes. Despite his complaining and the heavy pack on his back, Frank was perfectly comfortable in the light rain, sitting with his feet in water almost to his knees.

Father Salvatore, on the other hand, just *had* to be uncomfortable in his vestments, light weight as they were. He was a big man, and the cassock covered him from head to toe. It didn't look like it was waterproof, either, which meant it had to weigh a ton with absorbed water. However, the only sign that he even noticed the humidity and rain was occasionally removing his glasses to wipe away the water droplets. His face was calm, and he continued to stand at the edge of the dock, looking out along the narrow canal leading to the Arritim city.

Frank noticed a faint ripple, about a quarter klick down the water-way. As it approached, he could see the characteristic 'V' shape of a boat wake. As it approached the dock, the vessel raised slightly out of the water. It was open at the top and filled with water inside. The Arritim communities were largely aquatic, thus their conveyances remained open to the water except for the minimum streamlining required to reduce resistance. The boat—if it could be called that and not a submarine—rose up to the level of the dock and approached to within a few decimeters. There was a driver and one passenger. Much the same as Frank's own party, but while the passenger and Father Salvatore could converse; Frank had little in common with the boat driver, and nothing to say in this meeting. His role would come later.

The passenger rose and stepped out of the water-filled interior onto the dock. He bowed and offered a 'hand' to the Padre. Salvatore, on the other hand, dropped to one knee and kissed the large ornate jewel affixed to one digit of the alien appendage.

"Your Eminence."

There was clearly some form of starfish in the aliens' develop-mental past, hence the nickname 'Stars' for individual Arritim. The three upper appendages—two 'arms' and a 'head'—were conical projections from a circular central body. Each ended in small bone-less digits—and yes, there were ten per limb. Frank knew from the colonist database that the digits on the 'head' were specialized sen-sory organs, while the ones of the arms served the same function as fingers. The lower limbs were hidden within a garment that looked remarkably like water-filled coveralls, reminding the human colonists of pictures of Old-Earth farmers. Most of the central body, contain-ing the mouth, brain and respiratory organs, was concealed beneath the fluid, but a pair of eye stalks poked out above the surface and continuously scanned the area. The digits of one limb held a small plas-and-metal object, and from this issued a synthesized voice.

"Rise, Father Salvatore, and be at peace. Tell me, what do you hear from Nuova Roma?"

"Thank you, Your Eminence. The news is mixed. The Terran Holy See remains adamant that the Soglio di Pietro remain on Earth and threatens excommunication of Nuova Roma. Even though His Holiness emigrated to Nuova Roma, the Terrans have declared the Stellar Catholic Church heretical. They have their own troubles, and can do little to assist us. We have arranged for a single company of mercenario, and must find a way to get them into Commu'neDi when they arrive."

"That is unfortunate, Teofilo. My source tells me that the Arezzo General Pompe'oCo brought a thousand souls to discipline us, but cannot control them. It would be most regretful if Rome chose to do the same."

"These are turbulent times. The Terran Church senses that it is losing influence. There are those who protest that the races of the stars—even humans—cannot be of true faith for they have never trod the same ground as the Savior. The Holy See has many cardinals who are ready to agree and declare us *all* heretics."

"It is much the same with us. The General has been calling for the return of the Epichysis and the Telum for several years now. He has been telling the Commons that Arrita'yTer has 'stolen the history' of the Arezzo homeland.

"Dark days, then. He has over a thousand in his force. How can we resist?"

"'At least a thousand souls' according to the reports. Of course, I fear for their souls if they are following Pompe'oCo. I have dealt with him before, and he owes his allegiance to the highest bidder, and not any Divine Direction, no matter what his propaganda says. There are rumors that he has not paid his mercenaries, either. If he does that to his followers, they will revolt."

"In that case there is no more time to waste. I must get into the city, see the Holy One, and then we must prepare accommodations for our own mercenario." Salvatore turned to Frank. "Bless you for indulging an old priest Mr. Jefferson. If you are ready?"

"Oh, not so fast, Father, I have to go, you do not." Frank stood and reached into the heavy bag he'd carried down from the human settlement. He pulled an underwater breathing system that he would need for the trip in the Arritim 'boat.' I promised Bishop Crunelli that I would send you back. He'd never forgive me if I lost you."

"Ah, the impetuosity of youth. You may have me in years, but I know my duty, as well as you know yours, my son." The priest set his legs, and stared at Frank.

"Yes, of course." He reached into his pack and pulled out a second rebreather. "I promised I would send you. I never promised you would go." With that, he handed over the mask and offered the priest a hand to help him into the watercraft."

Father Salvatore's lined face crinkled into a grin. "Ah. Shall we go then?"

FRANK TRIED TO HIDE his unease as he waded down the 'street.' He and Father Salvatore had been in the city for over a week, and he'd long gotten over both amazement and feeling conspicuous, but tonight would be a bit different, and Frank's mission was critical to their own safety, let alone success. Father Salvatore was conspicuous in his cassock and vestments, yet human seafarmers were common enough that Frank was able to pass relatively unnoticed through the shallow canals that formed the thoroughfares of the alien city. The Stars averaged a few inches shorter than most humans, and preferred water to what would be waist level if they were human. Thus, the pedestrian walkways were about hip deep to a human, and easily accessible to the San Pietro colonist.

He was dressed in typical clothing for those who worked the sea platforms—a tight fitting singlet from mid-thigh to shoulders that kept the water out and his unexposed skin dry, topped by a mesh 'shirt' and head scarf to filter the sun. His feet were clad in light-weight neoprene moccasins that provided traction without adding weight or getting waterlogged. Unlike the humans, nearly all of the Arritim lived in Commu'neDi. Humans on the other hand lived in many places, the cool dry uplands, the hot, humid coast, the deep-sea platforms, and now the archipelago and shallow seas near the Arritim city. They were adaptable, and Frank's clothing reflected that adaptability to the point that he was actually pretty comfortable despite the heat and humidity.

Frank was still a bit bemused at the human and aliens sloshing through the water around him. Even though it happened decades before he married Betsy, 'bought the farm' and settled on San Pietro, it still hadn't been that long since the human colony and the Arritim had been at war over perceived 'invasion' of their colony worlds. The truth was that both colonies were planted at the same time, and the two races would not even have known the other was present except for a chance encounter. The archipelago and shallow seas around Commu'neDi were far enough from the settlement of San Pietro that it would have been decades before the humans ventured that far. To make matters worse, the two colonies were meant to be religious sequesters, and finding *aliens* in their respective hermitage had led to the short Heretic Wars. Only when an Arritim Prisoner of War discovered common ground with a San Pietrese priest, was a settlement reached. The peace turned into alliance and even friendship on common religious grounds—an issue which irritated the respective home churches on both Terra and Arezzo, the Arritim home world, leading to the current unpleasantness.

He reached his destination and entered the building through the water-level doorway. Like most Commu buildings, it was low, but wide, with three levels: one completely under water, the entry level half-filled with water to the same depth as the canals, and an upper level that could be kept dry for storage or human use. The Arritim used all levels, although humans preferred to get out of the water. A few buildings even had additional or enlarged upper floors to accommodate the humans with business in the city. This particular building filled a city block and had a roof access. Frank quickly moved to the uppermost level and looked out over the city. He could see the evidence of the siege off on the horizon—dark shapes and ripples from the submerged platforms. Occasionally there was a wisp of smoke, but that was probably from the Zuul, neither the Arritim nor their Arezzo cousins had much use for fire. There was also no need for Frank to hide from their own view of him; the Arezzo barely acknowledged that the uplanders existed, except to condemn their corrupting influence on the Arrita'yTer religion. Their biggest blind spot was anything more than a few meters above water—a fact that Frank and the Father had counted on for getting their own mercenary reinforcements into the city. He'd wait until dusk, then light the infrared marker for the stealth shuttle delivering the first of the Mercenario Svizz, as Father Salvatore called them.

As darkness fell, Frank could see the green beams and white tracers as the surrounding Zuul and Arezzo fired off their weapons. The last week had been filled with rumors—mostly that Pompe'oCo was losing control. The weapons fire seemed to be increasing, and suggested that there was some truth to the rumor. It was fully dark when he heard three clicks through the waterproof radio he was wearing under his head scarf. Even though he was toward the edge of the roof, he moved even further out such that the roof access was between him and the designated landing zone. A brief rush of wind and a shimmer in the air heralded the arrival of the stealth shuttle. After some muffled sounds and indistinct movement on the rooftop, one shadow separated itself from the others and came up in front of Frank.

"For the Grace, for the might of Our Lord" spoke Frank.

"For the Faith, for the Way of the Sword" replied a voice with the countersign. "I'm Captain Riedel. You are?"

"Frank Jefferson. I've been sent to meet you." Frank peered out at the still indistinct shadows moving on the rooftop. The Captain had night vision optics pushed up on his head, so the others probably had the same. "I see a maybe a platoon. Where are the others?

"Oh, hell no, this isn't even a platoon. The shuttles aren't big enough."

"A Mark Nine can handle two platoons and gear."

"We're not using Mark Nine's anymore, 'Prez.'"

Frank whirled to face the person behind him. He was about to lay into the newcomer for using that handle until he recognized the face behind the voice. His face lit in a smile. "Steel? How'd they drag your sorry ass down here? And why aren't you using Mark Nine's?"

Nicholas "Steel" Stihl laughed. "Same as you, I guess. I hadn't expected to see you here, either, Prez."

"Actually, I live here now. I 'bought the farm.'" He paused a moment, then clarified. "Colonization credits. Betsy wanted forty acres and a mule. They haven't decanted all the mules yet, but we've got a spread up in the mountains where it's cooler and drier."

"Betsy, huh. So, she waited for you. Lucky dog. Oh, and a farm sounds nice right about now."

"Yes, but you haven't answered my question. Why aren't you using Mark Nine shuttles? I cleared a landing zone expecting at least a Mark Eight or even O-I-V's!"

"We don't have them. The Company's not in great shape. We were on the wrong side in Zaragossa, lost half of our men, most of our CASPers. Your 'forty acres and a mule' are why most of us are here. One last job to earn colonization credit and then get the hell out of this life."

"Umm, okay. I didn't realize that was the Company at Zaragossa. On the other hand, I might know how you can get some of that equipment back..."

"Gentlemen. Focus," the Captain interrupted. "We need to secure a perimeter, secure the Principal, clear the area inside the perimeter, and then determine exfil. Once we get the Headquarters platoon down the Major can fill you in." He paused, as if listening to something. "Oh. That's f—-ed up. The Zuul have filed protest and Breach of Contract. The General has lost control of his mob."

Raising his voice slightly, he spoke to the troops on the rooftop: "Mission change. We need to get the rest of Second platoon down *now,* with First and Third down by daybreak. Clear the shuttle and send it back up. McCarthy! Alpha Squad arm up and on me." Turning back to Frank he explained. "The Major has been monitoring the Guild channels. He was expecting something like this. It just means we accelerate the schedule and we *are* bringing everyone down tonight. I think we'd better go see your Holy One right away."

Steel grinned. "So, does this mean you're back in the game, Colonel?"

The captain's head whipped around at the mention of the rank. "Colonel? What? Who?"

Steel pointed to Frank. "Lieutenant Colonel Franklin Washington Adams Jefferson. Call-sign 'Prez' since he was named for presidents of the old US of A."

"Full Colonel, Steel; and Benjamin Franklin was never President."

"Sure, but at least he got his face on the hundred-credit chit."

"YOUR HOLINESS, PLEASE KEEP your head down" Major Christopher DiNote told the Arritim priest. "We cannot be certain that there are not snipers within the city already."

DiNote, Jefferson, and the human and Arritim priests were on the top floor of one of the few three-story buildings in the city. The balcony was designed to not only provide a commanding view of the city, but also to provide the city with a view of the occupants of the balcony. It was this latter that concerned the mercenary commander.

For a race that has little use for fire, they are certainly embracing it now, Frank thought. Columns of smoke rose from several points around the perimeter of the city. In a purely human city, there would be shouting and crowds in the streets. The Stars had a high ululation instead of shouting, but it was largely inaudible to the humans. The depth of water in the streets had deepened as levees at the edge of town were damaged by the besieging army, making passage more difficult, but keeping the crowds down. Still, the locals were resisting to the best of their ability— the Arritim had changed more than their racial name when they left their homeland on Arezzo—they had no desire to submit once again to their distant cousins. In all, though, it was a remarkably quiet siege, save for the sound of distant weapons fire, and the occasional ricochet or stray projectile shot.

The priests had wanted to come up to the balcony to assess the conditions in the city themselves. As was fairly typical for both holy "men" they disregarded the risk to themselves, leaving that worry to Frank and the Major. A slight "tink" sound caught the Franks attention, and he looked down to see a deformed fragment of metal. He picked it up and held it out in his palm for the priests to see.

"Father Salvatore, Patriarch Clement, you really need to take cover. This is a railgun projectile. It's spent, which means the range was too far, but that won't be the case for much longer. We need to get you to cover before the skirmish lines ...sooner rather than later.

FRANK AWOKE IN THE dark. He blinked twice, and the chrono display in his contacts showed the time: 0423. *Oh-Dark-Thirty*. So, he'd been asleep for two hours. Mediating the argument between the two priests and the mercenary commander had taken them well past midnight. Two hours' sleep was enough to take the edge off of fatigue, but it wasn't *real* sleep...that or he'd gotten soft in his years as a farmer.

Something had awoken him, though, and as he searched his memory, he realized that he'd heard a squishing sound, similar to that made by water-filled boots. *Arritim? Or Arezzo?* He blinked, and then squinted, activating the night-vision mode of his contacts. *Strange, he hadn't worn a chrono in years, let alone a tactical vision system. He'd* liked *being out of the game, but apparently; the game wasn't out of him.*

Without moving, he scanned the room. *There!* It was one of the Stars alright, but not armed. The threat-detection readout in the corner of his visual field was yellow-green, no threats other than the strange presence.

"Colonel Jefferson?" The synthesized voice gave little clue as to the identity of the speaker, but the use of his old rank did. So far, only a few of the Company, Father Salvatore, and the Star's High Priest knew that detail.

"Patriarch." Frank gave the minimum response, waiting for the Holy One to reveal his purpose for disturbing Frank's sleep. "

"Colonel. I do not know these Men of Fire and Flame." The Patriarch continued. I do not know you, but Father Salvatore says you are a good man. I fear for my people. I fear for the Faithful, and am not comfortable with this plan. I should reveal myself to Pompe'oCo and let him take me and spare the city."

Frank sat silent. This was precisely what they had argued so late last night. DiNote favored booby-trapping the main avenues of advance, then setting up a hard line of defense around Patriarch. This would slow down the Arezzo, funnel them into zones where snipers could attrit the forces and smash them against reinforced defenses at the basilica. The priests had argued that the plan was too dangerous to the city's inhabitants. Personally, Frank thought that the Major's plan was ignoring the fundamental axiom of never assuming you had an unassailable position. On the other hand...

"Your Holiness..." Frank began, but was interrupted by a static sound from the Star's translator.

"That title is somewhat doubtful at the moment. Please, just call me Father Clement."

"Very well, Father, but I am not a Colonel at present. Just Mister Jefferson...or Frank." Frank paused a moment, then continued his original thought: "Father, you have no guarantee that surrender will save your people. The Arezzo forces out there are behaving in every manner consistent with fanatics. The General has stirred them up, and they will settle for nothing less than destroying you and your church. You may think you'll save lives by not resisting, but it is my professional opinion that the only guarantee of saving lives is to stop the enemy cold."

The electronic box produced a pretty good emulation of a sigh. Interesting that someone had programmed the translators in such a manner. "You may be right, Mister Jefferson, but I fear for my people. Mine and yours, for Pompe'oCo may not stop with just Commu'neDi."

"His troops won't be venturing up into the high plains, Father. Not easily."

"Not by themselves, but they've demonstrated a willingness to use orbital weapons."

That was true. It was why the full Company was not on the ground, including the CASPers. The shuttle carrying Headquarters Platoon had been shot down. It was next to last, with the CASPers scheduled to come down in the final pass. If Major DiNote hadn't come down as soon as he heard of the Zuul withdrawal; Frank might very well have found himself in command. He had mixed feelings over that possibility. He wasn't sure the Major was taking into account the fanaticism of the enemy, nor the obstinacy of the defenders.

"We need something different, Father. Something no one is expecting…" Frank trailed off. An idea occurred to him. It was something that had been nagging at him since he first heard that the Arezzo were bringing Zuul mercenaries to the planet. It had more to do with where he'd last heard of the Zuul…Zaragossa.

He stood, donned his boots and reached into the small locker at the foot of his cot. He'd brought it. Despite Betsy's protests and his own misgivings, he'd brought his uniform tunic, with the three stars and braid of a full Colonel's rank insignia. "Father, I think perhaps we should wake up the Major. I have an idea, and I suspect I'm going to have to pull rank to get him to go for it!"

"I STILL SAY WE fort up and make them come to us." The Major was insistent. "We can hold a fixed position against a thousand irregulars, no problem…and it won't even *be* a thousand because we're grinding them down as they work their way to us."

"At the cost of half the city. These people have to *live* here, Major. *I* have to live here when this is done," Frank clarified. "We need to draw them off. Make them think they've won, or at least are winning, and that their main target is not here. It's the only way to get them to leave the city alone."

"How? You just argued the priest out of surrendering himself on the basis that Pompe'oCo will kill everyone even once he has the Patriarch!"

"Misdirection, Sir." That was Steel. Frank had had to give him a brief outline of the plan, since everything would hinge on Steel's platoon. "If the Father is in Pompe'oCo's hands, he has no reason not to sack the city. On the other hand, if he has confirmed intelligence that the Patriarch is somewhere else, he'll pivot his forces to follow, leaving only a token force which we can easily clean up."

That gave the Major pause. He stroked his chin. "...and just how do you intend to get the priests—I assume you mean to everyone out, and not just the Patriarch—out of the city? If you hadn't noticed, we're somewhat surrounded. The Arezzo are aquatic, so underwater is out. Pompe'oCo is no idiot, so he knows that humans would take to the air. We've certainly seen that he has anti-air assets. How are you planning on getting them out?"

"For that, we need the CASPers," Frank said quietly.

"What the Hell?" Major DiNote exploded. "Our CASPers are in orbit! They're Mark 6's, we can't just drop them from orbit!"

"But what if you had Mark 7's?" Frank continued in that quiet voice.

"We lost our Mark 7's at Zaragossa. I thought you were better informed than that, *Colonel*!" The Major spat the rank title in disgust.

"...and who did you lose them to?" Frank was being extraordinarily patient. His face showed neither anger nor apathy, but his quiet demeanor was somewhat unnerving to onlookers.

"We lost them to the damn Zuul when we had to pull out of Zaragossa!" The Major was cooling down at bit, but it was more out of regret at the loss than disgust at the situation. "Damned incompetent Eatees, but we were hired by the wrong side."

Frank waited just a moment before dropping his final point. He wanted to see if the Major would fill in the gaps himself. "Remember the day you landed? The notice of Breach of Contract? "

Light was beginning to dawn in the Major's eyes. "The Zuul..." He swallowed, and turned toward Frank, for the first time with a look of appraisal and respect. "Do you think they still have them?"

"The letter of protest cited lack of payment, divided command, and the fact that the Stars had confiscated the six CASPers that the Zuul had brought with them intending to use as siege engines. They can't operate them, but they can slave them to a common command link." It was Steel's time to fill in the details, even though it was pretty clear that the implications were dawning on his commander.

"What about ammunition, then?" It was an honest question, not a challenge like the Major's former comments. "Surely the Zuul wouldn't have done much to rearm the CASPers. Not that I would trust anything the Zuul would use."

"All we need are small munitions. Grenades, Penetrators, just about anything explosive; HEAT would be nice, but not really necessary, and no long-range or orbital." Frank pulled out a slate with a list of armaments he needed, and handed it to the Major. "Call for a ballistic drop pod, have them place it in the Wet for recovery."

"The 'Wet?'"

"Bayou. Swamps. To the west back where this archipelago starts. We'll need to work from there, anyway."

"Very well, Colonel Jefferson. I expect I shall be relinquishing command to you, then." The Major had removed a small white baton from his belt, and was holding it out to Frank. "I'll have the adjutant draw up the Transfer of Command. Have you considered who is going to operate those CASPers, since my Squad is still in orbit?"

Steel laughed, turned his head and pointed to the control implant jack behind his ear. "That's where my heavy weapons platoon comes in." He turned back to Frank. "Welcome back, Prez. This should be fun!"

The major snorted and Frank rolled his eyes, but he accepted the baton and clipped it onto his belt.

"You want me to *WHAT?*" The disbelief was quite evident in Sergeant 'Bugs' Schmidt's tone, even though no-one could see his face from inside the CASPer.

"It's called the Buckley Maneuver. You launch a penetrator at the rock. You make a hole. You insert a grenade into the hole, back up, and blow the grenade. You drag the rubble out of the way, then rinse, lather and repeat." Steel's voice came from the second CASPer. "I'll be right behind you, breaking up anything too big to remove. If you get a particularly stubborn piece, we'll take it on together. You get a big rock, but you can get past it, do so. I'll take care of it."

"You're crazy, and so is the Colonel! We're below water level, the tunnel will flood!" That was Roeder—aka 'Roadblock'—in the third CASPer, the one tasked with covering their rear, at least until it was his turn to rotate up front.

"Exactly. That's the beauty of it. It carries the heat away when I fuse the walls; it washes out small debris and muffles the sound. We've got pumps for when we're done." Steel's CASPer turned and surveyed the area. A slight pop accompanied the *ping* of a projectile aimed at a crocagator that was getting a bit too nosy. "Now, get digging, Sergeant!"

'Liberating' the CASPers had been easier than they'd predicted thought. It mostly involved getting a squad close enough to enter the Command Override and erase any commands that the Zuul or Arezzo had entered in their attempts to utilize the human equipment. The Zuul had stationed the units in the shallows off-shore from Commu'neDi as part of their original siege line. Most of the Arezzo had long since moved into the outskirts of the city, save for a few technicians who still hoped that they could operate the CASPers. Evolution and intelligence had turned the radially symmetric starfish into a reasonable facsimile of bipedal, bilaterally symmetric humanoid. The main obstacle had been the human counter-intrusion software and compatibility with strictly human brain implants—an obstacle the mercenaries were happy to exploit.

The real problem had not been accessing the CASPers, but rather moving the Combat Assault System, Personal. They didn't dare use the jumpjets, and it wouldn't matter if they had. Zuul mercenaries were not known for meticulous maintenance and upkeep on their *own* technology, let alone something they could barely use. Only one armored combat suit had functioning jets, and three of the six had drained capacitors, one was even missing its cockpit cover and showed evidence of a catastrophic blowout of the ammo magazines. It was obvious why the Zuul had only used them as fixed position cannon—they weren't good for much more than that.

In the end, they'd scavenged canopy, spare parts and ammo, then sunk the three castoffs with thermite grenades on a delayed fuse. The working suits were removed by raft—the same way Steel and his platoon had arrived—to take advantage of the Arezzo's cultural nearsightedness regarding events above water. They'd returned to The Wet and waited for the drop pod carrying ammo, fuel cells, and pumps. Fully armed, and fueled, it was now time to dig.

FRANK FOUND THE PRIEST in the Basilica. It was hard to think of it as a church; it seemed more like an indoor swimming pool with an altar. Most of the humans had left the city, but a few had stayed to join the fight, so Father Salvatore had been hearing confessions from both humans and Arritim. The Arezzo mob had pushed back the Arritim into an area barely three blocks on a side. The Basilica sat on the highest ground of the island which formed the anchor for the mostly-floating city. At that, it was only about 10 meters above water level, but at three stories tall, it had a commanding view of the city...and the fighting. The same height made it a commanding target. Frank and Major DiNote had argued for a more peripheral, less conspicuous hold-out, but the priests had insisted.

"Father Salvatore. Please, it is time to go. Please tell the Patrician that we must ensure his safety."

"Your friends, they are here?" The priest had been showing his age, not to mention the wear of living inside a siege. He'd finally shed the cassock, wearing only the minimal vestments over a light seafarmer's garment. Even the stole and pectoral cross would have to be left behind when they evacuated.

"Not yet, but we must be prepared to move. The mob is getting close. The citizens cannot hold them. They've done enough and we've told them to hide and stay out of sight and be safe. It's up to the Company, now." Frank looked around for the Patrician. "Where is Father Clement?"

"He has gone to retrieve the Holy Relicts. If the Arezzo are indeed a mob, they will likely not recognize the Epichysis and Telum as valuable and destroy them."

"The Epi-whatsit and Telum? A telum is a sort of spear, right?"

"That is correct, Franklin. In this case, a spearhead; it is a true relict—a leftover from another time as well as a crystal formed inside of rock. The Epichysis is a vessel for holding oil, wine or some other liquid. A pitcher. On Earth, some might call it the Sangreal."

"The Holy G—? Um. Yeah. Okay, so that's what this is all about? Mystical artifacts with magical effects?"

"No, only mystery in the ecclesiastical sense. Unlike humans, the Arritim have a complete authenticated history of their church. The Epichysis was used to hold oils for interment rites, and the Telum was used to confirm the death of martyrs. No magic, just a powerful reminder that the Arritim believe in the same Divine Grace as we do."

"If it's so holy, yet so well documented, what's the fuss? Shouldn't they be in the hands of Father Clement's church anyway?" A faint rumbling shook the floor and Frank began to look around as ripples appeared in the water.

"The Arezzo do not think so. While most have rejected the Patriarch, some still feel that the Epichysis and Telum are their own historical artifacts. The rest feel that they symbolize a primitive superstition and should be destroyed and kept out of the hands of 'alien-loving heretics.'"

"O-kay. Now that sounds like what you said Rome was saying about *you*." The rumbling increased; it was now evident as a serious of thumps. Frank took the priest's arm and guided him to the edge of the room. "So, which side does the General fall on?"

"According to Father Clement, he wears the veneer of a believer, but his true motivation is to eliminate this colony. After all, the Arritim turned their back on their homeworld, and he thinks *that* is the true heresy. He wishes to destroy us, Arritim *and* human."

"Ah. Just another bully, then. I guess that makes my own motivation that much clearer." The water level began to fall, and Frank could see cracks in the floor of the Basilica. "Yup, right on time. Father, your ride is here. You'd better go get the Patriarch and his Holy Grail and get ready to go down that tunnel!"

STEEL, BUGS AND ROADBLOCK widened the hole and secured the follower line that they laid in place to guide evacuees through the tunnel. They'd given up on keeping water out of the tunnel—the Arritim would be perfectly comfortable in the water as long as there was light, and the few humans would use breath-packs. The only problem was figuring out who would get the fifty breathing systems they'd managed to collect.

"Bugs! You're going back down the tube; take Bravo Squad of Third Platoon on point. Get to the far end and secure it. I'm pulling Second Platoon off of the defense and sending them to guide and guard Father Clement and Father Salvatore. Frank looked around and counted mentally, Bravo was ten, the platoon another thirty, plus the human priest. "And...we have 8 more civilians; give them breath packs and flashlights. Captain Riedel, get your platoon and the civilians down that line. There's one more breath-pack; Major, I think that needs to be you."

"No, Colonel, as the senior officer, you have to preserve Command."

"Not me, Major. Wrong choice. The men don't know me other than as a plaque on the wall or stories told in a bar. Besides, I'm not active duty. If someone's going to make it through this and collect on behalf of the Company, it needs to be you. No argument. Go!" Frank paused a moment, and looked at the second CASPer. "Roadblock! As soon as the last person goes down the tunnel, block off this end. You're the road-block for real."

As Frank turned toward the exit, he was stopped by the surprisingly gentle touch of the armored limb of the third CASPer. Steel's voice came over the comm implant that Frank still wore despite years away from the Company. "You realize that when Second pulls off of the line, it's going to weaken. We might not be able to hold."

"Then we hold long enough for Roadblock to collapse this end of the tunnel."

"That was pretty novel idea, having us dig a tunnel."

"Not really, I got the idea from some books I read and a song I heard when I was young. Besides, the Stars pretty much *only* think about open water. They know that humans utilize the surface and the air above, so they would've expected us to make an aerial escape. Only a desperate man would tunnel underground, and the Stars could *never* conceive of tunnels inside solid ground. It worked."

"He's got a guard of forty-two…"

"…along a secret avenue. You heard that song, too. How many left outside?" Frank asked.

"One hundred fifty-five, plus you and me," came the reply over the comm.

"Okay, then, history repeats. We're the One Hundred Eighty-Nine, and there's no question but that we're in the Service of Heaven!" In a quieter voice, he added, "and the General is just one more bully that needs to be stopped. For our homes and families."

Frank stepped out the front door of the church, and positioned himself at the top of the stairs leading down to the water. He pitched his voice to activate the Company comm channel.

"Gentlemen. Time to stand fast."

A MIXED GROUP OF humans and Stars gathered in front of the ruined church, it's far long since extinguished, and the stains of blood and soot long washed away by the frequent rains. Father Salvatore and Father Clement stood directly in front of the obelisk on which were inscribed, starting from the top, one-hundred and fifty-five names, and then further down, another forty-two names were added to the memorial so that all would remember the sacrifice of the Company.

Major DiNote knelt in front of Betsy, presenting her with both the flag of the Schweitz Company, for Frank's service, and the American Flag for his country of birth. "For no greater love...In grateful remembrance." The words had changed, for few nations claimed the obedience of those who fought on their behalf.

Schmidt and Roeder stood at attention in full uniform to either side of the priests. Their uniforms bore two new devices: The Christian Cross symbol bisected by a spear point on a field of red, gold and blue signified that they were now members of the Arrita'yTer Guardians. A smaller version served not only as a campaign ribbon on the uniforms of the surviving members of the Company, but also signified that they were now landowners on San Pietro. Major DiNote had received the necessary release to muster out all survivors and then reconstitute the guard force under the employ of San Pietro in exchange for their land-grants. In a very real way, all one-hundred and eighty-nine had 'bought the farm.'

After the ceremony and brief homilies by both human and Arritim priest, Father Salvatore took DiNote aside. "One thing I never asked, Franklin was neither Deutsch nor Schweitz. How did he come to be part of the Mercenario Sviss? You yourself are...Italiano?"

"Ah, yes. Well, I suppose you'd have no reason to know. We're not all from Schweiz Colony. In fact, most of us enlisted for Colony Credits. Neue Schweitz could take a few, and others could cash out and invest in Terran Outbound—land grants as long as you swear to defend them. That's what Frank did...how he ended up here...and why he felt obligated to fight." The Major, soon to be Captain General of the 'Custode Sviss' Executive Protection Company, sighed. "As for me, Italian roots, Catholic even, but I'm from New Jersey. Just like Frank was from Texas."

"So, why do you do it? Why did he do it?"

"As I said to Betsy. 'No greater love.' Sometimes it's the only way to stop an enemy force. Not to mention that there's just something in our psychology that can't abide a bully."

Six

Best Laid Plans

AUTHOR'S NOTE: THIS WAS one of the earliest short stories I wrote. It was intended to be the opening of a novel. Unfortunately, the larger story has never quite taken shape the way I'd intended. It still sits on my to-do list, plotted and outlined, but far down the list of my other writing projects that need to come first.

Still, the opening was pretty well self-contained. So, I pulled it out, polished it up, and submitted it a couple of times early in my writing career...

...and it was rejected.

Ten years and more than 30 short stories sold (not to mention seven novels and editing two anthologies of my own) I know what the flaws were. It was early in my writing experience, I didn't understand the market, and frankly, I hadn't developed my style yet.

I revisited the story for this volume to introduce the "establishing an interstellar colony" part of the book and to pose the question: What happens when a team of explorers arrives at a world to prepare it for eventual colonization—knowing full

well that it's a one-way mission, and there may be no support for families for years to come—and one of their members is pregnant?

It is said that no plan survives contact with the enemy. Sometimes, nothing can survive contact with the best laid plans.

Part 1: Stowaway

"WHAT THE HELL?" THE voice rang out from the next compartment, the one that monitored all of the cryo pods.

"Captain?" I asked, my voice loud enough to carry over faint machinery noises and through several partitions.

"How the hell did she get pregnant in hibernation?" I could hear Captain Batel stomping around in the next compartment, still muttering and cursing.

I was about to go get up and go see what had caused the outburst when several alerts showed up on my board. *Excalibur* was moving through a region of increased proton flux.

"Alert. Strong solar wind with varying magnetic flux encountered." The cool voice was designed to be calming yet cut through any background noise.

"Thank you, Arthur," I said, responding to the ARTificial HEURistic intelligence handling most of the ship's operations until we woke up the rest of the crew.

I wanted to go find out what had the captain so worked up, but I was still in the process of checking ship's system since wake-up a week ago. The Storm Cellar Remote Access Monitor was a poor substitute for the engine room or my bridge engineering station, but until I verified that *Excalibur's* crew habitat areas were, in fact, habitable, the captain, chief medical officer and I were confined to cramped quarters.

"Wally, can you spare a monitor for the readout of Pod Nine?" A warm, calm voice asked just as I felt a soft hand on my shoulder.

"Um, Katrin, space is kind of limited in here. Especially with Arthur posting alerts on heavy plasma." I pointed to a plot of *Excalibur's* course toward the center of the Gliese 876. A spiraling plume of ionized hydrogen, helium, carbon, and oxygen was displayed in flashing orange. Fortunately, we'd pass out of it on our way in-system. We were well shielded her in the core of the ship and I wouldn't be suiting up to go outside and inspect the habitat ring for a couple of days.

Katrin spun my chair around, looked me in the eye, and smirked. "Chief Engineer Darnett, are you telling me you can't spare a five-centimeter section of screen to pull up a cryo pod monitor?"

"For you, Chief Medical Officer Karras, anything." I reached behind me, not needing to see simple controls to pull up the med-bay monitors. After all, that was the real function of the SCRAM, it monitored the cryo pods of our one-hundred-fifty hibernating crew members during our fifty-year trip. I was only using it as an Engineering station because it was so damned cold in the rest of the ship. "What's the problem, Sunshine? Did I just hear Herself say someone was pregnant?"

"See for yourself. Pod nine. I must check other patients. Oh, and turn up the heat." She wasn't kidding. The rest of the ship wasn't ready for us to spread out...yet, but even here in the Storm Cellar,

it was cold. After all, fifty years of space-ambient temperature outside this heavily-shielded section took time to warm up. Moreover,
whatever heat we managed to generate had to go toward gradually
warming up the whole ship. It wasn't a fast process, and frankly, it
shouldn't be.

"Just don't steal my blanket," I told her.

I'd known Katrin a long time, and in all that time, she was always
complaining of being cold. It didn't matter—she wore sweaters and
carried blankets to tropical islands. Right now, she was dressed like
a North Sea fisherman in a heavy blue-and-white sweater and black
wool pants. The contrast with her brightly colored fuzzy socks was
amusing, especially since those were being worn *over* her thin ship-
shoes! I'd asked her once if there was a reason why, and she said it
was just fast metabolism. I wasn't entirely convinced, but she'd been
tapped for CMO of *Excalibur*, and headed up the crew selection
team on Earth. She knew her business, and I was just an engineer.

Katrin reached out and grabbed the corner of the blanket covering
my lap and legs as she spun, laughed, and sailed out of the compartment into the short corridor leading to the other cryo pod bay.

I could still hear the captain over the muted alarms, beeps and pings
of the ship systems. She'd gotten more creative in her comments, so
I figured I'd best get on top of the situation.

Right now, Captain Batel, Katrin, and I were the only crew
awake on *Excalibur*—besides Arthur, of course—but while certainly
"awake" and "crew", the ART-HEUR occupied no space, consumed
no food, water, or oxygen, and certainly didn't require body heat.
We were still a couple months out from Gliese 876, and the three
of us were the first ones to be awoken by Arthur following system
arrival protocol: Wake up the Mission Commander, Chief Engineer,

and Chief Medical Officer first to assess the ship and hibernating crew, and decide when (and whether) to start waking up essential personnel.

"Arthur, give me a priority checklist and include pod nine status in that list."

"Engineer Darnett, you are currently on item seventeen of forty-two on the Week 1 pre-arrival checklist. The next high-priority item is visual inspection of core Life Module crew areas, the interior and exterior visual inspection of the habitat ring, and the deployment of accelerated heating for the Life Module. At list item nineteen, you, Captain Batel, and CMO Karras will decide whether to begin awakening the Planetology and Biology section leads to assess the suitability of the Gliese 876 planets for colonization."

The AI paused, then resumed, its voice measured and even. "However, I believe I should call your attention to the condition of the inhabitant of pod nine, as it seems likely to be the source of concern to Captain Batel and Dr. Karras."

"Fine, give me the rundown, Arthur," Wally sighed, not bothering to hide his exasperation.

"The 'rundown,' as you so quaintly put it, Engineer Darnett, is that Dr. Kosov's pod is indicating she is pregnant."

"Wait. What? How?" The words tumbled out of me before I could stop them. My gaze snapped to the five centimeters of screen Katrin had mentioned, immediately hunting for pod nine. The display was narrow, barely enough for the basics, so I reached out, fingers skimming over the control surface, expanding the medical readout and shoving aside the image of the solar storm straddling the ship's course.

The crew record appeared: Nikki Kosov, our lead xenobiologist. Low pod numbers, section head, should have known that, but my brain was still sluggish, still dragging itself out of cryo-hibernation.

Sure enough, the vital signs showed two heartbeats. "She passed preflight medical—they would have noticed!" I blurted.

"I know you are aware hibernation in a cryo pod does not entirely halt aging. *Excalibur*'s pods are actually complete Doc-in-the-Box medical treatment and stasis devices. Medical cryostasis slows metabolism to the point that the patient accumulates one day of biological aging every two hundred days in stasis. Dr. Kosov's pod confirms uninterrupted hibernation since Luna Station departure. That totals fifty-one Earth years. She has aged ninety-three days."

"She's six months pregnant!" That was Katrin, her voice echoing from the next compartment.

"Dr. Karras is correct, Engineer Darnett. Pod nine's readout is consistent with one hundred eighty-one days of pregnancy. This suggests she was eighty-nine days pregnant when she entered the pod."

"Three months. That would have been just before Alex died." Nikki's husband, Alex, had been killed in a jet crash two months before the team left. The Alliance of Space Agencies replaced him with his backup and wanted to scrub Nikki as well, but she argued. She and Alex had trained together, planned for this, invested nearly five years. She wasn't going to let it go. Psych and Medical cleared her, so she entered hibernation with the rest of the hundred crew members for the thirteen-lightyear, fifty-year, one-way run to Gliese.

"That's not right. How did we not know she was three months pregnant at departure?"

"Now that her condition has been discovered, I have access to a previously restricted block of memory. Dr. Kosov reprogrammed her Doc to suppress alarms and bury the evidence from everyone, even me. I was only able to access the data when the CMO set the pre-wake-up status for the department heads." There was a faint, almost apologetic note in the computer's synthesized voice.

"She isn't a department head. Mission planning team, yeah, but she should be deferred until general wake-up rotation for arrival. Right?"

There wasn't enough space in the Storm Cellar or the core's Life Module to wake everyone, not unless they wanted to stack bodies and call it insulation. We could handle more once the habitat ring was pressurized and rotating, but we wouldn't be doing that until we entered orbit.

Protocol said the three command leads were to wake up forty days out. That was a five days ago, and the CO, CMO, and ChEng—Captain Batel, Katrin, and me—were awake and working on our pre-arrival checklists. A week or so later, the three section heads from planetary sciences (bio and geo) would be awakened, but only once the command triad confirmed ship's integrity. Additional crew came online as needed, but never more than four or five at a stretch, not until the hab ring was up to temp, spinning, and Katrin and I signed off on habitability. Even then, with all hundred crew, the hab ring was going to be tight.

We'd need to only wake up the actual colony-building teams once their predecessors went planetside.

"No, and that's part of the problem. Pod nine is signaling for an immediate wake-up now that it's aware of her condition. Programming's been tampered with, and her medical records were falsified. Dr. Karras wants you to run diagnostics for the entire cryo array, figure out how this slipped by everyone's notice. She needs you to rule out instrument failure before she does anything else."

"And when, exactly, am I supposed to do that? On top of everything else falling apart?"

There was a sharp, ambiguous sound on the comm. If I didn't know better, I'd swear the AI had just sniffed.

"Not my fault you humans needed fifty years of sleep to get here. Besides, I'm the one running your planetary survey."

IT TOOK SEVERAL MORE days of warming the Life Module before I could finally move to the primary engineering substation near the ship's core. Not quite the bridge, not main engineering either, but a definite upgrade from the emergency console in the Storm Cellar. With the extra power and time, I queued a full cryo pod diagnostic for Katrin at the medbay command console. The results came in as a trickle, line by line, and as I waited, I caught myself scrubbing a hand over the stubble on my scalp.

Cryo pods had been standard equipment on long-haul routes for decades before our launch. The commercial version, commonly known as a "Doc-in-the-Box" med pod, was the norm for small crews or solo flights, and its track record went back even further. Nikki's pod didn't show anything out of spec. All the readings matched expected numbers.

I was so absorbed that I nearly jumped when Hugh van Alst's unmistakable voice sounded behind me:

"You're so predictable. Did anyone ever mention that you rub your head when you're thinking?"

"Only right after my hair is cut. Katrin did it for me last night."

"Only? I've never seen your hair longer than what, six millimeters?" He laughed.

"Eight," I admitted, grinning. "And you're saying yours is longer?"

"Well, let's just say I've been out of the military longer than you." There was a rasp of humor in his voice.

"Right. That explains the beard. Do you really think five years makes a difference after you add fifty more on top?"

Hugh didn't answer immediately. Instead, he pointed at one of the external displays. "So, what are the planetary survey results?" I got up and helped him into the other seat. He looked a little better than death-warmed-over, but that wasn't saying much. He'd brought two blankets—a Katrin touch, most likely. He handed me one, and draped a red, blue, and yellow-striped blanket around his own shoulders.

As he settled in, the comm chimed. "Good morning, Dr. van Alst. I hope you had a nice nap." The ship's AI's warm tenor managed to sound almost amused.

"Arthur." I did my best to sound severe for Hugh's benefit. "Do I have to check your programming? Are you developing an unauthorized sense of humor?"

"No, Wally. Just a very good simulation, as you should know." There it was again, the faint amusement. "Gentlemen, here's your System Report:

"*Excalibur* is twenty-eight days from intersecting the orbit of the third planet of Gliese 876. The primary is a K3V orange dwarf, main sequence. Habitable zone lies between 0.3 and 0.5 AU."

Hugh scrolled through the summary. "There are four planets: two rocks, two gas giants. Hot rock at 0.05 AU, superjove at 0.2, subjove at 0.4, cold rock at 2.5."

Arthur filled in more: "G-One is hot, dry, airless. G-Two has rings but no major moons; most likely stripped by tidal forces from the primary. G-Three has three significant moons: Alpha, airless; Beta, reducing atmosphere; Gamma, oxidizing atmosphere. G-Four is mixed rock and ice, inside the asteroid ring, and more like a large comet than a dwarf planet."

Hugh and I said it at the same time: "Gamma."

It was possible. We might not have to spend another fifty years chasing some marginal system. But there was something about Gliese 876...something just out of reach. Was it the K3V designation? Orange dwarf? Something else? I frowned, but the thought dissolved.

"Darnett," came the captain's voice over comm. "Plot course for rendezvous with G-Three Gamma."

IT HAD BEEN A busy month. The majority of the crew were still in cryo, and the resources to support the colony still in storage. Rather than filling the hab ring with people who would just sit waiting for months, the captain had only authorized releasing a total of ten mission crew until we got closer to our destination. It also put off the decision about what to do about Nikki.

"Okay, Arthur, that burn should put us in a Trojan orbit about Jolly." The green cloud bands of the sub-jovian-sized gas planet had earned it the nickname of "Jolly Green Giant." Katrin had renamed the habitable moon "gamma" to "Sprout" for what she told everyone were "very good reasons."

"Yes, Wally. We will be in a stable co-orbit sixty degrees with G Three until the Captain decides on approach. Please be aware, the captain has given orders to awaken the third shift. Except for Dr. Kosov. Announcing the burn, now.

"*EXCALIBUR* CREW, SECURE FOR MANEUVERING. MANEUVERING BURN IN thirty MINUTES. LIFE MODULE SPINDOWN COMMENCES IN five MINUTES. MICROGRAVITY IN ten MINUTES."

"Wait, you said she's not waking Nikki?" Wally asked.

"No." That commanding alto voice could only be Herself, entering the bridge from behind me. "We don't know cryo effect on gestation. Six months to dirtside. Can't afford distraction."

"Nikki's our xenobiologist, we're going to need her." I halfway agreed with the captain, but still felt a need to stick up for Nikki since she couldn't do so for herself.

"No. Consulted Cassie. Final Decision." A woman of few words, fewer pronouns, and no explanations, she turned and left the bridge.

CAS-E, the Command Analysis Simulation Expert was Earth's answer to a twenty-six-year round-trip communications lag. The crew had no way to "call home" for political or military directives, so the command hierarchy back on earth, the Alliance of Space Agencies, or ASA, gave us Cassie, an AI Expert System distilled from a century of historical command decisions. In theory, the CAS-E would return an expert opinion for any simulated crisis in less than a minute.

"Arthur, can you connect me with Katrin?"

"Yes, Wally. Dr. Karras said you would call. She suggests that you and Professor van Alst discuss this in the theater during the maneuvering burn."

The 50-seat theater served as a briefing room, entertainment room, and acceleration seating. The walls and ceiling were covered with swirls of colored cloth in brown, green and blue tones that the psychologists assured us would help stave off claustrophobia and homesickness. The captain wasn't there, naturally, so the room only contained nine people. Hugh, Katrin and I sat together, with a couple of our assistants nearby. Four other crew members of the Biology section, were clustered in another section of the room. With only ten people moving around in the Life Module, it was still cold, even without opening up the hab ring. True to form, Katrin was wrapped in a soft, cream colored cashmere blanket, and had brought a gray-green tartan blanket for me and the red-white-yellow Hudson's Bay blanket for Hugh.

"I think she's crazy." That was Koshilie, one of Hugh's Planetology techs.

"Herself?" Hugh asked.

"No, Nikki. How did Medical and Psychological Assessment not pick up on her pregnancy? We know she protested being kicked from the mission. She would've *known* she was pregnant at the time. To fool MedPsych and reprogrammed her pod to lie to Arthur and the rest of us she had to have been a bit psycho."

"*I* was MedPsych," Katrin said, defensively.

"Actually, you and I were onboard *Excalibur* by then with the rest of the command staff," I clarified.

"Captain Batel has been talking to Cassie a lot." Katrin told us. "She's been skipping meals and exercise. She's not sleeping enough.

She keeps putting me off when I try to talk about her health—and Nikki's."

If Batel was spending a lot of time discussing with Cassie and neglecting herself...that wasn't good news.

"What's the solution, then, terminate the pregnancy?"

"No. It should be Nikki's decision." Katrin was emphatic from within her blanket.

"Wake her up? Keep her on board until the baby is born? Then let them be the first permanent settlers on the Sprout?"

"Irresponsible. Selfish." Koshilie muttered.

"Is there any chance she was awake on the trip out?" Hugh had a thoughtful look on his face. "Wally, you were up."

"Yeah." I answered with a tone of disgust. It had not exactly been a pleasant experience. "Three times. No one else."

"You're sure of that?"

"Yeah. I'm sure. Who'd want to?"

"I would," Hugh said.

"Really? Picture this: You wake up in the cryo bay. It's dark—no lights except your pod. It's damned cold. You're naked stepping out of your pod. The thin air sucks your body heat away and it's hard to breathe, like...Everest hard."

Katrin shivered just hearing about it.

"Right. I didn't have Katrin's blankets, either. The air pressure was at fifty-percent Earth-normal with lots of helium, but that's not enough oxygen, so the vents are adding Oh-Two to make it breathable. The problem is, the air's coming from tanks that have been a space-normal for years. It's snowing in the cryo bay—not water, but Cee-Oh-Two. You have to hurry to get into your shipsuit, thermals, and vac suit because you don't know if there's air outside the Storm Cellar."

"Sorry, Wally, but protocols state that if outgassing doesn't impair core functions, repairs are deferred until the crew is awakened. You were safe in your medical stasis." When Arthur spoke, its voice seemed to come from right beside them despite the emptiness of the room.

"Exactly. The first time, we still had ambient in the Core's Life Module. No gravity, though because the drive was off.

"That was why Arthur woke me. We were out in the Oort Cloud, and the drive ingested too much of something that wouldn't fuse. Probably supernova remnants."

"That shouldn't..." Hiro started to say. He's my Second Engineer, for comms and survey. "Oh. Oh! Iron."

"Right. Interstellar gas has lots of heavy atoms. The Oort Cloud concentrates them. So, the drive burped, and I had to clear it and perform a restart.

"I couldn't get to the engine room because all bulkheads are closed in-flight. That's particularly true of the rad shielding. With the drive off, we were on emergency power, and it was easier to walk outside of the hull than to pressurize the spine of the ship and open all of those shielded doors.

"Walking through The Black knowing you are all alone is...nerve wracking."

"You had me," Arthur said, with just a hint of petulance.

"Yes, and you're the only reason I'm as sane as I am."

"Doubtful," sniffed Katrin.

I stuck my tongue out at her, and she smiled. Hugh rolled his eyes at us. Hiro scoffed, and Koshilie started to turn pink.

"So, I lived in a vac suit and slept in the Storm Cellar's Doc-in-the-Box for two months while I purged the drive, restarted it, then monitored for another four months to ensure everything was back to normal. With no one around, and only machinery and drive sounds, you start to see and hear things. Even an unimaginative engineer like me starts to imagine things – I half expected to see a cat."

"What?" asked Koshilie.

"Shh. It's a movie reference." Hugh shushed her. "He's acting 'Old' again."

I gave Hugh a sour look. "If I may continue? Right. Six months of cold, thin air, *dry* air, headaches, nosebleeds, and loneliness. I went back to my pod for twenty years, then out again for turnover, and the final course correction at T-minus five years.

"Turnover was shorter, but no less problematic. The cryo bay was in vacuum and I had to direct Arthur to make repairs before I could even get out of my pod. Fortunately, it was just outgassing, and Arthur only needed to replenish the air. It was noticeably colder, but at least I didn't have to do the vacuum shuffle or wrestle my way into a suit while sucking vac."

Thinking back on it, the situation had been helped by the cryo bay and Life Module design. My pod, along with the captain's, the XO's, the CMO's, and the deputies' pods, were all housed in an isolated chamber, deliberately small enough to be over pressurized even in case of rupture. Suit storage was next to our pods, minimizing exposure if we did need to suit up in low or no pressure. Someone had planned ahead.

I finished by asking, "you tell me; who would put themselves through that on purpose?"

"Hmph." Koshilie's mind was clearly made up.

Hiro raised his hand, tentative, but immediately put it down when Koshilie stared at him.

"Engineers," Katrin snorted.

"I've gone through every record and log," I said. "After I found out Nikki's pod data was tampered with, I had Arthur run a full diagnostic, then checked it myself. No one else was awake during the trip."

Hiro looked uneasy. He was Alex Kosov's replacement. "This is somehow my fault, isn't it?"

"No, Hiro, it's mine. I was Alex's Best Man. I introduced them. I've known Nikki for years. I was awake three times. I could have checked her Doc... In fact, I did check her Doc."

"No, Wally. You couldn't have known." I'd started rubbing my hand over my buzz-cut hair again. Katrin caught my hand and pulled it under her blanket. "The software block Nikki inserted in her Doc only released when I input my master code for Department Head wake-up. There was no way for you to tell unless you physically examined her. You. Could. Not. Have. Known."

I exhaled, heavy, my mind shifting back to the captain.

"We need Ewan."

"The quack?" Katrin's tone sharpened; first hint she held any of our crew in less than the highest regard. "What for? You? The captain? Nikki? No. I am the Chief Medical Officer. I will talk with Captain Batel and make sure she is okay. She's overdue for her physical."

"Ewan could help. He's a psychologist."

"No, he is a zoologist. He just studied sociology and psychology 'In Case We Encounter E.T.' He is a quack."

"You're beautiful when you're jealous."

"Too little oxygen, too much libido." She slapped my hand and gave me a gentle shove. "I should have adjusted your pod."

"I know *I'd* feel better talking to him."

"Talk to ART-HEUR. It's better trained."

CHIME. "*EXCALIBUR* CREW. TEN SECONDS TO MANEUVERING THRUST."

The next thirty minutes were nothing but being slammed and jostled in our seats as the ship settled into orbit. When it finally ended, we had arrived at our new, permanent home. There was no going back now.

Part 2: Worldbuilding

FOR HALF A STANDARD year, the crew went to work on the system. Humans, AI, bots, drones—the lot of us. Surveys, probes, satellites for the moons. We laid the groundwork and got ready for the next round. *Excalibur* shifted position twice: first from the trailing trojan of Jolly—G-III—then into a close orbit around Jolly itself, and finally out to the L2 point beyond Sprout—G-III-Gamma. They wanted to park right over the moon, but Jolly's tides were brutal. Any close orbit meant constant corrections. There just weren't any stable Keplerian orbits that close. L4 and L5 would have been better, except those Lagrange points were already choked with debris.

For the last month, Colonel Riedel—Executive Officer for the mission, and now in charge of surface ops—kept running sampling flights down. Planetology and Biology teams went groundside in suits, gathered what they could, and brought the samples straight back to Life Module's xenobio lab. The planners had decided early on: after the first couple runs, quarantine wasn't worth the hassle. We were going to be here for a while.

Today was different. The whole team was shipping out for good. Hugh, Ewan, a handful of geologists and biologists. They were all heading down to Site One, the first real base on the surface.

"Darnett. Report to cryo bay, soonest." The comm was sharp, no time wasted. It seemed Captain Batel had made her decision.

I got there fast. Main cryo: ninety-four pods lined up, silent. All dark except the handful reserved for command. Ninety-three pods: empty. One was humming, online. Katrin and Captain Batel were waiting next to pod Nine. Captain in full uniform, every crease sharp, hair perfect, boots gleaming. Katrin looked like she always did off-shift: purple fleece, Med blues, fuzzy socks. Hard not to see the contrast.

"Yes, Ma'am?" I said, stepping up.

Batel looked at me, then the pod, then Katrin. When she sighed, it sounded almost painful. She didn't want this. I could tell. I wouldn't have, either.

"Wake her. She stays on ship." Batel's tone said it was final. "Prep for birth. Afterward? She handles her brat, not us." And with that, Captain was gone, leaving Katrin and me in the corridor, staring at Nikki's Doc, locked in Pod Nine.

I ALWAYS FIGURED ORBITAL duty would stick to me. Our assignment: get a working colony infrastructure up and running at Gliese

876. Infrastructure—not a full colony. A hundred people can't do more than seed a planet.

Once we proved the place was livable, we'd signal Earth. They'd send a real colony ship, but it'd take thirteen years for the message to make the trip, then another fifty for the ship to get here. Maybe longer, if they hadn't even started picking or prepping the colonists.

It was a lifetime mission, any way you looked at it. We had to last, self-sufficient, for the next sixty-five, maybe seventy years. The docs and stasis pods would help slow down aging, but we'd probably end up cycling through ten- or twenty-year stretches of sleep, just to make sure somebody was awake when the colony ship arrived. Worst case, the infrastructure had to be tough enough to hold until the new colonists showed up, even if we weren't around to see it.

While the scientists and techs scrambled in the dirt, *Excalibur* had her own job. We were the communications hub, the "eyes in the sky"—keeping watch on the colony, the planet, and the system for anything that looked like a threat or an opportunity. Once the colony got going, we'd be the base for exploring the rest of the system.

With all those jobs, somebody from Command or Engineering had to stay in orbit. The captain might drop down for a survey or inspection, but as Chief Engineer, it was my job to keep the ship alive for seventy years, until relief arrived.

The funny part? I started out in geology and comp sci, then moved to astrophysics for grad school. I was always hooked on stars, planets, whole systems. I wanted to be an explorer, so I branched out from pure physics, made sure I could fit any science team, go dirtside.

My postdoc, cybernetic control systems for astronavigation, landed me on the *Excalibur* design team. It was the job of a lifetime, and I knew it was my chance at reaching another star and setting foot on alien soil. When I made the mission roster, I got tapped as lead engineer for propulsion and AI systems. Then I got the ChEng slot...and found out I'd be staying on the ship. Somebody had to, and as Chief Engineer—and the only design team member on the crew—it was me. The logic was, everyone else could be spared, even if that meant I was the only one left up here.

There's a downside to being indispensable.

In retrospect, it could have been worse. Once groundside was fully settled, *Excalibur* would push further into the system, and there would be more to do than stare at bulkheads. I wouldn't be alone for most of it; there'd be a command team presence—a captain, second, or third officer. XO had groundside as his domain, and he'd stay down there unless a supply or medical run dragged him back to orbit. Medical rotated, too. Katrin or one of her deputies would be up here, and a small science group would cycle through planet and star surveys.

And then there was Nikki. Veterinary degree, EMT certs, and captain's orders keeping her on the ship. No groundside rotation for Nikki, but orbital medical? Absolutely. I had hoped a med rotation would mean time with Katrin, but if Nikki was out of the loop, Katrin would be spending even more time down on the planet.

I glanced down at Nikki's pod, all this running through my head.

I'd been Alex's Best Man. I'd introduced him to Nikki.

It wasn't exactly a debt, but there was something there. Obligation, maybe.

Nikki would wake up, stay on *Excalibur*, have her baby, and raise it here. Just by being close, I'd end up part of that kid's life.

Was I prepared for that? The whole help-raise-a-child thing?

Not even close.

But I turned to Katrin anyway. "Okay. Let's do this," I said, and held my breath.

I WAS ON THE bridge, watching a thirteen-year-old newsfeed from Earth and keeping an eye on the systems. Technically, I could have done that anywhere—the SCRAM, my quarters, even the zero-gee head—but I always liked the bridge for this.

It was the kind of compartment you'd see in a sci-fi movie, even without windows or a central Captain's Chair. Instead, it was tucked into the core of the ship, just forward of the non-rotating Life Module. Two seats, a U-shaped console, flat screens and touch panels of every size wrapping around. You could stand behind the seats or use the fold-down jump seats if you wanted, but that wasn't the main draw.

The main draw was the view. I sat at the focus of the spherical volume, with a full projection of the ship's three-dimensional surroundings mapped onto the wall. Sprout was below, Jolly to one side, and Gliese 876 was at my back—or that's how it felt from where I sat.

It was glorious. Sitting there, at the center, it felt like I was the ship itself—or at least standing on the hull. I could toggle the view to show the exterior from any point on the outside, if I wanted. Or I could swap in anything else: skiing in the Alps, Document MED41-11 Detailed Schematics of the Ion/Fusion Drive, Arthur's operating system...

...and do it without giving up and the view.

I was paging through the newsfeed from Earth. Thirteen lights was a long way for a signal to travel; text was easier on bandwidth, easier to error check and correct. Besides, Earth wouldn't even know we were awake for another twelve or thirteen years. Nikki was in the other chair. Katrin and Arthur had decided she and the baby could tolerate a few hours of nullgee every day. I'm still not sure where Arthur found the name for his "Family Practice" instance. He told me "Dr. Welby" was traditional, though, so who was I to argue?

Naturally, Katrin would be handling the delivery, and she was not exactly thrilled about the AI. I could have sworn I heard her mutter, "He's not a real doctor, just plays one on the vid."

"Wally, did you see this physics article?"

"Not yet. Still working on 'Ringo's History of the Twenty-First Century.' How does he get away with writing a history when the century isn't even two-thirds over?"

Nikki made a noise halfway between a laugh and a snort. "For us, maybe, but not for him. Don't forget the travel time."

"Oh, yeah." I said, feeling kind of foolish. "It's easy to forget that. So, then you were saying?"

"Well, speaking of time, this article's about us, or at least about the telemetry Arthur sent back during the flight out here. It says this physics whiz-kid was analyzing the data and found something interesting anomalies about thirty years into our trip. He used the readings to come up with a new theory of space-time."

"Better than Bose-Einstein? I'm still looking for wormholes."

"Yes, better. He says that even though our trajectory from Luna to Gliese was smooth, the telemetry shows there were a lot of tracking errors along the way. He thinks they're not actually errors at all, but evidence that space-time itself is wrinkled and folded. He claims it should be possible to tunnel through those folds, cut transit time, and shorten the distance."

"How long before he can get that working?"

"There's an engineering guy here—name of Cochrane. He says, fifteen years and he can deliver the first Folded Space drive."

"Cochrane? You're kidding. Like, Star Trek Cochrane?"

"What? No, James Cochrane. Not Zefram. No subspace, no warp drive. Anyway, he's the engineer. The physics prodigy, the one who came up with the idea, is named Sunday, or something like that."

"Hah. As if anyone's going to remember that. I'll bet they still call it the Cochrane drive. The 'Sunday Drive' just doesn't have the same impact." I tried to laugh, but it came out as a whistle. Funny how easy it was to forget about gravity until you didn't have it. "So, anyway, we don't have to lose any sleep for another fifteen years. Now, listen to this:

'The twenty-first century didn't go the way anyone expected. No Moon colonies, no commercial space stations, no mysterious alien monoliths...'"

"Unnh."

"Don't you like it?"

"Unnk. Unnh."

"Nikki?"

"It's time. Call Doc, baby's coming."

I punched a pre-arranged code to alert Katrin, then helped Nikki out of her seat. In the core of the ship, with zero gravity, I could guide her toward the hab ring lift, then carry her the rest of the way outward. When we exited the lift, Katrin was there with a gurney—and a crowd. We rushed to the Hab Ring med bay and got Nikki onto the delivery bed Katrin and Arthur had set up for her, just in time for Arthur to make a ship-wide announcement.

CHIME. "*EXCALIBUR* CREW. PREPARE FOR IN-
CREASED GRAVITY IN HABITAT RING. INCREASING
SPIN IN SIXTY SECONDS. GRAVITY WILL INCREASE
TO ZERO-ONE-POINT-TWO-FIVE GEES OVER THE NEXT
THIRTY MINUTES."

"Can it, Arthur. There are only eight people on board, three of
us in here, four just outside the door, and Herself walked onto the
bridge as we left."

"Sorry, Wally, but you know the rules. After all, you helped write
them."

"If all you two are going to do is fight, you can both go outside and
join the others."

"Sorry, Katrin. I... Hey, Arthur can't go outside!"

"Hmph. He should."

"Now Darlin'," This was a different voice from the AI speakers –
somehow it felt more, well, *fatherly*. "Don't upset the mother."

"I can do this myself, Arthur. I don't need your meddlesome program."

"Ah'm jus' tryin' to keep y'all relaxed." What had Arthur done? A
NorthAm *Southern* accent? No wonder Katrin didn't like Dr. Welby.
She barely tolerated AIs to begin with, but a patronizing Southerner
was pretty low on her list. Except for *me*, but that's a different story,
I wasn't really *Southern*, I had a *much* more checkered past than that.

The centrifugal force we thought of as gravity increased as the Hab
Ring spun up. Katrin was using a trick they'd learned in the asteroid
colonies – support the mother upright, increase the gees at just the
right point, and the delivery went much easier – and faster.

In fact,...

"It's..."

"…A BOY."

Nikki named him Jack. She said it was Alex's nickname. Bestowed by Alex's father, it was short for "Jack in the Box." Alex was technically our second Engineer, but he'd also shown talents as a Programmer, Crafter, Carpenter (assuming we ever found a tree), and Builder. "Jack of all trades" would have worked too, but Nikki's insisted that Jack in the Box was more appropriate—always moving, always questioning, always pushing to do the next big thing.

Nikki's sense of humor was always a bit sly, and I wasn't sure I believe the bit about Alex's nickname. On the other hand, the description sure fit this squirming baby who'd just popped up out of nowhere.

Jack was a quiet baby. Cute. Cuddly. Smiled, burbled, and laughed more as he grew. Everyone took to him right away, except for Captain Batel. I think she was uncomfortable with the whole idea. I know she wanted kids, to raise a family on a frontier world—she'd confided as much to me several years before launch. She wasn't really a cold, hard, professional. It was that she felt this mission didn't have room for the commander to find a mate, let alone raise a family.

We were on a one-way trip, and we knew it.

Now, though? It was almost like being uncles and aunts. Nikki wouldn't have to do it alone. We were establishing a colony, after all—even if no one had expected children for several more years. Once the infrastructure was in place, families would be permitted. Not quite expected, but the mission parameters would be loosened.

In that respect, little Jack Kosov would simply be the first.

For more than a year, Nikki handled all her work remotely. She was officially the mission's senior xenobiologist, and her job would have started the moment life was discovered on Sprout. Now, though, she had to rely on others for sample collection and have everything sent up to the ship for analysis.

To be fair, the orbital lab was a major upgrade over anything on the planet. It spanned an entire section of the hab ring, laid out as a multi-level facility with variable gravity zones. Nikki had it to herself, and she made the most of it. Still, she wanted to go down and see things directly. In a rare mood, the captain agreed. That's how Katrin and I ended up on-duty with Jack for two weeks, while Nikki finally got her surface rotation.

Captain Batel had been scheduled for groundside leave, so fifteen days ago she'd piloted the number two shuttle down with Nikki and the tertiary shift. With a good chunk of the crew now on the planet, I was holding down dual posts as both Chief Engineer and First Officer. Katrin kept her role as CMO. Hiro got bumped up to First Engineer, reporting to me. The skeleton crew rounded out with Koshilie, Gil—a comm tech—and then two astronomers and two planetary scientists, all focused on prepping probes for the orbital survey of G II's rings.

Before launch, the planners had been clear: rotate every team, always have rescue and backup standing by at another location. Surface ops were divided between two colony sites: one set in a green valley, the other higher, windswept, up on a plateau. A third station sat between them, mostly a depot for emergency shelters and rations.

Colony planning was straight out of Earth's cautionary records. The first NorthAm colonies? Vanished. Words like "Croatan," "Roanoke Island," and "Lost Colony" still echoed in the files.

So, thirty people at each main colony, ten more at the emergency depot, and ten on the ship (eleven, counting Jack). Crew rotations meant another twenty cycled between orbit and planet on the three surface shuttles: Ajax, Bravo, and Charlie. We did have a fourth shuttle, Echo, but it was strictly orbit-to-orbit: satellites, probes, that kind of thing. One ground shuttle was always stationed on the surface; one kept in orbit. Whenever a ground shuttle moved, the orbital shuttle detached and stood ready as a rescue fallback, just in case.

Safety was the prime directive. We were ready for anything.

Or so we told ourselves.

I WAS MONITORING AS usual, one eye on the comms and the other flicking through colony feeds stitched alongside the usual system metrics. The main display showed Sprout from geostationary orbit. Site One: dense blot of green in the northern quadrant. Site Two: a thousand klicks west, just coming around Sprout's limb—a broad, flat patch of brown. A small window at the bottom piped in live sunspot telemetry from Gliese 876, a trickle of numbers and graphs courtesy of the science team.

"*Excalibur*, Bravo." The comm from Captain Batel's shuttle was crisp and clear.

"Go, Bravo." I straightened, my attention shifting to the right-side console. "Arthur, give me the..." The display flickered, shifting to shuttle trajectory: altitude readout, orbital insertion, all tagged M-13, bold and blinking.

"Launching in T-minus two. Flight path will be TSTO."

"Copy, TSTO launch in two." I tracked the path on screen, over-lays updating in real time. "Looks like you're set for standard approach, M-thirteen. We'll see you in a few hours, Captain."

So Batel was taking her time. She usually chose an SSTO—single-stage-to-orbit—a punishing vertical boost, hard and fast, up in fifteen minutes if you could stomach the gees. TSTO, two-stage-to-orbit, was gentler: fly horizontal for altitude, then boost. Mission regs liked TSTO for safety, but unless you were hauling cargo or coddling equipment, nobody bothered. SSTO burned more reaction mass, but that was mainly water, and Sprout wasn't short of water.

Batel, who usually ran hot, usually opted for speed. And yet, here she was, choosing slow and steady.

"Ackno…" Hiss. Crackle. The comm sputtered, then dropped out.

"Bravo, *Excalibur*. Repeat last, your message cut out."

Crackle. Dead air.

"Wally."

"Yes, Arthur?"

"There is a problem. Satellite H-1A reports increased activity on Gliese."

"The sunspots?"

"Yes, Wally. We're seeing a flare, possible CME."

"Damn." The response might have sounded mild, but Momma had raised us with strict, old American South manner. Dad was a pilot, an engineer, and Australian. He knew quite a few colorful ways to swear, plus I'd spent my life in and around the military. But we typically didn't do so with an audience, and *never* around Momma, a habit that stuck with me.

Except in emergencies, or very stressful situations.

This was shaping up to be one of them.

The H-1A hung out there in the emptiness between Jolly and Gliese, just another Helios-class solar observer, dutifully streaming data back to Arthur and the science team. We'd had our eye on a new patch of sunspot activity for a couple of weeks now, but this wasn't the familiar pattern from Sol. Not even close. In two years at Gliese, we hadn't seen anything like Sol's sunspot cycle, which honestly had been a relief; Jolly and Sprout didn't have much in the way of magnetosphere, nothing to blunt the solar wind. Gliese 876 was supposed to be a mild little orange dwarf, steady output, quiet flares, nothing to write home about.

But now we were expecting a solar storm, and something about that nagged at me, like a splinter at the edge of my thoughts.

Solar storm. That was it. *Excalibur* had flown through the tail end of a solar storm coming into the system, a thick, wild stream of charged particles blowing out from the star. Now Arthur's feed showed Gliese 876 right in the middle of a large flare—and a CME, a coronal mass ejection. Full-on stellar plasma, protons and even heavier charged ions, snarled magnetic fields, radiation by the bucketload, all of it headed right at us.

We'd just cleared Jolly's shadow. *Excalibur* and Sprout were wide open and dead center in the path.

"When?" I asked. "Arthur, what's the window?"

He didn't answer for half a second. Then the sirens went off, sharp and immediate, almost drowning everything else. Arthur's voice barely cut through: "Now."

I didn't bother to hold back. "Shit."

Part 3: Survival

THERE WAS A LOT you could do with a virtual keyboard and the holobox, but I'd always insisted there be a physical override. It looked like any other blank patch on the console, which was the point—you wouldn't spot it unless you knew, or unless you tapped just right. Then it slid aside with a soft click, and there it was: a big red button. I'd told the designers: "if it's silly and cliché but it works, then it's not silly. It just works."

I pressed the button. My own voice—not Arthur's, mine, from the recording I'd made five years ago, or maybe fifty-five (it all blurred, planning for this long)—blared from every speaker on the ship: "EMERGENCY. ALL PERSONNEL TO STORM CELLAR. THIS IS NOT A DRILL." After that, I started juggling half a dozen things at once. Each hand worked different sets of controls, some physical, some virtual. It wasn't a remarkable talent, but it had its uses.

First order of business, break into the intercom: "KATRIN. GET YOURSELF AND JACK TO THE STORM CELLAR. I DON'T CARE WHAT YOUR PROTOCOLS ARE. DO THIS NOW. HIRO, KOSHI, GIL, SCIENCE TEAM, DROP WHAT YOU ARE DOING AND MOVE. WE HAVE RADIATION NOW, PEOPLE!"

At the same time, I triggered a system override, putting Arthur back into the autonomous mode he'd used inbound to Gliese. If the crew went down, Arthur could run the ship alone, keeping the rest of us alive.

Third task: I turned most the bridge walls and ceiling into a shifting mosaic of video windows. From either seat, you could catch a hundred different views at a glance; the inputs cycled through a thousand sensors, telescopes, satellites, and planet-side cameras, all choreographed for maximum information density. The walls glittered and flashed.

Fourth, I routed the H-1A feed to a five-meter segment of the main screen. The data confirmed it: big CME, already detached. We were less than five light-minutes from Gliese—the solar wind was practically on top of us.

Fifth: I brought up the feeds for the shuttle pads at both colony sites. Only one pad was occupied. Bravo was already airborne.

Damn.

The kaleidoscope of images showed Katrin and the others running for the storm cellar. Katrin held a wriggling bundle, which had to be Jack. Now it was decision time. A shuttle in the air during a storm left me with no good options.

Up top, the crew was ducking for cover. The ground teams should be all right—they could dig in, and the habs were buried deep. The shuttles were supposed to be hardened, but mostly for launch or docking, not flying through a saturating particle storm. If Bravo got EMP'd in-atmosphere...

The priority was shielding. People were squishy and needed to be protected behind shields that could absorb or deflect the radiation and particles. Water was best; ice, even better. The ship had plenty of both, plus frozen stock for the colony. The Storm Cellar was in the middle of all that ice.

Our technology was both more robust and more fragile. Systems might glitch, but we had backups and spares in shielded storage.

Excalibur's critical hardware (Arthur's core, the engines, the shuttle controls) was "hardened"—shielded and resistant to electromagnetic pulse. The surface teams had underground spaces for storage and protection from atmospheric storms.

The shuttles, though, were never meant to be out in the open during a solar event.

With magnetic field to speak of—for both Jolly and Sprout—the solar wind would punch straight into the atmosphere. Shuttle Bravo had launched into a literal storm, and now the clock was running.

"Wally, it's Katrin. We're here in the Storm Cellar, where are you?"

Her voice came through the comm a little rough, but at least it worked. I checked the display, just as the radiation numbers started to climb. Not great. I didn't have any standout options: I could duck into the Cellar with Katrin and the others, or head for Medical and get myself locked up in a Doc for some shielding and a rad flush, or I could just suit up right here, on the spot.

Huddle. Hide. Suit. Pick one.

Twenty years in uniform. I wasn't trained to hide. One of my shuttles was out there somewhere. That helped make the decision.

"Katrin. I'm suiting up. I'll be okay. Just stay in the Cellar until the rads settle down." That place was stocked to supply a hundred people for a week. Nine and a toddler could probably last for months.

"Koshilie has Jack. I'm coming back out."

"No. Stay there. A whole lot of people are going to need you soon, and Jack needs you, too. Don't leave the Cellar."

"Eddie!"

She was close to panic now. It'd been years since I'd heard her call me by my real name, not the nickname derived from my Academy callsign "Wallaby."

I cut in before she could get going. "Hon, not now. I'll be fine. Bravo launched, and they're probably gonna need back-up."

Nothing for a second, then: "OK. Go now, be careful."

"I will, love. Keep everyone safe."

Sixth on the list (sixth? or was it seventh? eighth?) I put Charlie and Echo under Arthur's control. If I made it, one would be ready for launch. If I didn't, Arthur would run a rescue. Mostly.

Last bit. Suits were stashed everywhere, since nobody ever knew where they'd be when the alarm hit. Every locker had emergency suits, basically Mylar bubbles with a helmet, and then the full custom jobs. There was a locker in the projection wall, right across from the bridge hatch. I undid the buckles, pushed off, and drifted over. My suit: deep green, sized for me. Dark red and black for the captain. Two emergency bubbles stuffed underneath.

One of the displays glitched, caught my eye—the bridge rad counter. Even smack in the middle of the Life Module, the numbers were ticking up—fast. Not dangerous yet, especially once I was suited up, but I'd probably lose my lunch, maybe some hair. The suit's thigh pocket had an injector loaded with antirad and antinausea. Before sealing up, I jabbed it in my arm and hit the release. At least I wouldn't puke in the suit, not for a day or so.

Time to clear the Bridge.

THAT WAS ON ME. I should have caught it, I mean, astrophysics degree, right? The clues were all laid out, clear as day, back in that plume we crossed two years ago. I couldn't stop thinking about it. Gliese was classified K4V. Main sequence, orange dwarf.

Of course.

Dwarf stars, especially the cool types, never just sit there. Sol's a yellow dwarf, and even it throws out flares and CMEs like it's on a schedule. But the K and M classes—the oranges, the reds—they'll go quiet for centuries. Sometimes longer. And then, no warning, they'll flare. Or eject a CME. Or just... brighten, all at once. Orange and red dwarfs don't burn much hydrogen; it's helium, heavier elements. That kind of fusion is messy. Heavy elements clog things up, slow them down, then let them surge through all at once. Like a bad case of indigestion.

Gliese had it bad. And it burped.

We'd seen those signs on approach—the spiral of high-energy protons, tossed out by the previous burp, just over two years back.

I was still on the bridge when the streak lit up Sprout's upper atmosphere. Could have been a meteor. Maybe aurorae. But that didn't fit.

It was probably Shuttle Bravo.

No—it was Bravo.

SHUTTLE BRAVO LAUNCHED FROM Site Two at the exact moment Arthur's CME warning hit the comms. Captain Batel was at the controls. Nikki, Hugh, and eighteen others crammed aboard, packed shoulder to shoulder. Twenty-one people in a shuttle nominally designed for sixteen and a pilot. All headed back to Excalibur on monthly rotation.

Ten minutes after the alert, I was suiting up. Bravo had climbed to 3,000 meters, still ascending.

At the fifteen-minute mark, I'd dosed myself with antirads and sealed my helmet. Bravo was passing 5,000, accelerating past Mach 2.

The shock front from the particle wave slammed into the upper atmosphere. Aurorae flared everywhere. The horizon flickered and rippled with light. With no ozone to absorb the worst of it, high-energy reactions between atmospheric gases and solar particles raged unchecked. The EMP arrived as a bright shimmer—a sudden pulse overhead.

Shuttle controls were rated for re-entry plasma and the vacuum of space, for cosmic rays and solar wind. Not for sitting dead center as an electromagnetic pulse took shape.

I watched the monitor, piecing together the rest. The shuttle kicked and shuddered as charged particles hammered the air. Crew and passengers would see flashes, streaks or sparks in their vision. Dizzy, confused, maybe even blacked out for a moment. Batel throttled up, punching through the turbulence. G-forces stacked up.

Then, whether by intent or failure, the main boosters ignited—the vertical stack, designed for launch or orbital insertion. Those boosters were rated to push past Sprout's 9.2 kilometers per second escape velocity. They weren't meant for horizontal flight, or for Sprout's thick air below twenty thousand meters.

The shuttle itself? Not built for Mach 30, powered, in dense atmosphere.

Shuttle Bravo's trail ended in a scatter of bright sparks.

I couldn't leave the bridge. Not now. I kept searching for any trace their escape system had triggered. I tried to reestablish a tightbeam optical link to the colonies. I monitored Gliese, and watched the storm, waiting for the particle count to drop enough to even consider launching a rescue.

I waited—and hated being unable to act.

To do—anything.

I stayed there at the bridge, twelve hours, while the highest-energy particles battered *Excalibur*...

...and me.

I spent another full day on the hull, patching sensors, antennae, communication lasers, fixing microfractures in the plating. As the particle count ebbed, Arthur's radiation-hardened bots took over. I returned to the bridge and rode out the rest of the storm. In the end, I spent another two days in the suit, knowing the Gliese 876 colony mission had failed...

...and feeling that I was to blame.

At some point I stopped talking to Katrin and the others in the Storm Cellar. I sat, oblivious, eyes locked on the display—a shifting prism of images, tuned to trigger only the critical, to avoid a neural crash.

I didn't hear Katrin come up behind me. The solar storm had passed, and radiation levels dropped enough for Arthur to call her up to the bridge. He was worried. I'd stopped talking to him, too.

Katrin unbuckled my helmet, wiped sweat and hair from my face. She held my head in her hands, kissed my forehead, and hugged me as tight as you could, with someone still half in a vac suit. She didn't say anything. She just got me to stand up, steered me to my quarters, out of the suit, cleaned me up, bundled me in a blanket. Then she sat beside me and held on as I cried. After an hour, she gave me a sedative and left me to a long, dreamless sleep.

"WAKE UP, SLEEPYHEAD. Is work to do." Warmth beside me; familiar, solid. I reached for her, then froze as the memories caught up, sharp as a med injector. "No, is okay. They are safe." There were times when her old Russian speech patterns came through.

Safe. Or at least as close to safe as we ever got.

Maybe that wasn't fair. Conditions were as good as they could be, given everything. But there was still work to finish. Today was our last day in orbit of Jolly.

What was it they called Apollo 13? A successful failure?

Yeah, that was us. We'd rescued thirty people; lost forty. You can't build a colony with that few, but you could explore, map a system, and send all of that back for next time.

I quit thinking of myself as the villain months ago, but I never bought the hero talk, either. Sure, I was the one who figured out we could rip the cryo pods from the main bay and pile them onto Shuttle Gamma. Twenty-six survivors groundside, seats for sixteen, room for twenty pods in the hold.

Multiple trips were still necessary. No way to spare the hours per run to dismount and remount all the pods.

Site Two was the worst. We went there first: high plateau, no mountain shadow, no caves, zero ozone. Col. Riedel got the team into a building with a sublevel, bulldozed the upper floors flat, then smothered it with dirt. I went down with five pods, Hiro and Gil. Hiro would rip out the site's two Doc-in-the-Box units and set them up in Gamma's hold. Gil, the colonel, and I dug the survivors out. Six scientists and a farmer, all bad rad poisoning, but alive. Col. Riedel didn't make it. He'd driven the bulldozer. Too much sun.

Site One was better. They'd found caves during early surveys. Ewan got the warning in time. Most of his group made it into the caves. Nineteen ambulatory, four heavy rad cases—including Ewan. I wanted to overload the shuttle, pull everyone in one trip, but Hiro offered to stay groundside with the ambulatory until I could swing back.

Site Three? Not a real colony site, just a depot. No survivors. No remains, either.

I half-expected "Croatoan" carved into a tree or painted on a shed. It would've fit. The universe has a sick sense of humor, and a pointed message about best-laid plans.

So: chief engineer, then first officer, now acting captain. Mission in shambles. One hundred crew down to forty. Sixty dead. Only seven truly healthy, the Storm Cellar group, minus Hiro, who got exposed helping me after the storm, and Gil, who needed a Doc to reconstruct his ankle after a pod bounced loose in Shuttle Gamma. Eleven survivors already in cryo; they'd need indefinite Doc time, safer to let the pods handle it. Nineteen from the surface, plus Hiro, Gil, and myself, needed Doc time too, but we could cycle through while prepping *Excalibur*.

Well, mostly. Katrin had me on an IV while I ran things from the bridge, managing my shrunken command.

Jack? He was fine. The bright spot. He was ours now; all of us. His new family.

Katrin adapted Nikki's pod for Jack, since it was tuned to the closest DNA match. She said something about mine and gave me a look. She had him prepped for cryo. I questioned it, but she and Dr. Welby both agreed it was best. Arthur told me, privately: whatever we did, Jack should sleep through it all.

Decision time.

Two options: return to Earth, or wait for the colony ship, sixty or seventy years. Either way, everyone would need to be in cryo.

I asked for input, but as acting captain, final call landed on me. No matter what, *Excalibur* would be set for hibernation: minimum fifty years. If we waited, I'd have to pilot her out to the edge of the system, away from rocks, radiation, debris.

I made the call to go back. No guarantee Earth would send a ship at all. I'd fired a tightbeam seven weeks ago, but it wouldn't reach Earth for thirteen years. By then, they might write us off. Forget Gliese. Forget us.

We were all still young. Jack had a whole life ahead of him. I owed the crew that chance.

I owed Jack.

Katrin loaded everyone into their pods, started hibernation. It's been just the two of us for over a month now. She's staying awake with me for the next six months while I set up return flight. I didn't argue. If she hadn't needed to get Jack to the Storm Cellar, she might not be here. If she wasn't here, I don't think I could have managed. Given all that, I don't think I could stand to be alone, either.

"ARTHUR, GIVE ME A countdown for boost."

This was it—the long burn. We'd just cleared Jolly's orbit, setting our own course around the sun we'd called home for almost three years. This was too complicated a procedure to use a secondary station. The bridge had too many bad memories, though, so Katrin sat with me.

I started on pre-burn checks, but Arthur overrode me: "Wally, stop. I've locked your console."

I frowned. "Why am I locked out?"

"There's a command override," Arthur replied, voice tight in the way it always got when something unexpected landed. "Incoming message."

"From who?" I asked.

"Whom," whispered Katrin, but she smiled as she said it.

Arthur didn't answer right away. "Tagged from Earth," he said finally. Definite edge now. Not something he said every day.

Katrin gave a dry laugh. "Old news. Thirteen years old at least. Ignore it."

"Arthur, we'll listen after the burn. Return control and start the countdown."

"No, Wally. It's a command signal. My autonomous functions are restricted." He almost sounded sorry. "Embedded override directive: Maintain Position. IFF and voice channel attached. Would you like to hear it?"

A voice from Earth. Not text—a voice. Across thirteen light years. Just the idea of a clean signal was nearly impossible.

"IFF reads as '*A.S.A.S COCHRANE.*' Does that help?" Arthur asked. His tone faded out, like he was waiting for something else.

Cochrane. I blinked. Suddenly the name came with a rush of memory—the whiz kid, the engineer, our telemetry data. Fifteen to make a revolutionary star drive work. Not fifteen from when Nikki read the article, but fifteen from when it was written. Thirteen years for the message to get here.

Fifteen years was now.

I started to laugh. Shaking my head, not quite believing it.

Katrin was beside me, hand gripping mine in anticipation.

"Arthur, play it."

The bridge filled with static, then a clipped, urgent voice: "*Excalibur*, this is *Cochrane*. We will match orbit with you in two days. STAY THERE. WE'RE COMING TO GET YOU."

Katrin started laughing with me, the sound bouncing off the bridge walls, sharp and bright and full of relief.

Seven
Appleseed

AUTHORS NOTE: IN 2020, Sandra Medlock and I created the shared-world anthology titled *The Founder Effect*. Sandra and I created the world, the setting, and a few key events, and wrote some wrap-around continuity for the stories.

The anthology was well received. It told a consistent, continuous tale of how the acts of colony founders might be viewed through the lens of myth and legend. We had a wonderful mix of experienced and new writers; several had their first short story publication in that volume. Aside from the concept development, worldbuilding, (editing) and connecting text, though, neither Sandra nor I had stories in the volume.

Still, there was a story I wanted to tell. Baen Books gave me the opportunity to write it and publish it on their website to coincide with the paperback release of *The Founder Effect*. Once again, I drew from history—this time, the story of John Chapman (a.k.a. Johnny Appleseed). A man some might consider an ecoterrorist for his habit of planting non-native crops.

In this tale, the struggling human colonists keep finding groves of Earth fruit trees on their world. The man responsible

is labeled a subversive and a terrorist, but his actions give the colonists much needed hope, nourishing both their bodies and their minds.

Great things can grow from a tiny apple seed.

"Izzy, do you have a minute?" Jan knew that Isaac hated the nickname, that was one reason he used it. However, this might not be one of those times. The senior data tech from Logistics and Supply had a serious look on his face as he floated in the doorway of the Sensors and Tracking office.

"Not really, but you look like I need to, Janny." Isaac used Jan's least favorite nickname in response, but again, there was no rancor . . . just a slight irritation.

"Well, it's the trajectory data from Ceres Station. There's a serious downtick in arrivals and departures." Jan held up a databord to emphasize his point. Isaac could see nothing but columns of numbers on the 'bord's display screen.

"That's Traffic Deconfliction stuff, Jan. What does it have to do with Logistics?"

"It's an odd pattern, Isaac." The very fact that Jan wasn't calling him by a nickname was a tell-tale that he was worried.

"Well, it's a pattern. Something strange."

"Show me."

Jan touched his 'bord, then flicked his fingers in a gesture toward the wall screen in front of Isaac. The numbers now appeared on the screen accompanied by a graph of inbound and outbound trajectories over the previous twelve months. "See here?" A bargraph appeared showing totals per month, declining toward the present. "A thirty percent decrease, and it's all in trajectories inbound and outbound from the Belt."

Ceres was the primary supply base for the independent miners and prospectors working the Asteroid Belt. Every one of the stakes in the Belt needed resupply, approximately every three-to-six months. A decline in ship traffic meant that they weren't resupplying at Ceres.

But there wasn't any other location to resupply other than Earth or Mars . . . was there? Belters wouldn't willingly enter The Well just for groceries.

"What does Ceres Logistics say?" Isaac asked his counterpart.

"Earth shipments are on schedule, but the warehouses are starting to back up. Stuff is not being distributed outbound as fast as it's being supplied. The weird thing is that the major difference is in produce and consumables."

"What? We've never seen a surplus of fruit and vegetables! Ceres is usually right on the fine line of shortfall—only the L4 and L5 farms keep that from happening. It would drive the prices sky-high if not for the price controls ordered by Congress three years ago." Isaac thought for a moment. "Okay, Jan, so why did you bring this to me?"

"Well, Isaac, I was hoping you could run some tracking and figure out where the Belters are going for their groceries—if not Ceres, then where? We need to know in order to ensure that it's safe . . ."

". . . and job security has nothing to do with it."

"Well, once that big colony ship out at Mars is finished, stocking it is going to use up everything we've got. There won't *be* any surplus; it'll be a logistics nightmare." Jan shuddered. "That's why we need to figure this out. It could mess up all of the planning."

"Entry Squad, this is Eagle One. Sound off."

"Eagle Five, ready."

"Eagle Four, ready and waiting."

"Eagle Three, planting daisies and watching the grass grow."

"Eagle Two, about to put a stiction boot up Eagle Three's ass if he doesn't watch his comm discipline. E-Two ready."

"Eagle Six, this is Eagle One. Carl is being a pain in the ass and is about to *earn* a pain in the ass, but we're ready to enter."

"One, this is Six. Clear to enter."

"Go, go, go. Execute entry plan alpha."

"Five, in and clear right."

"Four, in and clear left."

"Three, in and *Oh my god, it's full of stars!*"

"Two, in and clear straight. Oh. Oh my."

"Eagle Six, this is Eagle One. You're not going to believe this, sir, but the asteroid's been hollowed out and turned into a biosphere. There's soil, plants, even trees."

"Eagle One, are there lifesigns?"

"Sir, this entire place is lifesigns."

"Not what I meant, One. Are there any people in there?"

"Negative, sir." The comm was silent for many seconds as the squad leader checked his sensors. "There's insects in the soil and on some of the plants. Something small is flying... honeybees?" After another pause, he continued, "not even a mouse, sir."

"Understood, Eagle." A new voice had come over the comm. The sergeant recognized it as belonging to the lieutenant colonel in charge of the Marine patrols for the outer Belt. "It was a long shot, anyway. Tracking says there's been minimal activity to this rock in the past year. Foxglove and Gladius platoons have found the same thing—hollowed-out asteroids with full biospheres inside. RTB and get prepped for a six-day high-gee boost. There are several more promising targets about ninety-degrees' rotation from your AO."

Two of the other three squads of Eagle platoon were securing the entry and docking structures on the exterior of the hollow asteroid, while the third was checking on a few rocks in the near vicinity. The new orders meant that they would return to their patrol ship, along with the other two platoons of Charlie company, Fourth battalion, Five-Oh-First regiment of Lunar Marines. Their next destination was one-quarter of the way around the sun from their current position. It would require nearly a week at one-and-a-half gravities of acceleration, and the same amount of deceleration, to get there in time to meet up with the rest of Charlie 4/501. Even though all Marines trained at a minimum one-gee, their bodies would require preparation for the extended load.

Command was hot to get them onto the next target.

What was with these hollow worlds, anyway?

"Sensors and tracking. Isaac."

"Have you seen the latest, Izzy?"

"Hi, Jan. Nice to hear from you, too. How are Maureen and the kids? Enjoying the new posting? Thanks, Lorraine and I are fine. Jakob starts at the Academy in Harriman Dome next month."

"Umm. Oh. Sorry, Iz. It's just that there's a new report in from Cybele."

"Cybele. Three-hundred-kilometer C-type in Outer Belt? Okay, I heard something about—Hey, isn't that where they found the kids last week?"

"Yeah. Hollowed-out and bio-formed just like the rest, but this one had people living in it. There were a few older rockrats, some whole families, and lots of dependents."

". . . and the new report? Don't keep me waiting, Jan."

"Oh. Sorry. Well, the report said that one of the older folks said the habitat was set up by someone named 'John Chapman.'"

"Chapman, huh? That name rings a bell."

"GENERAL ISHIHARA, HOW IS the search going?"

"Mister President, there is nothing new to report. So far, the Patrol has located seventeen unregistered biospheres—thirteen uninhabited and four inhabited ones. I need to caution you that we have surveyed less than ten percent of the Belt, though.

"The Trajectory Deconfliction division claims that each of the uninhabited spheres has been visited at least once since we started tracking six months ago, but that they have not yet been able to track those ships to its next destination. In each case of the occupied worlds, the residents claim that they were told of the biosphere by a man who called himself John Chapman, and that they could move there as long as they 'promised to tend the orchard.'"

"John Chapman. Why do I recognize that name."

"Johnny Appleseed—a legend in colonial America, Sir. Planted apple trees. I'm rather surprised to be saying that to an American President, Sir."

"Oh, I know the legend, General—for that matter, it's more than legend, it's history. Appleseed planted hundreds of nurseries, mostly apple, but other fruits as well. They stretched from Pennsylvania to Illinois and he actually tended them himself. He was a preacher and his travels allowed him to return and tend to the nurseries for decades." The president paused and chuckled at the expression on his chief of staff's face. "Well, I *was* a history professor, General. So, this person or organization styles itself after Johnny Appleseed?"

"Individual, as far as the reports go. All of the people interviewed provide the same description."

"So why do they say he's doing this . . ." The president gestured vaguely.

"Terraforming, sir. The witnesses said he's establishing these worlds to preserve Earth's fruit trees."

" . . . and *that* sounds familiar, too, although that movie is over one hundred years old by this point."

"Yes, Mister President. It doesn't change the fact that he's violating the Planetary Protection statutes, though."

"Stupid. The laws, not this Appleseed person; but then again, if he's supplying the rock rats, he probably doesn't care about Earth laws anyway. Still, the Alliance is fragile enough as it is."

"We'll find him, sir. It's just a matter of time."

"I'm certain that you will, and a smart man will be ruined, I'm sure." The President sighed. "Keep me posted, General."

THE GAVEL SLAMMED. "Siôn Céapmann, aka John Chapman, you are charged with violations of the Planetary Protection treaty, the

Luna-Belt trade pact, and the Food and Drug Act of 2120. How do you plead?"

"Not guilty, your honor."

The defense attorney had wanted the trial to be publicly streamed on the 'net, but the prosecutor invoked federal security concerns. That didn't keep the proceedings from being viewed with interest by several governmental agencies on private channels.

"So, this is the guy responsible for the hollowed-out asteroids?"

"That's what they are saying. He hollowed out carbonaceous chondrites, turned the slag into soil and atmosphere, installed light-pipes, then planted trees and other plants."

"He couldn't have done it alone."

"That's pretty obvious, but no one has come forward and he's not talking."

"Huh."

Elsewhere . . .

"He screwed up a decade of logistic planning. We *knew* that *Victoria* was going to need provisioning, and we planned for it. That's why we got the contract. He screwed it all up. Ceres has overflowing warehouses and produce rotting in the cryo-prep area. He's a menace."

"Technically, he made our job easier, we always ran short on fresh produce for the belters."

"Who cares about the belters? Scarcity drives the prices up. The *Victoria* contract was supposed to set us up for the next decade; now we'll be lucky if we just break even over that same number of years."

In Mars orbit . . .

"I like this Chapman, person. You say he's a plant geneticist, Adam?"

"Best I ever met," said Adam Walker. "I tried to recruit him for the TRAPPIST-2 mission, but he turned me down. I ran his name anyway and apparently the psychs had their own reservations."

"Hmm, perhaps we can make him an offer he can't refuse," mused Keegan Coran.

Later . . .

"Mister Chapman, this court finds you guilty. You are sentenced to life imprisonment on Earth. Since you have spent most of your life in reduced gravity, and this would essentially be a death sentence, the Court has considered the alternative that has been presented by Mister Coran." Gavel bangs. "You are hereby sentenced to exile in the form of the TRAPPIST-2 colony mission. You will be remanded to the custody of the Colony Foundation in the person of Mister Adam Walker, where you will be immediately placed into cryo-suspension until the mission arrives at its destination. Since we have your recorded assent to this sentence, we feel that we have offered sufficient clemency to fulfill our humanitarian obligations. As such, we have a Finding from the President that there can be no appeal without reinstating the original on-Earth sentence." The gavel banged again. "This court is closed; members of the jury, you are dismissed."

THE MAN WAS ESSENTIALLY naked except for a light mesh singlet holding the sensors in place. He sat up and looked around. There were five other individuals within sight, also just getting out of their cryopods.

"John Chapman?"

He nodded, not yet able to bring himself to speak.

"Welcome to Cistercia. You and the others in this cohort are part of Terraforming Team Six. You will have your work cut out for you."

"W—wh—why?" he finally got out.

"I don't have all of the details. I was simply told that the expected advanced terraforming did not happen. We're carving this world out all by ourselves."

John swung his legs out over the edge of the 'pod. *Full gravity. We're on the planet already.* "Gravity?" he croaked.

"Don't worry, you've had one hundred seventy years of medical treatment in the cryo to strengthen your bones and circulatory system. Any weakness you feel right now is strictly muscular. It will dissipate in a couple of days." He was handed a bulb of opaque liquid. "Drink this. It's protein, electrolytes and a mild stimulant. Think of it as a coffee smoothie."

John did as he was told. *A new world, a new biosphere, and one that wasn't supposed to require environment suits—or, at least that was what it was supposed to be.* "Atmo? Temp? Water?" The cool liquid was easing the dry soreness of his throat.

"Earth normal within ten percent all around. This is Antonia, we've been onsite for about two years getting the habs set up. It feels like subtropical Earth–Florida or the Mediterranean—oh-two is a touch high, but it's moist enough that there's not much fire hazard. We're also near a river delta, and just off of a large bay, so we have freshwater and low-saline shallows available. There's rainforest equivalent well to our south, cloud-forest in the highlands to the northeast, and grasslands to the northwest." The man recited the conditions without obviously consulting the databord in his hands, so he must be involved in either the terraforming or science groups.

"Sorry, but you are?"

"Oh, yeah." The speaker tucked the 'bord under his left arm and held out his right hand. "Emílio Belo, supervisor for Terraforming Section B; that's groups five through eight. Yours is the second cohort we've decanted today." Releasing John's hand, he consulted the 'bord. "Once your cohort is ready, I'll take you over to the dorm and we can get you kitted out. Your personal cargo kilo is in the drawer under your pod, and your allocated cubic meter of effects will be delivered to the dorm later. We're all in dorms for the time being, but you'll be assigned to a remote facility within a couple of weeks. Again, welcome to Cistercia."

"Absolutely amazing." Belo looked over the field of small trees, each about a meter in height.

"They are a fast-growing variant. That means less time until they flower and fruit, but they won't live much more than ten years. The trees—and the fruits—will always be small because of that fast growth, but at least it will provide fresh fruit." Chapman beamed with pride, but then his face fell. "Unfortunately, they will need to be replaced sooner than ten years. The downside of this strain is that it depletes soil nutrients in a few years... and they need *Earth* nutrients. The Cistercian soils are not enriched enough to grow any of the strains we've tested so far."

"That shouldn't be a problem. We'll just terraform more hectares of land. Until then, these will make excellent luxury goods in the marketplaces."

Chapman's expression darkened. "What we grow here is supposed to be for *everyone*."

Belo laughed and slapped Chapman on the shoulder. "And they will be. Eventually."

When the supervisor left the test nursery, John turned to his co-worker, Maile Kalani. "Luxury goods. Typical bureaucrat thinking. What we need to do is develop a strain that thrives on native soil and does the transformation for us. These trees and their fruit should be for everyone."

Maile nodded. "I've heard this argument before. I've *made* this argument before, remember?" She was native Hawaiian; an agronomist in the Green Sahara project before joining the colony mission. "Look, I studied plants that could turn a bare rock lava field into grasslands, pineapple fields and macadamia groves. We never quite managed to transform equatorial Africa back into fields and forests, but we learned a lot. We'll make this work."

John grunted and turned back to the grove of young trees. He took a sample container out of a pouch on his belt and scooped a small amount of soil into it. He repeated the process at several points across the field, and then proceeded into the defoliated perimeter and into the native Cistercian growth past the quite literally terraformed fields of the agricultural research center.

Maile shook her head as she watched him move off. *He's obsessed with fruit trees and making sure every single colonist can have their own garden complete with fruits and vegetables. Well, I suppose that's a pretty good obsession.*

She heard a faint buzz behind her and turned to see a small honeybee settling in on a flower in an adjacent plot of hibiscus shrubs. Technically, they weren't food plants, but rather were interspersed with the plots and groves to encourage pollinating insects. "The fact that they smell nice doesn't hurt," she muttered to herself.

"The bees are doing fine. In fact, they're doing better than our best projections." She hadn't heard Cruz Fernandes, Team Six's apiarist, come up beside her. "I'm fairly confident that there's hives out in the outback by now." Cruz waved vaguely at the low native growth beyond the terraformed region.

"That would be good, especially if . . ." she trailed off without finishing the thought.

" . . . especially if Apple Tree Johnny goes through with his plans."

"Shhhh. That's not something to spread around."

"Hah! As if no one knows."

"Well, as far as we can tell, Emílio doesn't know. And if he doesn't know, the colony leadership doesn't know."

"Those fools?" Cruz phrased it as a question, but it wasn't really. Everyone on the terraforming and agriculture teams knew that something was out of synch between colonists and colony administration. "How in the hell did we end up with an eco-idiot as mayor?"

"Especially on an interstellar colony mission?" Maile asked in turn.

"Exactly. Rumor has it his father bought his selection."

"Who's his father, anyway?"

"Actually, no one's really sure, some say Keegan Coran, the Foundation CEO, some say he was a high muckety-muck in the FEFfer movement."

"Fix Earth First? But they *hated* the mission."

"So, what better way to make sure we fail? If the sabotage didn't kill us, the government would."

"True. Which is why those of us who know John's plans aren't telling," Maile concluded.

"Okay, let's call a break." The men climbed out of the ditches and off of the heavy machinery and headed for the shade of the trees lining the sides of the roadbed.

On Earth, crews would have set a course and programmed a Road-Builder2150 or similar fully automated device to clear the ground, prepare the base and leave behind a weatherproof surface for suitable wheeled and ground-effect vehicles alike. The loss of the automated heavy terraforming equipment meant that the Cistercian colonists had to revert to techniques used throughout the late Twentieth and early Twenty-first centuries. They had plenty of heavy construction equipment, but it meant that the road-building crews had to actually operate bulldozers, excavators, pavers, and yes, picks and shovels. The overland road between Antonia and New Virginia would take a decade to complete at this rate, so the crews made sure to pave right up to the ground that they cleared, as soon as they cleared it. The result of that policy was that homesteads, ranches and farms followed close behind the leading edge of the road. With "civilization" so close behind, many of the crew lived close to the leading edge of construction, so the actual "construction camp" was fairly small, but well-supplied.

However, they were not so well-supplied that Nguyen Phan's lunch went without notice.

"Apples? Full-size apples! Where did you get apples?" one of the other construction crew asked quietly.

"What, Newby has apples?" Hector Santos' voice was not so quiet, and several heads turned to listen.

"Quiet!" hissed Gernot, the one who first spoke.

"Well, of course," answered Nguyen. "There's a grove of apple, orange and pear trees on my father's farm." He was new to the crew, just turned thirteen, and part of the first generation of children born on Cistercia. No one was very old on the crew—except for Mister Santos—because frankly, the colony couldn't afford idleness from anyone capable of working.

"Your dad planted them?" Paola asked. She, too, was new to the crew, and also from a farm sited about ten klicks back from their current location. "You'll have to tell my grandfather how he got them to survive. Grandpops wants lemon trees so that he can make his family's traditional limoncello.

"He didn't plant them. They were there when he cleared the land."

"Nonsense. Earth fruit trees don't grow in this soil. They certainly don't grow out in advance of the terraforming perimeter." Hector was not only foreman of the ground-prep part of the road-grading crew, but he'd originally been part of the crews that cleared native Cistercian life out of the zones that were marked for agriculture. "Earth and Cisty life don't grow in the same places. The terraforming eggheads said it was something about extra 'tides and nuclei or something like that."

Nguyen looked up at the sky. There *were* two moons up there... "Tides? But we're nowhere near the ocean?"

"Not that kind of tides, Newby. The science-y kind... And no, I don't know any more about it. I only know what the eggheads said—" He broke off as one of the members of the vegetation-clearing team came running up.

"Mister Santos, we have a problem with the trees."

"What problem? Either cut them down or bulldoze them."

"No, it's not that. These are *Earth* trees!"

"MY GOD, JOHN, YOU look horrible."

"I've been camping. Lost my gear in a storm a month ago."

"You've been gone for almost three years. People have been looking for you."

"I've been tending my nurseries."

"Yes, that's why they've been looking for you—"

THE GAVEL BANGED. JOHN winced; it brought back bad memories.

"John Chapman, you are charged with resisting arrest, failure to register your whereabouts with the Committee for Public Safety, and fifteen counts of violating Antonia Terraforming Ordinance 10-50 5.3, regarding commingling of Terran and Cistercian lifeforms." The judge paused, looked at the gallery and saw the nod from the Mayor. "How do you plead?"

"... he performed unsanctioned genetic splicing on Cistercian and Earth plants..."

"... he's insubordinate. He listens to orders and instructions only when they suit his own purposes..."

"... well, he didn't resist arrest exactly, it's just that no-one wanted to get that close to him..."

"... there's groves of apple, cherry, pear and citrus trees halfway to New Virginia..."

"... we had to re-route the overland highway five times to avoid digging up orchards..."

"... we're starting to find Terran growth all through the wildlands, now..."

"... I mean, just *look* at him! Does a reputable scientist come to court barefoot and in clothes that are frayed at the ends of the pants and sleeves? This man is no more a scientist than—than *you* are, Your Honor! ..."

"... what my esteemed colleague *should* have said is that my client cares more about science and feeding people than about his own appearance..."

"MISS FOREWOMAN, WHAT ARE the jury's findings?"

"Your Honor, on the charges of resisting arrest—we find John Chapman not guilty. On the charges of violating Terraforming Ordinance 10-505.3—not guilty. On the charges of not reporting his location—guilty..."

Gavel bangs. "Miss Foreman, ladies and gentlemen of the jury, the court thanks you—"

"Your Honor, we're not done. The Jury wants to add that we think the registration regulation is stupid. The rules limiting the planting of Earth crops are stupid, and frankly, we suspect that the Mayor..."

Gavels bangs repeatedly. "Enough. Jury, you may not editorialize in my courtroom. You are dismissed."

"MISTER CHAPMAN, YOU HAVE been cleared of all charges except failure to report your location to the proper authorities. Since we cannot sentence you to anything like returning you to Earth, you will wear a tracking bracelet at all times, and are banned from travel beyond the city limits.

"And keep in mind that the court is aware that this is your second strike. If you persist in defying authority, we *will* put you back in cryo—indefinitely."

"MISTER MAYOR! MISTER MAYOR! A statement for the news-briefs, please." The reporter held a databord up so that its pickups would record the politician's image and words.

"Why certainly, Janet. I would like to say that City Hall is somewhat displeased that the jury has acquitted the so-called 'Apple Tree Hero.' Rest assured that this man is no hero. We are scrutinizing his activities and backtracking his movements while he is off the grid and are certain that he has violated many more laws and ordinances than the paltry few presented here. Trust me, we will stop this terrorist in his tracks!"

Multiple voices clamored for attention.

"Yes, I said what I meant. John Chapman is an ecoterrorist. He is now, and he was before we left Earth and Mars. He has no regard for the consequences of his unrestrained genetic monstrosities..."

An object flew out of the crowd and hit the mayor on the side of the head. Security guards immediately closed in and hustled him off the entry steps of the municipal dome. More objects continued to fly, pelting the mayor and his security team.

For the most part, the fruit squished when it hit, seeing as it was largely rotten—that is, except for the dwarf-apples which were still mostly solid. The fruit had come from the city leader's own commissary supply. No one wanted to pay the commissary's exorbitant prices when the city market sold fruit at less than a tenth of the cost. Hence the rotten surplus that constituted a classic protest against oppressive authority.

"It might be time to activate Operation Trudovik," the mayor muttered to his chief aide once they had escaped the crowd.

MAILE KALANI WAVED TO the crowds at her inauguration. She scanned the gathering looking for a particular face—long stringy hair and a lined, weathered face. John Chapman wasn't a young man when the judge on Luna had sentenced him to exile, and he'd spent most of his twenty years on Cistercia out in the fields and forests. She hoped he was here. He'd been one of the major reasons for it.

The demonstrations following Mayor Ivanoff's accusations of ecoterrorism had brought about a major change in government. The mayor and his Committee for Public Safety cronies had left on the next shuttle, destination unknown. Over the next few months, nearly five hundred others left Antonia, cutting the colony's population by nearly one-tenth. Strangely enough, the workforce was not greatly reduced, since the people who went missing were predominantly from the science, education and administration offices.

In their absence, many of the regulations which had limited colony growth, including the expansion of the farming and ranching lands, were repealed. There was considerable progress in adapting Terran lifeforms to grow in Cistercian soil without pre-conditioning, and a new Office of Forestry was established to foster and guide the industry that was transforming the native plains and forests with Earth-Cistercian hybrids.

John would love it—if he were here. Maile scanned the crowds again but didn't see him. Oh, there were still reports of Apple Tree John sightings, and nearly every month someone reported coming across a previously unmapped grove of fruit trees. Just last week they received a report of a brand-new nursery with seedlings that couldn't be more than two months old.

He was out there, and the whole colony was thankful.

Maile proudly brandished and then bit into the fresh apple a staffer had handed her. It was the symbol of her campaign, and it never failed to get an enthusiastic reaction from the crowd.

Thank you, John, wherever you are.

A STATUE STANDS IN the Municipal Park in Antonia of a thin, raggedly clothed man of advanced years. He has one hand upraised, holding an apple. The other hand is down at his side, holding a gardening tool. One foot is raised and resting on a rock. A plaque attached to the rock reads:

Apple Tree John: Siôn Céapmann, plant geneticist, agronomist, nurseryman, who took the name John Chapman in honor of the legend of "Johnny Appleseed." Born 2131 CE, Rinehart City, Luna; died Cistercia, date unknown. Chapman defied authorities on Earth, Luna and the Belt by creating unlicensed asteroid biospheres containing plants and trees adapted to grow in low-gee, low-oxygen and low-nutrient soils. He joined the TRAPPIST-2 Colony Mission in lieu of a life sentence for violating Earth-Luna-Belt ecological laws.

Chapman is credited with developing plant varieties that would grow in Cistercian soils without terraforming and is suspected of being responsible for spreading groves of fruit trees throughout the wildlands outside the colony perimeter. He is often associated with apples and apple trees, even though he always took care to promote all manner of flowering fruit and nut trees and shrubs. This statue marks the location where Mayor Maile Kailani launched her Appleseed Campaign to oust the corrupt of administration of Mayor Filip Ivanoff—the success of which Mayor Kailani attributed to the example set by Chapman.

-*Encyclopedia Astra*, Gannon University, Antonia, Cistercia, AA212.

Eight
To Light Up the Night

By Robert E. Hampson and Brent M. Roeder

AUTHORS NOTE: THIS IS one of only two short stories I ever co-authored. I paired up with Brent Roeder, a/k/a the Evil Penguin, a long-time friend and colleague in science. Brent wrote "The Legend of Beaver Flight," for *The Founder Effect*. It is framed as a memorial service for spacers who lost their lives escorting the final lander—twenty-five thousand colonists in hibernation—to a mostly safe landing on the planet *Cistercia*. It's a tale of heroism wrapped in reverence.

I liked the final scene so much, I incorporated it into the epilogue for the anthology.

In 2020, Baen published *Give Me LibertyCon*, a charity volume to fund a scholarship set up in the name of superfan, TVA engineer, and LibertyCon founder Timothy "Uncle Timmy" Bolgeo. In 2023, *Onward, LibertyCon*, followed, honoring Uncle Timmy's daughter Brandy, who now runs the convention in Chattanooga, TN every summer.

I was asked if I wanted to contribute to *Onward, Liberty-Con*, and talked it over (as I often do) with Brent. He was the one who suggested we add to the legend of Beaver Flight, with a tale set before the memorial had become the stuff of legend. Our main character is none other than Brandy Bolgeo, who honors the fallen heroes by offering her community a way to light up the night.

"SAN SALVADOR, THIS IS Beaver Lead. I have made it to the controls and am preparing to eject fuel tank. Godspeed and safe landing, San Salvador. Beaver flight is cl..."

From the civil defense speakers, the replay of the last broadcast from Beaver Flight during the landing of the San Salvador ended with a brief burst of static. After a minute of silence, a voice came back over the speakers, slowly reading out the names of Beaver Flight. The voice paused, then spoke the final words of the annual Landing Day Ceremony. *"Beaver Flight, this is Beaverton Ground Control. The lander is down with all souls safe. Prepare for Landing Beacon to guide you home on my mark..."*

***

"Do you think they'd be proud of us? Do you thing *he* would be proud of us?" Brandy Bolgeo quietly asked the friend sitting with her to watch the closing of the Landing Day ceremony.

"I certain hope so." Jaqueline Rabinowiscz murmured. In a stronger voice she answered, "I know what Gil would say to you in particular. 'While Beaver Flight got us down safely, it's still a miracle that they were able to get us down to a hard landing on this island.

Don't get your nose out of joint just because Antonia and Roanoke look down on us for having gaps in our tech base. You've done a lot to rectify the situation, even with all of the trouble of the past few years.' He'd be proud of *you*, Brandy. I'm proud of you, too."

"Even if all you have is nails – you can always design a better hammer?"

"Exactly. Be proud. We're growing faster than the other colonies. More importantly, we're *thriving,* thanks to you."

"Don't sell yourself short, you played a role, too." Brandy countered.

"I remember..." Jackie said.

THE MAN KNOCKED ON the door to the den before opening it. He stuck his head in and called gently into the dimly lit room, "Ms. Jaqueline, you've got a visitor."

"What is it, Argi?" the Widow Rabinowiscz asked.

"It's Li Sihai. He's come straight from the BuRP emergency meeting. Said there's things going on that affect the ranchers and farmers, and that you need to know right away."

"Bring him in, Argi," Jaqueline said with a note of resignation in her voice as she reached to turn up the lamp.

Argi led Sihai into the room and to the pair of chairs before the desk the Widow Rabinowiscz was sitting behind.

"Mrs. Rabinowiscz, I'm sorry to intrude," Sihai started.

"Please don't, Sihai," she said standing up and extending her hand. "Call me Jackie and forgive my manners. How was your trip? Would you..."

He made a gesture cutting off her pleasantries, "Please, Mrs. Rabinowiscz. I think the resources committee is making a grave error, Ms. Bolgeo argued against it, but the mayor was determined. I need your help before it is too late. *We* need to fix things before it gets too late."

She sat back down in her chair behind Gil's desk and waved for the two men to sit as well. "I haven't been paying attention since Gil passed and you took his place, Sihai. Tell me what's been happening."

"Well, ma'am, we have to go back to when Gil represented us in the Bureau of Resource Planning, and truthfully, it's not my story to tell – you really need to hear it from Brandy..."

"Argi, can we send a truck for her? If it's this serious, then I agree, we should get her here."

Argi hid his smile behind a hand across his mouth. He hadn't heard that tone in Jackie's voice since before Gil's funeral. "I'll have her here by dinner, Miss Jackie."

THE WHITE STREAMER STRETCHED from a point somewhere behind the stage and raced into the night sky. The trail faded but was quickly replaced by a red starburst pattern as the firework burst into brilliant color. The muffled 'boom' arrived before the individual lights began to twinkle. Every year, the residents of the settlement honored the memories of the brave "Beaver Flight" orbital tug pilots who'd made it possible for the colony to exist at all. The celebration of Landing Day involved picnics, community games, a thankfully brief speech by the mayor, and a re-broadcast of the radio communications detailing the heroic sacrifice by Beaver Flight pilots who'd guided the colony lander to its best possible rest. The night ended with the "Landing Flares" – a fireworks display signaling an end to rest and relaxation, and a return to the hard work of life in Beaverton.

The final colony site on the world of Cistercia had been held in reserve for twenty-five years to ensure that the other colonies had taken hold. Twenty-five-hundred colonists remained in cryo about the lander *San Salvador* as insurance against the failure of the first two settlements. A full complement of infrastructure-building machines rested in its hull, waiting for their turn to establish a home for Humanity on the new world of Cistercia. Whether it was the long delay, or neglected maintenance, or some unforeseen circumstance that caused it, *San Salvador*, destined for the "Paradise Colony" on the tropical shores of the subcontinent-sized island Aopo, had malfunctioned, running short of fuel and nearly crashing down on a rocky island ten miles offshore.

The hard landing of the San *Salvador* had crumpled the lower decks, damaging or trapping much of the heavy machinery, limiting Beaverton to a technology level akin to the early twentieth century on Earth, as opposed to the fusion power plants, automated terraforming and construction of the other colony sites, Antonia and Roanoke.

BRANDY BOLGEO, LEAD ENGINEER for the electrification project in "Paradise Valley" on the eastern side of the Aopo mainland, was sitting with friends watching the commemoration of the miracle that heralded the founding of their community. With her were Gill and Jaqueline Rabinowiscz who owned the largest of the cattle ranches in the Paradise Valley, and Li Sihai, owner of the first farm to start producing taro and other fast-growing foodstuffs to supplement the limited rations to survive the crash landing.

The conversation had turned to the challenges in keeping technology going – and even expanding – without the "luxuries" of the large machines still trapped (and damaged) within *San Salvador* years after landing. "I guess I'm just second guessing our progress a little bit after that conference call with the other colony sites. I'm not used to being looked down like I'm some country bumpkin," Brandy said.

Gil snorted, "they've just got their noses out of joint because even though a bunch of our heavy equipment and supplies were damaged in the landing, we're growing faster than they are, even though they have an intact tech base while we've had to adapt."

"I wouldn't have thought it before landing, or for quite a few years after, but I think having gaps in our tech base from the damage has actually been to our benefit," Jaqueline said with a chuckle.

"Really?" Sihai asked with a surprised tone.

"Really," Jaqueline said more firmly. "Everyone at Antonia and Roanoke are concerned with keeping their tech base going that it makes them think of everything from that perspective. When trying to solve a problem they always look for the high-tech way as opposed to the best way."

"If the only tool you use is a hammer, then everything starts to look like a nail?" Sihai asked.

"Exactly," Jaqueline agreed.

A sudden increase in the rumble of explosions drew everyone's full attention back to the sky with the four of them watching the final minute of the fireworks display enraptured.

"Alright, I think it is time for bed," Gil said with a wistful tone as he gazed at the sky lit only by stars. "Brandy, Sihai and I have the annual Beaverton Resource Planning Committee meeting tomorrow, and you know Mayor Donahue expects everyone to arrive bright-eyed and bushy-tailed."

"I think he must have a bit of a sadistic streak setting the meeting for seven in the morning the day after Landing Day," Jaqueline chuckled.

"I agree with you, and I think the rest of the committee would, too," Sihai said.

"Well, I will just let the head of the Paradise Valley Authority and the joint heads of the Paradise Agricultural Association go catch some rest," Jaqueline said, going up on tip toe to kiss her husband on the cheek. "I think I am going to go catch up with the Urbaneks, as I don't get out to Beaverton nearly as often as the rest of you."

The residents of Beaverton were self-reliant, but with a strong sense of community. It would likely be more than a century before additional colonists arrived from Earth – if at all – and Antonia and Roanoke were many weeks' journey away over rough seas. The strength and hardiness were necessary to survive – the community was necessary to *thrive*.

BRANDY PAUSED ON HER way into town to look up at the massive crane being erected on the hull of the San Salvador. The salvage crew was getting ready to remove the forward left engine. With it out of the way, it would be easier to access the forward equipment hold. The hold entrance was inaccessible due to the combination of the terrain and the crumpled lower decks.

The collapse of the lower decks protected the precious human cargo, but it meant that large equipment and supplies intended to allow installation of modern technology were damaged – some irretrievably. Beaverton been forced to adapt a mixture of low, modern, and hybrid tech far below that of their sister colonies at Antonia and Roanoke. Beavertonians stubbornly refused to abandon their landing site and move to the "civilization" of the other cities. They made do with what they had, and worked to recover, rebuild, and repair what they could.

Shaking her head and amused at her woolgathering, Brandy continued into the lander. Interior cargo holds, storage spaces and crew compartments had been converted to offices, classrooms and meeting rooms. The Beaverton Resource Planning Committee (BuRP to the general public, much to the annoyance of many committee members) was about to have its annual in-person meeting in one of the larger rooms. The "RPC" (the committee's *preferred* abbreviation) was always scheduled the day after Landing Day, to ride on the upswell of community sentiment and take advantage of the influx of residents for the annual celebration and remembrance. As head of the Paradise Valley Authority for Flood Control and Power Generation (or PVA to the general public), Brandy was there to report on dam construction and electrification on the western half of Aopo –"Paradise Island."

"And with the Atkins River Dam ahead of schedule, we were able to start early on the initial stages of the Moops Valley project. This leaves us with a major decision to make about the electrification project," Brandy said, signaling for the next slide in her presentation.

The timetable that had been projected on the screen was replaced with multiple images from within the San Salvador's cargo hold.

"As you know we had eight high-capacity hydro turbines in the cargo hold, which the mission planners thought would be more than enough to last us until we were able to build modern ones of our own. Three of these came through undamaged, the first of which we used in the Cajon Dam for the initial electrification of Beachhead Town on Paradise. The next two were planned for the Atkins River and Moops Valley Dams," Brandy again gestured for the next slide to be displayed, this one a graph of estimated power usage and availability for multiple scenarios.

"This is where the good news comes in. We are taking parts from damaged turbines to see if we can assemble working models, even if smaller or of reduced capacity. We've been able to get all broken turbines stripped down and we have enough parts to build at least one, probably two, and a slim chance at three. The rebuilt ones are not going to be able to handle the high flow rates of the originals; thus, we shouldn't expect as much electrical generating capacity. While Atkins River is one of our best building sites, it doesn't have the water flow to make full use of an original turbine. According to initial plans, lower efficiency was better than nothing. Now we have an intermediate option, but it will affect the ranchers and farmers on Paradise."

"How do you mean?" asked Gil Rabinowiscz, representative for most of the ranching sector on Paradise.

"The next stage of electrification involves power to the scattered farms and ranchers, as well as building up the Beachhead and industrial grid. The generator house at Atkins River will be finished in about five months, and we can begin building the generator house at

Moops Valley about a month after that. It should be finished roughly a year from now. We also have two new turbines ready now, but the first rebuild will take between twelve and eighteen months. It should go faster after the first one, but we will clearly have Atkins River Dam finished before a rebuilt turbine is ready. Installing one of the two original turbines commits the station, we can't go back and swap it out later. So, we need to decide whether we install a new turbine at Atkins River once it's done or leave the generator house empty for up to a year waiting on the rebuilt unit. If we wait, we delay increasing our generating capacity, but will be able to increase capacity by having a good turbine for a full-power, third installation later. If we don't wait, we get power sooner, but reduce our eventual maximum capacity."

"And the sooner we can electrify the irrigation pumps, the better," Li Sihai added. He was Gil's counterpart, representing the farmers on Aopo. Paradise Valley was on the windward side of the island, and a tall spine of mountains – the Ko'Olina Heights – blocked the moisture-laden trade winds from the west. Even more than the ranchers, the farmers needed electricity in order to expand outward from the narrow, fertile margins of the rivers.

"Is a way to speed up the timeline for Moops Valley?" Gil asked.

"Yes, and no," Brandy answered. "There's three parts to that time-line: Building the generator house, clearing the overland path to the dams, and transportation and installation of the turbines. We've been able to airlift the construction materials via the cargo heli-copters, but as you recall from the dam at Cajon Gorge construction, the turbines are too large to be airlifted. They will need a clear over-land path from the coast."

"Do they have to go from the coast, or can they be taken part of the way up-river?" Greg Donahue, Mayor of Beaverton and RP chair, asked.

"We looked at that possibility, but the only potential landing spots on the Atkins River are either inconveniently placed to start an overland path to the generator house or would need so much improvement that the distance saved wouldn't be worth the effort."

"Unfortunate, but that makes sense," Mayor Donahue acknowledged.

"Turbine rebuilding, transport, dam construction and building generator houses are all fixed durations. Where we can save time is in clearing the paths – it's not just cutting brush, but stringing power lines and stabilizing the soil for heavy vehicles. We add roads where necessary, plus transformer stations and maintenance sheds where needed. We also pre-position the junctions for spurs and residential connections. Until the turbine houses are finished, there's been no reason to speed up the roads and power lines, so I only have a ten-person team working on them. In addition, we aren't building separate roads to Atkins River and Moops Valley. The best route to Moops is from the Atkins Dam site, which decreases the total distance we clear and improve. It can be sped up but will require additional manpower. As-is, Moops is scheduled for completion after Atkins, and there's been no real benefit to throwing additional effort into it since the dam, generator house and roads will all complete at the same time.

"But you still have to resolve the question of which turbine we install at Atkins. When do we need to decide?" Gil asked unhappily.

"Best to have a plan within three months, four months at the latest," Brandy answered.

"Well, that's not as bad as it sounded at first," Gil said in a mollified tone.

"What option do you recommend?" Donahue asked.

"Let me put it this way, Cajon Dam has an eighty-five-meter drop, and a turbine capable of generating 1200 megawatts. It typically operates at seventy-five-percent peak capacity. During high water flow, the excess is diverted into pumped storage and irrigation. Moops Valley will have a one-hundred meter drop and will likely get close to ninety percent of peak out of its turbine. Atkins River only has a fifty-meter drop and very little variability; it will likely top out at fifty-five percent of peak capacity from a 1200 MW turbine. The rebuilds, however, will probably only generate 800 MW at peak, making it well matched to Atkins, reserving a turbine capable of half-again as much electrical generation for a site further up the highlands, or even on the Windward side of the island. Atkins is fast and easy – not as easy as Cajon gorge, but it's accessible. The best option for Atkins is a rebuilt turbine, even if it means a delay. It's just that it means we don't bring additional generating capacity online until we finish Atkins and clear the way to Moops."

"Rabinowiscz, you represent the agricultural stations. What do you think?" Mayor Donahue asked turning to the rancher.

Grimacing, Rabinowiscz shrugged and answered, "it sounds like we should follow Brandy's recommendation. I think it is the best option, but it is going to be inconvenient to wait eighteen more months for electricity that doesn't come from batteries or generators burning fuel we need for the farm equipment."

"Do you think the rest of the farmers and ranchers on Paradise will go along with it?"

"When I explain it to them, I think they will," Gil answered.

"All right," Mayor Donahue said turning back to Brandy. "Go ahead with your recommendation. We can revisit if we must, but absent any objections today, let's move forward." He looked down at his notes, shuffled them, then looked up at the rest of the committee. "Now that we're done with the PVA report, Dr. Schoeffel will report on community health and the clinic expansion process. Kim, come on up."

As the ferry approached the Beaverton pier, Brandy sat up in the lounge chair. She'd been trying to catch a nap on the top deck and had gotten comfortable for the ferry ride. Reaching for her boots and socks, she grimaced down at her toes trying to remember when she last had time to get a pedicure. A near-constant sense of urgency continually warred with delays and difficulties, so she doubted she would find any time soon. This was the second time in the last three months she had been called back to Beaverton for a meeting of BuRP. Given that the regularly scheduled annual meeting was only two weeks from now, she figured it was just another in the series of "emergencies" that seemed to be business-as-usual for the colony.

The first emergency meeting had been in response to the cattle failing throughout the colony due to "failure to thrive" – the scientific farming term for "nobody knows what's wrong." It was a serious problem for the colony – especially the farmers, which was why they'd met. None of that had affected her projects directly. As she looked up from picking up her boots, she got a sinking sensation that this new emergency, whatever it was, would impact her more severely. There was a car on the pier with a driver standing next to it holding a sign. There were only two other passengers, and they both had bicycles. It was only a mile walk from pier to lander – if they were sending one of the few private cars for her, this had to be really bad.

"THANK YOU FOR ATTENDING everyone," Mayor Donahue said. He spoke over the individual conversations and gestured for everyone to sit so that they could begin the meeting. "Let's get right into it. Dr. Schoeffel, brief us on the problem we face."

As he stood, Brandy noticed that Schoeffel's warm smile and friendly expression were absent. "There's a problem with the farming plan that needs to be addressed. We need more milk."

"I don't understand Doctor," Victoria Elliott, owner of Elliott's Explosives. "I thought BuRP announced a new plan with the farmers after the last emergency meeting. Besides, what do I have to do with milk production? I make explosives for infrastructure projects; I don't make milk."

Li Sihai stood up and called out, "You don't make milk. You compete with my fields and goats for nitrates." With Gil Rabinowiscz's passing, Li now represented al of the agricultural concerns on Paradise.

"Mr. Li is correct," Dr. Schoeffel said. "When the cattle failed to thrive, we were concerned that we could feed ourselves; we now know we can do this. However, the new problem is providing enough milk for our expanding population. In particular, we are seeing an increase in birthrate as we establish more farms, ranches, and local industry. As the community grows, so does the birthrate. We are currently riding a baby boom, and we need to provide for them."

"I'm sorry, Doc, but I'm not following how this is a problem now," said James 'Wrecks' Snover, the salvage team chief.

"If I can interject," Donahue said, "We didn't realize there was a problem until we looked at the time-tables for human population growth compared to livestock population growth. The latter necessitated examining nitrate availability in relation to growing food for the sheep and goats that will replace lost milk production from the cattle. Caprinae need less fodder from Earth plants; goats can even survive by foraging Cistercian native plants in areas where even sheep would have difficulty. They certainly need less fodder than cows, but weight-for-weight, they are less efficient at producing milk. This means we need to grow more Earth plants per gallon of milk than we did with cows. For that we need the nitrates for fertilizer."

"Nitrates which *I* need to manufacture explosives," Victoria said, with dawning understanding in her voice.

"That explains the problem," Snover said. "But why is it one right now?"

At a gesture from Donahue, Li stood up. "We don't have many sheep and goats right now. As a food source they were only secondary. We need to start a massive breeding campaign, and just like any other scale-up – we need to prepare the basic stocks, first. We were *going* to scale up flocks to match the amount of fodder we could produce. Instead, we need to scale up fodder production *before* we increase our flocks. Instead of ramping up demand for nitrates over time, we need them now, so that we can plant now and be ready for the next breeding cycle."

"This is why we've called all of you here today," Mayor Donahue interjected, taking back control of the meeting. "We have a plan on how to handle this but need to hammer out the details."

"Levitt," Mayor Donahue said turning to Jeremy Levitt, the chief construction engineer. "The new chemical plant at Beachhead City is dependent on electrification from the dams. What's the timetable on that?"

"We're a little behind schedule, but I've already been working with James..." Jeremy paused to nod in the direction of the salvage chief. "... to reprioritize the parts we are shipping over. We'll have the ammonia facilities up before the rest. It will take time to get the rest of the plant up, but the ammonia section should be ready to go about the time we get electricity. It will be just anhydrous ammonia at first. We can use it to enrich recycled waste to serve as fertilizer for now. Ready-to-use fertilizer variants will take longer."

James coughed to gain attention. "We've also been working with the machine shop here on the lander to modify equipment for the farmers and ranchers to apply the anhydrous ammonia."

"Next item," Mayor Donahue said checking his notepad. "Bolgeo, where are you on getting the turbines installed at the dams?"

"We're behind schedule," Brandy admitted with a grimace. "The cattle die-off pulled manpower from every project. Every bit of our timetable ended up taking a hit. We have the road to Atkins built, and the power lines are in place. The dam is done, and the generator house is as complete as it can be without the turbine. We're behind on both the clearing and wiring to Moops Valley. The dam is curing and only the foundation for the generator house is in. The rebuild of the turbine for Atkins River is also behind schedule, and from what it sounds like from what James and Jeremy said their project might be interfering with the turbine rebuild."

"Unfortunately, Brandy is right. We've had to pull people from other projects to help with the chemical plant. The turbine rebuilds got sacrificed because we were planning for installation at Moops Valley, first. The rebuild for Atkins River got put on the back burner."

"So, we have a dam with no turbine, and a turbine with no dam?" Donahue asked. "Why is that a problem? Why not swap the turbines? For that matter, don't we have two intact turbines in the cargo hold?"

"We might have been able to do that a year ago. It's what we talked about right after last Landing Day. Atkins River Dam does not have as high a pressure head as either the existing dam at Cajon Gorge, or the new one at Moops Valley. Once we decided to use a rebuilt turbine to matching dam flow rate with turbine capacity, we committed to that generator house configuration." Brandy agreed hesitantly. "If we swap the turbines, we not only waste more than forty percent of the capacity of the generator – *permanently*, but I might also add – we have to completely remodel the generator house at Atkins. The other limitation is that we don't simply unwrap a turbine and install it. There's several months' preparation and conditioning to pull it out of the shipping container."

"How long to finish Moops Valley?" Mayor Donahue asked.

"That one is mainly manpower. We can speed up the build on the generator house, and the concrete will be ready for pressure loads in a month. Clearing the road is the problem – more manpower, plus explosives. From what I'm hearing, that's the real limitation. With the current crew and at normal explosive use, we are about three months from completing the road, plus a month to float, transport and install the turbine. Four months at the earliest until we have power. The original timeline was to bring Moops Valley online on

Landing Day, with Atkins River six months later. We're behind that estimate by at least four months."

"Hmm, as opposed to power in a month if we just install the Moops Valley turbine at Atkins River," Donahue mused.

"Not entirely correct, but if we had to force it, we could meet the timetable, give or take two weeks."

Donahue turned back to Jeremy Levitt, "When will the chemical plant be able to start up production and how much will you be able to produce?"

Jeremy and James exchanged reluctant looks, before Jeremy finally spoke. "We will be ready to produce anhydrous ammonia at half capacity in three weeks, no more than four. The rest of the plant will not come online for several more months after that. On the other hand, we're estimating a ton a week for the first six-to-ten months."

"Elliott," the mayor started, "what's your stockpile of nitrates and explosives like."

Victoria paused while she checked her notes, "We have just under half a ton of black powder finished, just over a ton of filtered saltpeter and with our most recent delivery we are sitting at about four tons of nitratite that we will be processing into saltpeter. We can expect shipments of nitratite to remain at about two tons a month for the foreseeable future without much room for expansion of mining operations. Of course, that's not counting the fireworks that we've already manufactured for Landing Day."

"Li, what's that look like compared to your needs?" The mayor asked.

Sihai didn't say anything for a minute as he worked away at a scratch pad, but finally looked up with a grimace. "With the ammonia plant production and using all of the saltpeter that Victoria has, should be just enough to get everything planted and fertilized in time."

"Is there any slack in that timetable?" Brandy asked.

"We don't have to start the planting process yet as it's not time, but we'll need to prep the soil, which means we need fertilizer in about two and a half months," Sihai answered.

"We're going to have to go with installing the turbine we have at Atkins River to be on the safe side," Donahue said. "The timetable is too tight for anything else."

"That's a waste of time and effort. We have to tear down and rebuild the generator house at Atkins, and even then, the Atkins River doesn't have the flow rate to fully power the chemical plant and the other industry we planned to build at Beachhead," Brandy informed the mayor. "Not only that, but we also permanently lose the option to install the higher-output turbine in a more suitable site."

"Once you finish the path to Moops Valley, you can install the next available turbine. That will provide the power you want for Beachhead and the leeward shore," the mayor answered.

"That's short-sighted and will severely cut our future growth ability," Brandy objected. Several of the others nodded in agreement. "Without a high-output turbine, there's no hope of a settlement on the windward coast of Aopo for decades. Give me the manpower and we can get the path to Moops Valley cut and the turbine installed in time. The saltpeter that Victoria has in stock will buy us the time to get Moops Valley fully operational. It will also provide enough power to the ammonia plant and partial electrification of the grid until we get the rebuilt turbine installed at Atkins River."

"Either way, that means I'm not going to have raw materials for explosives until the chemical plant comes fully online to produce nitrates and nitratites instead of just ammonia. Not only is that going to slow down road clearance and building, but it also means no fireworks next year," Victoria said.

"I'm sure everyone will miss the fireworks next year, but that's not as big a concern as proper nutrition for our children." Turning back to Brandy, Donahue continued, "I'm sorry, it's too risky. We must prioritize survival of the community; installing the existing turbine at Atkins River will ensure that. We'll worry about the future once we solve the problems of today."

Donahue looked down at his folder of notes. He closed it with a firm slap of his hand on the table. He stood up and glared at the room, as if daring them to speak any further. "We know what we have to do. Let's get to it."

BRANDY LOOKED ACROSS THE sitting room at Jaqueline Rabinowiscz after completing the summary of events the past year. "I'm sorry to have wasted your time – I appreciate Sihai wanting me to fill you in, but there's nothing I can do. I know this seriously changes the plans for electrification of farms and ranches. We just don't have the resources."

"Dearie, you just leave that to me."

"BRANDY? THERE'S SOME PEOPLE here to see you."

It had been a week since the ranch foreman Argi had dragged her to the impromptu meeting at the Rabinowiscz farm. Jackie was a dear friend, and she missed Gil, but that was time she simply did not have to spare. She was leaning over a table spread with the blueprints for the generator facility at Atkins River, wishing Mayor Donahue here – she'd put him to work demolishing the old sluice gates and water channels leading into the generator house and rebuilding them. If she was feeling generous, she might lend him some help.

There was nothing about this job to make her feel generous, tough; if he wanted this done, he could damned well do it himself. It wasn't that the building was too small, on the contrary, it was the same as every other generator house. The difference was that the penstocks – the input channels for the water – needed to be custom designed to get the maximum energy transfer from the fifty-foot pressure head off the dam. That involved pipe diameters, air bleeds, calculating vertical and horizontal distance for optimum slope, and so on. What was suitable for an 800 MW turbine was simply not appropriate for a 1200 MW turbine. Since the original, undamaged turbines shipped from Earth were meant for higher water flow, there were two choices for modifying the penstocks – increase diameter to increase water volume or decrease diameter to increase flow rate. She was still waiting for a response back from the hydrologist she'd contacted at Antonia University as to which way they should go. Meanwhile, they needed to dig up the channel and uncover the concrete pipe before it could be modified.

Brandy looked up. "Unless it's Professor Song with my calculations, I'm kind of busy here."

"It's Jaqueline Rabinowiscz. She has a bunch of farmers and ranch hands with her."

She sighed. Without looking up, she said, "Please offer her my apologies, but there's nothing I can do. I really need to keep working on the redesign for Atkins. My hands are tied by the 'Burpee's decision.'"

A voice behind her spoke "Honey, I know you're busy. We've come to help."

"Help? Digging channels and rebuilding the penstock? We've got the workforce for that, although I'd rather make Mayor Donahue do it all himself."

"No dear, we're here to finish the road to Moops Valley. You said that if you can get the road finished you can install the big turbine there, first, right?"

"Moops Valley? But... we still need to clear the terrain, and Victoria said that explosives are in short supply. Donohue is certainly not going to authorize the diversion after telling us to just go with Atkins and not Moops."

"Not to worry, the farmers and ranchers are all donating some of their black powder. We need to save enough to fend off the urswolves, but frillhorns don't need more than a loud shout. We can make do. I trust you to make the most of the labor and supplies."

"Oh. OH! Oh, ma'am, thank you so much!"

"Ma'am? How long have we known each other, Brandy?"

"A long time, Jackie. Thank you so much. Won't you get in trouble, though? With Donohue, I mean."

"Pfaw, Donohue and the rest of BuRP are so caught up in survival, that they are forgetting that it's not enough. We can't just survive... we need to *thrive*."

THERE WAS NO CAR waiting this time when the ferry reached the dock in Beaverton. That was just fine with Brandy; she'd come in a day early for the BuRP emergency meeting – the new mayor, something-something Litchford – wanted to be briefed on resource utilization and allocation. She'd never met the former deputy mayor, mostly just seen her from afar during the Landing Day ceremony. With Donahue recovering from his accident, Acting Mayor Litchford needed to be brought up to speed in a hurry.

With much of the worry and hectic pace of the past year behind her, she might even have time for a spa day. The Landing Spa wasn't fancy, after all, Beaverton and Paradise didn't really have an "upper class." That didn't mean the hard-working people of the colony couldn't enjoy the artificial hot spring or the occasional manicure and pedicure. Brandy was staying with the Urbanek's, so maybe Tara would be interested in going with her.

On her walk, she passed the lander. The crane was now working on dismounting the forward right engine. The port side cargo holds had been emptied in the year-and-a-half since that engine had been removed. Now they needed to switch to the opposite side and begin the salvage of the heavy cross-country transportation elements. Neither Beaver Island nor Paradise had terrain suited to maglev, but if they could salvage the heavy construction equipment, they might be able to use it to build better roads, and maybe even a cogwheel rail line up to the Ko'Olau Heights, and then over to the windward side of Aopo. It would certainly be more efficient than the catamarans and canoes in use by those few hardy souls who'd elected to try building on the far side of the sub-continent.

As she passed the lander, James Snover came out of the "public works" office nestled up against the hull. He waved in her direction and hurried over to greet her. He was a big man, and always seemed to be a bit out of breath. Brandy wasn't sure if that was necessarily exertion or enthusiasm, as the engineer always seemed to be proposing newer, faster, more efficient – and more power-hungry – projects.

"Hey, Brandy. I have an idea for reducing the dependency of outlying ranches on vehicle fuels. We can build better batteries now that we have the chemical plant online, and even fuel cells. The thing is, we're going to need more electricity in the short run, but I have a plan for that as well."

"*More* electricity? You've got the output of three dams going now! Cajon is a 1000 MW unit, Moops is 1200 and Atkins is 800. Why do you need more than three thousand megawatts?"

"Well, we have to share all of that, of course. Beachhead industry is growing, and farm and ranch usage is building up, especially now that they need to fence in the frillhorns. I only want some way to handle surges, and as I said, I have an idea for that."

"Okay," Brandy sighed. "let's hear it."

"Well, we have one of the lander engines dismounted, and the other one's coming off this month, right? Those two weren't damaged in the hard landing, that's why we can dismount them so easily. Anyway," Snover continued, breathlessly, "with the chemical plant now at full capacity, we don't need all that anhydrous ammonia for fertilizer or Elliott's explosives. With ammonia we can make hydrazine, and with hydrazine..."

"We can run the lander engines, just like they used to run natural gas through jet engines back in the TwenCen on Earth to generate power during peak demand. Yes, I get it. It's an idea, but those things burn so much fuel in one go; you could power the entire planet, but only for a few seconds. Do you know how much hydrazine that would take?"

Snover's face fell. "Oh. Yeah, I guess you're right." He brightened. "But I think I might be able to scale down an engine from one of the shuttles or a helicopter!"

Brandy patted him on the shoulder. "That's better. I doubt the new mayor will allow you to divert one just yet but having a source of on-demand power generation isn't such a bad idea."

"Yeah, thanks, Brandy. You're the best!"

As the big man walked away, Brandy thought of his idea. Foolish, yes, but wouldn't that be a sight! One of the lander engines burning full power would certainly light up the night.

THE BURP MEETING WAS low-key. Mayor Litchford was mainly interested in learning, not in giving commands or making immediate decisions. The committee gave updates, and for the first time in two years, it seemed like there were no crises looming on their horizon. There were still shortages – with the diversion of chemicals to fertilizer over the past year, plus paying back the farmers and ranchers for the "loan" of their private stocks to finish the road to PVA/Moops Valley, black powder was still in short supply. Elliott's Explosives was still reporting not enough for fireworks at this year's Landing Day festival.

With all that they had overcome, the loss of the annual fireworks display seemed like a trivial matter. Still, Jackie Rabinowiscz's words came back to Brandy: *We can't just survive... we need to* thrive. She stood up and got the mayor's attention. "I... may have an idea about that. Actually, it's Mr. Snover's."

James looked up in surprise, wondering what the idea was. He then obviously remembered his conversation with Brandy, because he smiled the biggest smile. "Oh yes, what if we could light up the night on the next Landing Day?"

"SAN SALVADOR, THIS IS Beaver Lead. I have made it to the controls and am preparing to eject fuel tank. Godspeed and safe landing, San Salvador. Beaver flight is cl..."

From the civil defense speakers, the replay of the last broadcast from Beaver Flight during the landing of the San Salvador ended with a brief burst of static.

After a minute of silence, a voice came back over the speakers, slowly reading out the names of Beaver Flight, "Beaver one, Mark Cramer. Beaver two, Brian Johnson. Beaver three, Vanessa Pearson. "Beaver four, Jack 'One Cajon' Murray. "Beaver five, Scott Atkins. "Beaver six, James Copley. Beaver Lead, Chris French."

After another minute's pause the final part of the annual Landing Day Ceremony. "Beaver Flight, this is Beaverton Ground Control. The lander is down with all souls safe. Prepare for Landing Beacon to guide you home on my mark. Go for beacon, mark."

Unlike previous years there was no eruption of the fireworks. For years, the "landing flares" had been the traditional way for the residents of Beaverton to mark the way home for Beaver Flight. Instead from the city square a rumbling and glow began as the salvaged

Engine Number One came to life. Suddenly the glow surged and was replaced by a pillar of fire which leapt up into the sky.

Encyclopedia entry for Beaverton:

Beaverton: The town of Beaverton is a legacy to wresting victory from the jaws of defeat. Every year, on the anniversary of the near disastrous crash of the *San Salvador* lander – carrying all of the supplies and colonists for Beaverton – the townspeople hold a memorial service for the brave tug pilots of Beaver Flight, who saved the lander at the cost of their own lives. Their sacrifice stabilized the ship enough to land all colonists safely, although they lost some supplies and all of their heavy equipment. The ceremony started solemn, and eventually turned into a day of celebration with picnics, speeches, and fireworks. When several critical components for fireworks were not available, an enterprising power engineer had the idea of using one of the wrecked lander's engines, plus a small amount of fuel intended for supply shuttles, to continue the celebration. This event paved the way for the modern Landing Day celebration – see "The Loss of Beaver Flight" {supplemental}.

-*Encyclopedia Astra*, Gannon University, Antonia, Cistercia, AA212.

Afterword

As with the previous volume of Journeys Beyond the Known, several of the stories here have appeared as part of other worlds and universes. "The Suit," "Cheating the Odds," *and* "Rescue Ops"—were a fun exercise in writing the kinds of characters and stories I grew up reading in Tom Swift, The Hardy Boys, Boys' Life magazine.

"In the Dust" is similar, I think, given that it conveys the world of a young man with a hobby no one understands. As one of the readers of *Fantastic Hope* told me, there were tears of nostalgia and *hope* evoked by the story.

Sadly, those types of stories are rare in modern fiction—where kids grow up and become adults far too quickly. I try to recapture that spirit, of the aforementioned books and the Heinlein juveniles, where I can. I hope to bring you more such stories—novellas, and perhaps even a novel or two—in the coming years.

"Appleseed" and "To Light Up the Night," gave me the opportunity to revisit the world Sandra Medlock and I created for The Founder Effect. While "Best Laid Plans" is not a *Founder Effect* story, it is in the same spirit, the hard work and legends of colony founders, and the hard

Music also plays a role in my creative process. Quite often, I write and edit while listening to music on headphones. I'm especially fond of the genre often referred to as "modern classical" or "epic"—stirring themes and soaring vistas that seem to match the tone of my stories. That said, I have very eclectic tastes, including the Swedish metal band Sabaton, with their songs of heroes and historical events. "Unto the Last, Stand Fast" was the first story I sold that used a Sabaton song as inspiration. It certainly won't be the last.

Whenever I write short stories, they're seldom actually very short. You'll likely notice that my natural writing length seems to fall around 10,000 to 12,000 words, as demonstrated by several of the stories here. Hitting the 5,000–8,000-word range is actually fairly rare for me—and something that I keep working on. But if it means I give you more story, then so be it.

It's fun.

And there are so many more of these stories flitting around in my head.

I don't plan to stop anytime soon.

Acknowledgements

As always, there are so many people who gave me the opportunities to write and publish—bringing me the enjoyment of storytelling, and hopefully bringing my readers and enjoyable story to read.

First up, I'd like to thank Kevin Steverson and Chris Kennedy for the opportunity to "play" in Kevin's Salvage Title universe. Thanks to Chris again, as well as Mark Wandrey for the chance to write in the Four Horsemen Universe—in particular, my very first story in the 4HU —and then inviting me back to contribute more!

Baen publisher Toni Weisskopf and contributing editor Gray Rinehart were the ones who gave the valuable feedback on In the Dust.

Thanks to my friend and co-author, Brent Roeder. You've put up with a lot from your grad school advisor, who is also your friend and co-author. Also, I never realized how many of our friends we tuckerized in that story!

Special thanks to Sandra L. Medlock, my sister, co-author, co-editor, and the editor who makes my stuff look good. The world we created for *The Founder Effect* still lives!

I'd also like to thank William Alan Webb and Kevin Steverson for many, many conversations on constructing and marketing these books. Bill is the one responsible for showing me how to add the little graphic details to the text, as well as composing the covers and full-page illustrations.

Finally, thanks to my family for putting up with my writing, especially my wife Ruann who is a fierce protector of my time. Thanks to Mom, my biggest fan, and Dad, my hero and role model. Thanks to Sandi for expert editing, and my sons, for putting up with my stories and puns.

Finally, thanks to my readers and fans. I hope you enjoy the stories.

Connect with
Robert E. Hampson

http://REHampson.com

About the Author

Robert E. Hampson, Ph.D. is a national bestselling author and world-class neuroscientist whose stories traverse science fiction, military adventure, post-apocalyptic scenarios, speculative fiction, and even hard-SF style fantasy. Drawing from more than 40 years in scientific research, he crafts universes filled with carefully constructed ecological, technological, and political systems, infused with rich character dynamics and moral complexity.

Rob is dedicated to meticulous worldbuilding and rich characters. His stories engage readers with gripping tales that blend emotional realism with speculative imagination to create a thoughtful blend of scholarly depth and subtle wit. His stories explore themes of survival, rebellion, redemption, and legacy. His creative universe includes heroes facing complex challenges and antagonists possessing relatable depth. Worlds where hope surfaces even amidst the darkest situations.

When not dictating and refining his literary projects, Dr. Hampson continues to explore the intersections of neuroscience, technology, and storytelling, consistently delivering compelling fiction that resonates intellectually and emotionally.

For more information visit: http://REHampson.com

Baen Books by Robert E. Hampson

Across an Ocean of Stars

ISBN 978-1-964856-07-0

NATIONAL BESTSELLER!

After the end of the world, a tropical paradise might just be the hardest place to survive.

The virus robbed humans of their higher thought processes, turning them into uncontrollable savages. The Hawaiian Islands are separated from the rest of the world by thousands of miles of ocean, but that couldn't stop the virus. Civilization fell, and it fell HARD.

Can paradise survive the end of the world?

High atop a dormant volcano, a team of scientists preserve the last remnants of higher technology. Off the coast of Kauai, a flotilla of survivors must decide whether to return to their island, or make their way to another location, risking pirates and nature on the gamble of safer shores. On the central plateau of the Big Island, a group of ranchers want to rebuild civilization... but to do that, they'll need to reunite a people scattered across an ocean of stars.

https://amzn.to/4kZnthh

The Moon and the Desert

ISBN 978-1-982192-49-5

What would it really take to make the Six Million Dollar Man? A medical thriller on earth and in space!

Glenn Armstrong Shepard had his sights set on going to Mars as a flight surgeon, but a training accident on the Moon left him crippled. Now he has a new plan: to be fitted with bionic prosthetics and come back even stronger.

Fate and the Space Force have other plans, and Glenn is grounded. Another doctor—his ex-fiancée—takes his place, and Glenn will have to fight to prove he can be an astronaut once more....

https://amzn.to/4kYFpse

The Founder Effect

ISBN 978-1-982125-09-7

ANTHOLOGY EDITED WITH SANDRA L. MEDLOCK

AWARD-WINNING AND BEST-SELLING AUTHORS CONTRIBUTE NEW STORIES: All-new fiction from Dragon Award winner and New York Times best-selling author David Weber, Dragon Award nominee D.J. Butler, best seller Jody Lynn Nye, indie best sellers Chris Kennedy and Mark Wandrey, and more. Also featuring an introduction by multi-award-winning and New York Times best-selling author Larry Correia.

It is 2185 CE. Humans now live throughout the Solar System, but their most ambitious adventure is about to begin. The starship Victoria will carry over 10,000 colonists to a new world outside the Solar System. The larger-than-life exploits of those colonists will become legendary. The colonists will build a new civilization, and the actions of a few individuals will become famous—and infamous—forever marking their new colony with the Founder Effect.

Contributors: Larry Correia, Mark H. Wandrey, Les Johnson, Christopher L. Smith, David Weber, Daniel M. Hoyt, Brad R. Torgersen, Monalisa Foster, Sarah A. Hoyt, Chris Kennedy, Vivienne Raper, Jody Lynn Nye, Brent M. Roeder, Catherine L. Smith, Philip Wohlrab, D.J. Butler

https://amzn.to/44QbcqP

Stellaris: People of the Stars

ISBN 978-1-481484-25-1

ANTHOLOGY EDITED WITH LES JOHNSON

THE STARS WILL CHANGE US.

STELLARIS: PEOPLE OF THE STARS is a collection of original science fiction stories and nonfiction essays speculating about humanity's far-term expansion into the universe beyond the limits of our solar system—with an emphasis on the changes humans will undergo as a species as we make this happen. Is interstellar travel so far beyond our current imaginings that it will take a fundamental transformation of humanity in order to make it possible? And, if so, will we remain Homo sapiens or become a new and unique species—Homo stellaris (the People of the Stars)?

Herein are original science fiction stories by award-winning authors such as Kevin J. Anderson, William Ledbetter, Todd McCaffrey and Sarah A. Hoyt, supplemented by accessible nonfiction essays describing the science behind the fiction from people who should know—Sir Martin Rees (Astronomer Royal of the United Kingdom), Mark Shelhamer (Chief Scientist for the NASA's Human Research Program), and more.

This collection of original stories and essays was inspired by a gathering of scientists, science fiction authors, and futurists at a series of annual meetings held by the Tennessee Valley Interstellar Workshop. Let their speculations, imaginations and boundless sense of what's possible. Take your own journey beyond the edge of the solar system in STELLARIS: PEOPLE OF THE STARS!

NEW STORIES AND ESSAYS FROM TOP AUTHORS AND EXPERT SCIENTISTS. Explorations of how interstellar travel may affect humanity by best-selling authors and scientists:

Sir Martin Rees, Kevin J. Anderson, Sarah A. Hoyt, Mike Massa, William Ledbetter, Todd McCaffrey, Kacey Ezell and Philip Wohlrab, Dan Hoyt, Les Johnson, Robert E. Hampson, Mark Shelhamer, Brent Roeder, Jim Beall, Cathe Smith

https://amzn.to/4mexGr1

The Wrogul's Oath Books by Robert E. Hampson and Sandra L. Medlock

Four Horsemen Universe, *Seventh Seal Press, Chris Kennedy Publishing*

Do No Harm (Hampson, Kennedy, Medlock)

ISBN 978-1-950420-11-7

WHEN TODD'S CRITICALLY DAMAGED ship dropped out of hyperspace near the Human colony world of Azure, he had no memory of his past. He didn't know who he was, or even what he was, and the Humans didn't either. That didn't stop the colonists of Azure—they took him in, anyway...even though they didn't understand how he could do some of the things he could do.

Todd and his descendants consider themselves Human—eight armed and water-breathing—but Human, nonetheless. After seventy years living among Humans, Todd's descendants are going back out into the Union to make their mark—from fifteen-year-old Verne, who's a little short to be a mercenary, to Harryhausen, who wants to be the most famous PI in the galaxy. Eventually they learn that the rest of the Galactic Union knows them as Wrogul, intelligent octopus-like beings known for science and the ability to perform surgery like no other race can.

These Wrogul do more than just practice medicine, but they still intend to do no harm. Unfortunately, the Humans, whether they have two arms or eight, have powerful enemies...and the Wrogul may have no choice.

https://amzn.to/455Fx3f

And Break It Not (Hampson and Medlock)

ISBN 978-1-648551-92-5

THE PLANET OF AZURE is nearly idyllic—there is a high standard of living, industry is booming, and the two races—Human and Wrogul—get along well with each other most days.

But underneath it all, there is tension between the races. Despite having no reason for it, the Humans don't always trust the Wrogul, and there is a faction within the Wrogul community that doesn't want its young growing up "Human."

When a large group of Wrogul move into the ocean and strange things begin happening—weird lights seen in the depths and sabotage at the mariculture stations—the Human's distrust becomes outright suspicion of treachery.

As things spiral out of control, another force enters the system—a group ostensibly sent by the UN on Earth to inspect the crops being grown on Azure—which threatens to destroy everything the Humans and Wrogul have worked for.

While the Wrogul still intend to do no harm, the Humans have powerful enemies in the galaxy, and, this time, the Wrogul may have no choice about whether to join the front lines with their Human friends. Will the threat of a common enemy break the relationship between the Humans and Wrogul...or break it not?

https://amzn.to/3GYsgBO

As My Witnesses (Medlock, Moores, and Hampson)

ISBN 978-1-648554-17-9

AZURE COLONY AVOIDED THE larger conflicts of the Omega War and Guild Wars, only to fall prey to rogue mercenaries. Now they're rebuilding, but strange forces are at work. New friends on the ground and mysterious lights in the sky promise "interesting times" for the Humans and hyper-intelligent Wrogul of Azure.

Meanwhile, mercenary leader Verne and Peacemaker Harryhausen resume their search for the ancestral home of Azure's Wrogul. They encounter distrust, deceit, and misdirection from the all-powerful guilds, but they manage to learn of sightings of Wrogul-like aliens. Their strongest lead takes them to a forgotten system where a lost Human colony coexists with a strange alien race with remarkable similarities to the Wrogul.

But when they find the colony is in the middle of a civil war, they're forced to make a choice—do they choose sides or stand by while the colonists slaughter each other?

https://amzn.to/3U036pb

This I Swear (Hampson and Medlock)

ISBN 978-8-893192-01-8

Azure is a paradise—balmy breezes, lush jungles, and warm, turquoise seas. But peace is an illusion... and memory can be a weapon.

For over a century, the Wrogul—intelligent, four-limbed cephalopods—have called Azure home. Alongside their human neighbors and a growing chorus of species, they've endured mercenaries, galactic intrigues, and a brutal protection racket bent on exploiting their world. Yet one mystery remains: the Wroguls' own past.

Aboard the starship Nautilus, a Wrogul-led crew journeys into the unknown in search of their origins. What they discover is not a lost homeworld, but a hidden colony—where Wrogul and humans suffer alike, and the villains may not be who they expected.

Back on Azure, danger multiplies. A shadowy real estate syndicate is quietly seizing land. Whispers of rebellion echo from deep-sea Wrogul colonies. The Crusaders arrive with fire in their rhetoric and warships in orbit. And an ancient intelligence offers its services—but can it be trusted?

The Wrogul are determined to uncover the truth. But it might be better for some answers should stay buried...

From the reefs of Azure to the edge of the Peco Arm, This I Swear is a sweeping science fiction epic of memory, identity, and sacrifice—where alien legacies collide, and the cost of peace may be... everything.

https://amzn.to/3U0cuJu

Journeys
Beyond the Known

Available from Amazon:

Journeys Beyond the Known Series

From National Bestselling Author Robert E. Hampson comes **Journeys Beyond the Known**—collections of science fiction and science fantasy exploring the human condition through the lens of biotech, space exploration, and strange futures.

Tinker, Tailor, Bio, Spy

Brain & Brain Press
   Seven tales of cells, circuits and cyborgs
   From battlefield surgeons to post-human colonists. Explore the line between body and machine, memory and manipulation. A line where humanity must embrace the future...or lose it.
   Available in eBook, Paperback and Hardback editions from Amazon.
   https://amzn.to/3UbxPQg

Where the Light Still Reaches

Brain & Brain Press

Eight stories from the edge of exploration

Venture into deep space and distant futures, chronicling the legacy of pioneers, the courage of survivors, and the quiet triumph of those who refuse to be forgotten.

Available in eBook, Paperback and Hardback editions from Amazon.

https://amzn.to/3Hjd7Lp

When the Stars Forget Us

Brain & Brain Press

Eight visions from the edge of magic, and the end of science

Wander the borderlands between science and sorcery, offering seven visions of apocalypse, myth, and transformation—where magic rises, science fractures, and unlikely heroes carry the fire.

Available in eBook, Paperback and Hardback editions from Amazon.

https://amzn.to/4mt5C3J

A Hero Rises

BRAIN & BRAIN PRESS

Six portraits of uncommon valor and courage in the face of the unknown

Travel the paths of heroism, great, small, and everything in between—where people find a way to do the impossible—not always because they want to, but because they have to.

Available in eBook, Paperback and Hardback editions from Amazon.

https://amzn.to/46GgjLo